William Henry Sallada

Silver Sheaves

Gathered through clouds and sunshine. In two parts

William Henry Sallada

Silver Sheaves
Gathered through clouds and sunshine. In two parts

ISBN/EAN: 9783337343880

Printed in Europe, USA, Canada, Australia, Japan

Cover: Foto ©Andreas Hilbeck / pixelio.de

More available books at **www.hansebooks.com**

SILVER SHEAVES:

GATHERED THROUGH

Clouds and Sunshine.

IN TWO PARTS.

PART FIRST:
CIVIL AND MILITARY LIFE OF THE AUTHOR.

PART SECOND:
MISCELLANEOUS COLLECTION OF PROSE AND POETRY.

———————

BY

WILLIAM H. SALLADA.

SECOND EDITION

DES MOINES:
PUBLISHED BY THE AUTHOR.
1879.

PREFATORY.

ABOUT nine years ago the author published a short history of his military career, which met with so much favor that the edition was soon exhausted, and after repeated solicitations from friends consented to re-write and enlarge the work. And now, in sending this volume out into the world, he does not expect to add much to the History of the War, either in learned disquisitions as to its causes, or brilliant narratives as to its progress; he only offers to the public the simple story of a Soldier-boy, who went forth in the glorious confidence of youth to dwell on the tented field and lift his willing hand in his flag's defense, only to meet a fate of which he does not complain, and yet a fate which, next to death itself, is the most grievous that may befall a man—the loss of his eye-sight.

The reader will find in Part First a faithful, thrilling narrative of thirty-three years of struggles and triumphs of an active life, under disadvantages of the most distressing character. A simple story, told as he would tell it to his friends around the fireside upon a winter night.

Part Second contains a fine collection of original and selected Poems and Essays.

Hoping to please and benefit the reader, we send SILVER SHEAVES adrift in its native guise.

DES MOINES, IOWA, August, 1879.

CONTENTS—PART I.

INTRODUCTION.

EARLY HISTORY OF THE AUTHOR.

CHAPTER I.

INCIDENTS OF TOWN LIFE.

CHAPTER II.

AN ANXIOUS YEAR.

CHAPTER III..

LIFE'S TURNING POINT.

CHAPTER IV.

ARMY INCIDENTS.

CHAPTER V.

THRILLING CAMPAIGN.

CHAPTER VI.

SUFFERING AND SORROW.

CHAPTER VII.

LIFE IN WASHINGTON.

CHAPTER VIII.

IN PHILLADELPHIA.

CHAPTER IX.

CIVIL LIFE.

CHAPTER X.

MOMENTOUS TRANSACTIONS.

CHAPTER XI.

LIFE IN THE WEST.

INDEX—PART II.

—

PART FIRST

CIVIL AND MILITARY LIFE

CIVIL AND MILITARY LIFE

OF

WILLIAM HENRY SALLADA.

INTRODUCTION.

BY J. M. DIXON.

MEN generally take an interest in the early history of those who like themselves have encountered the trials and misfortunes of life. We will introduce this little volume to the reader by giving a short sketch of the parentage and early history of the author. His father, Daniel Sallada, was born in Dauphin county, Pennsylvania, in 1816. At an early age his father died and his lot was cast among strangers. We need not trace the wanderings of his early life; it needs no comment, for as an orphan without home he was subject to hardship and misfortune. At the age of twenty-two he apprenticed himself to a shoemaker. After this he removed to Lycoming county where he formed the acquaintance of Maria Stover, of Lehigh county, Pa., and in July, 1845, they were married. On the 12th of July, 1846, their oldest son, WILLIAM HENRY SALLADA, was born, who, as the following pages

will show, is the author of this work. His father, by
his industry, energy and hard labor, provided a home
for his family in a beautiful valley lying at the foot
of Sugar Valley Mountain, near the banks of the Susquehanna. His mother was a woman of highly con-
sistent christian character, passionately devoted to her
family. His parents soon discovered that his intellect
was more than an ordinary one, and, anxious for the
development of his intellectual powers, they at an
early age engaged a boy to take him to school, where,
by his facetious nature and generous disposition he
soon won the love of both teacher and schoolmates.
His active mind soon drank deep of knowledge, and
it was with pride his parents noticed his early inclina-
tion for advancement in his studies. His natural abili-
ties afforded him superior advantage. His childhood
was marked by childish pranks: fishing and wandering
on the mountains were among his favorite amuse-
ments. An amusing little incident occurred in his
early childhood which will show that he was not of an
excitable nature, but rather cool and collected: At one
time his father's house caught fire; he was fast asleep
in his bed when the noise awakened him; he arose and
was proceeding down the stairway when his father,
unconscious of his presence and blinded by smoke
dashed a pail of water in his face, upon which he
coolly retraced his steps. After the fire was extinguished, and excitement abated, Willie was found fast
asleep covered up in his bed.

His first years were happy childhood years, gamboling with his sister and brother, the dark future as yet having never crossed his pathway. Oh, happy childhood days, too soon they pass from us, bringing in their stead the stern realities of life. To some joy and contentment, but to many afflictions and distress; but in all times we have the assurance that we have a friend who will aid and comfort us in sorrow and trouble—He will revive our drooping spirits, and will animate us with love, peace and happiness. Though at times our path seems dark and gloomy and thorns strew our way, yet we have the promise of a brighter day.

The morning of his life was as cloudless as a summer morning; his sun arose bright and clear. In most children we see the future man, so in Willie's active energetic mind was his future traced. Like most children he had a strong will, apt to love his own ways, and not easily pursuaded to do any thing contrary to his will. He never allowed himself to be overcome by petty troubles and was not easily daunted in his childish pursuits. Thus, how heedless we run on in disobedience and folly which we often regret in after years. The sun of our existence has just arisen, all is light and love, we little dream of what may befall us, and it is well it is so, else our childhood might be overshadowed, and the years that now are without care darkened with the thoughts of what is to come. The short hours of our infancy are soon passed, a mother's fond caress and smile, a father's care, are gone like a shadow that fleeth, and we are left to battle with life alone.

Has the time come to any of us that we have been sorry for past acts, when we would gladly have recalled words that had been spoken, could we have strewn some one's pathway with flowers instead of thorns? Oh how often we might have performed a kind act, or done a good deed, but the opportunity is past; how often in our childhood has our waywardness grieved a loving parent, or our filial love cheered her anxious heart. But, the wing of time is swiftly bearing us onward, our brightest hours have no abiding; but this life has its clouds and sunshine, its joys and its sorrows, its fortunes and misfortunes, its prosperity and adversity—all these we meet face to face in the battle of life.

> My happy childhood art thou past,
>   So free from sin and pain;
> Thou was too happy far, to last
>   Or to return again.
>
> One fading moment's mirth
> And boyhood's day is gone.

In 1852, his father hearing of the advantages of western settlers, and thinking to better his lot, removed to Mercer county, two miles northwest of Greenville, Pa.

This beautiful and enterprising town, of between three and four thousand inhabitants, is situated in the Shenango Valley. To the east and south, as far into the exterior as the eye can reach are richly cultivated farms, adorned with neat and comely buildings. The stately pine, and rugged oak with its magnificent branches nodding to the passing breeze, add to the beauty of the surrounding scenery, while in the northern suberbs is the Shenango river, which quietly steals its way southward through the western portion of the town. To the west rises a majestic hill that overlooks the town, and from this elevation you have a commanding view of the immediate town, with its grand structures and templed palaces; your ear is attracted by the busy hum of the town, and you see the heavily loaded boats slowly winding their way to their destined harbors, while on either side the swift locomotive, with its heavily freighted train, monopolizes the active routine of business.

In the vicinity of this place Willie's boyhood was spent in assisting his father on the farm and attending district school, where he received a limited education. If he had had the opportunity, and gone through a regular course of studies, his talented mind might have been largely developed. But circumstances were such that his course was ordered otherwise. At this time we may call him a mischievous boy; like most boys of his age, playing tricks and passing jokes seemed to afford him much amusement. It may not be out of place to state that at this early period of his boyhood he displayed a wonderful taste for war. He would organize little companies and spend hours in training them to his mode of dicipline—with his paper cap and wooden sword, and his little forces armed with wooden guns, would march with all the dignity and pomposity of a regular organized militia, never dreaming that this bright fancy in after years would waken into stern realities.

He showed great ingenuity, and nearly every piece of machinery which he saw, after a close examination, would imitate it with such perfection that it awakened the curiosity of those who saw him. His mind was uncommonly active; his busy feet in constant motion. He was always cheerful and happy. A busy life must be a cheerful one. A merry and cheerful countenance was one of the things which Jeremy Taylor said his enemies could not take away from him. It may at times seem difficult for the sweetest tempered to keep a cheerful countenance. When we are sick, what causes more unhappiness than peevishness? The loved ones who have the care of us are grieved at such unkindness. If we are unfortunate, why distress our friends by a recital of our misfortunes? Why not trust God, and be not afraid? Birds sing in a storm. Then, why not we, as God's children, even when we can see no ray of his love? Though He sometimes seems a hard and austre master, He is a kind and loving father, and friend; He doeth all things for the best, and is ever ready to cheer and comfort us in every affliction.

CHAPTER I.

INCIDENTS OF TOWN LIFE.

Civil War—The News Boy and his Employer—Commun-
ings with Nature—Sabbath Excursions—Melon Patch
and Revenge—Poisoned Blackberries—Anxiety to Enlist—Death of Mr. Walker.

The introduction to this work, as the reader is
aware, embraces all that portion of my life, beginning
at my birth, and terminating in my fifteenth year.
The period to which I have now come—that is, the
spring of 1861—signalizes a memorable crisis in the
affairs of our country. The secession of several of the
States followed by overt acts of hostility on the part
of the Southern Confederacy, inaugurated the most
formidable war of our history as a nation. The fall
of Sumpter thrilled all hearts, North and South. The
loyal States were ablaze with excitement, and companies and regiments were in process of organization
everywhere. Each succeeding act of the great military
drama, as the report of it flashed along the wires, and
was transmitted to the local journals, was caught up

with the greatest possible eagerness, and read with the profoundest interest. The fife and the drum constituted the music of the hour; and the earth itself resounded with the tread of armed men, advancing, with banners flying, to the battle-fields, on which the destiny of our government, for weal or woe, was to be decided.

CIVIL WAR.

At this exciting period, I was living in Greenville, in the employment of W. H. C. Walker, who was the proprietor of a book store, news depot, etc. At that time the little city of which I was a resident, had no railroad. Twelve miles away, at Jamestown, was the terminus of a road, which was destined in time to reach our place. Each evening, at seven o'clock, the stage from the railroad made its welcome appearance, bringing with it packages of the *Express* and *Courier*, daily papers of Buffalo, N. Y. The columns of these journals, filled as they were with stirring news from the seat of war, were the centers of popular interest and expectation. A rare harvest, indeed, was reaped in a pecuniary sense, by men who were engaged in the sale of daily papers.

THE NEWS BOY AND HIS EMPLOYER.

In Greenville, there were two competing news depots, the rivalry between which on account of the peculiar character of the news, was very sharp and exciting. The one belonging to Mr. Walker was three blocks distant from the Express Office, while its competitor was quite near. It was my duty, as a news boy, to station myself each evening at a point near the office, and when the stage came in, and the precious package of papers was committed to my charge, I would run with it to the store, where Mr. Walker, standing at the door, was waiting to receive it. The papers were speedily folded, as my employer was an adept in this business: and then the contest in the distribution began. We had a number of permanent patrons, whom we supplied each day; but the public anxiety to obtain the journals at the earliest moment was such that in most cases the news boy who found his way first to the purchaser was the one patronized. Despite the fact that our store was so remote from the express office, compared with that of our competitor, I managed to sell many more papers each day than were sold by the other house. I may be pardoned here for the statement that my activity and diligence, as well as my spirit of friendly accommodation, were highly commended by Mr. Walker, and by the many patrons whom it was my pleasure to supply with reading matter. I was frequently greeted with words of kindness and good will; and in this way I was stimulated and cheered in the performance of my duties.

COMMUNINGS WITH NATURE.

While not otherwise engaged my business hours were spent in the store, waiting on customers. My employer was a young man of much respectability and promise; he was a genuine lover of the beautiful in nature, and with this trait of character, it was my good fortune to be in full accord and sympathy. Often in the evening, when the work of the day was suspended, he and I would ramble away from the town to enjoy, in the silvery light of the moon, the grand scenery which spread out in panoramic beauty before us. It was here, while contemplating those familiar scenes which memory has enshrined, never to be driven from their sanctuary, we studied the open volume of nature whose revelations, if indeed there were no other volume, taught us to apprehend some of the attributes of the Almighty; or, in other words, led us in thought upward along the stairway of the universe, to the pavilion of Him who dwells in eternity.

SABBATH EXCURSIONS.

It must be confessed, however, that in spite of the sacred influences to which I have referred, many of my Sabbaths were spent in a very thoughtless manner, strolling over the country, without any definite object or aim, or propelling the light skiff, as it glided on the bosom of the river, regardless of the divine command, "Remember the Sabbath day to keep it holy." On other Sabbaths, not so thoughtlessly abused, it was a pure and rich enjoyment in my experience to visit the old hearthstone at home, around which were gathered the other members of my father's family to welcome my arrival among them. These visits were refreshing

events to me. Here I was the recipient of many kindnesses from brothers and sisters; and here too the be-
nign and gracious influences which comes to the boy
through the sacred channel of parental love and authority, was felt in all its fullness of affection. In connection with these home visits, I have here a little episode to record:

MELON PATCH AND REVENGE.

One of my brothers had cultivated, with much care,
a melon patch, designing to give me a delicious entertainment when the proper season came. The melons
had reached their maturity, presenting a luscious and
inviting appearance to all beholders. Having been advised of the repast that was intended for me, I repaired
at the appointed time to my father's residence full of
delightful expectation. What was my disgust and dis-
appointment, when I learned that on the previous
night some heartless freebooters had visited the patch
and deprived all other persons of any benefit from it.
In the bitterness of my heart I resolved to be avenged,
and learning that the son of a neighboring farmer was
guilty, in part at least, of the cowardly theft, I put my
designs of revenge into execution. Along with several
comrades I visited the patch of the farmer, but instead
of despoiling it we feasted on a few melons, leaving the
others to the owner.

In recalling this rather shameful affair, I desire to
state somewhat in extenuation, that the temptation to
be revenged did not originate in my own mind; that

dubious honor belonged to one of my companions, but I displayed cowardice and weakness in yielding to such temptation, no matter who started it.

Some days after this occurrence the old farmer, on whom I had retaliated in return for the act of his son came to Greenville. Through his son-in-law, who lived near him, and who chanced to see my companions and myself strolling about rather suspiciously on the day in which my revenge was accomplished—for it was in broad daylight when the deed was done—the farmer regarded me as one of the marauders. Inviting me to step aside with him he spoke of the deed which had been perpetrated at his expense, and concluded by expressing his strong suspicion that I was one of the offenders. I confronted the charge with a look which was intended to be one of injured innocence, and stoutly denied all knowledge of the depredation. Finding that the evidence was insufficient to convict me, and attaching some importance no doubt to my straight denial, he departed, leaving me to my painful reflections. As he went his way along the street, his venerable form burdened with the weight of years, and his white hair which was stirred by the passing breeze, excited in me, as I gazed, a feeling of respect and reverence, and this feeling was suddenly followed by the pangs of a sharp remorse for the cowardly part I had been playing. Incited by an honest resolution to repair the wrong I had done, as far as I was able to make reparation, I followed the old farmer, and, calling him aside, made a full retraction of the falsehoods I had uttered in his presence a little while before, and sincerely confessed my guilt, taking care, however, to conceal the names of my companions in the theft, standing thus alone in responsibility for the deed, of which others were guilty as well as myself. I begged his forgiveness with tears of penitent sorrow bedewing my cheeks. Fully imbued with the desire to make it all right, I proposed to pay for the damage he had sustained, and although I was allowed by my employer but a dollar a month, in excess of board and clothes, I paid the farmer three dollars for the mischief that had been done, and never asked my comrades to take from me any part of this financial burden.

That bad act of mine, taken in connection with its bitter but salutary results, taught me a lesson which has never been forgotten. It taught me to respect the rights of other parties; and more than this, it taught me that the spirit of retaliation, even when gratified to its fullest extent, brings remorse instead of satisfaction. From that day to this, I have been careful to suppress all desire to appropriate to myself the property of others, believing that the happiness of every-day life depends on the honest observance of the golden rule: Do unto others as you would wish them to do unto you.

POISONED BLACKBERRIES.

Nature had endowed me with a warm, lively and impulsive disposition. Imagination, as it usually is with the young, had full play; and my jokes and sportive sallies contributed, if they had no other effect, to the amusement of my patron and friend. When from any cause we were kept within doors in the evening, the time was occupied in relating incidents to each other, and in interchanging thoughts on various topics which suggested themselves to our minds. In this way whatever intellect I possessed received strength. My sphere of information was enlarged, and my ability to grapple with the great world, in the conflict of life, was maturing day by day.

Here I must relate another incident, which created, for the time, quite a sensation in the little circle in which I moved. It was often the case that friends from the country would kindly bring to us presents of fruits, and other delicacies of the season, which were always gratefully accepted. On one occasion a young lady brought us some blackberries, which were held in reserve in a basket behind the counter until such time as an adjournment from business would give us leisure to feast our palates. During the day Mr. M., a well known merchant, whose place of business was not far away, came into the store, and stepping familiarly, though somewhat carelessly, in the vicinity of our rich deposit of fruit, searching, as he was, for some desired article, he overset a vessel of fly poison, the contents of which fell among the berries. The accident was not observed by any one else; and Mr. M. omitting to mention the disagreeable circumstance, left the store shortly afterward. In the evening, when the customers had all departed, Mr. Walker and myself sat down to the delectable entertainment. The berries were very inviting, and having a great fondness for such fruit, I went to work with more than ordinary greediness, excelling my patron in making rapid progress in this feast of good things, when Mr. M. again entered the store. As soon as he saw what manner of business, or pleasure, was employing our time, he started back aghast, calling out at the same time to me:

"Will, stop eating those berries! Stop! Do not eat them, I would not eat them!"

Thinking that Mr. M. was trying to get off some practical joke, which was no uncommon thing in those times, I responded with great coolness:

"Neither would I."

Having made this remark, in imitation of the cant phraseology in vogue, I calmly proceeded to devour more berries. The merchant was in such a state of excitement and terror, that moments elapsed before he was able to explain the situation. Taking me forcibly by the arm, and summoning all his powers of utterance, he at last made us comprehend the alarming fact. We started up in dismay, and threw the poisoned berries into the street. Having eaten more of the fruit than my employer, I soon began to feel the effects of an active poison. I hastened off in the direction of a drug store, but before I reached it, a deadly sickness seized me, and I was compelled to stop by the way. Here an antidote was brought to me, which allayed, to some extent, the violent symptoms, but all that night I suffered dreadfully, and many days passed

3

away before I regained my former vigorous health.
Mr. Walker, having regaled himself more temperately
at the fly banquet, suffered much less than myself, and
was soon well.

ANXIETY TO ENLIST.

As stated in a former part of this chapter, the great
civil war was in progress. It was now raging in all
its fury; and every part of the country was in a condition of unrest and convulsion, as though an earthquake,
like that of Lisbon, was producing universal desolation. It may be that the aptitude, as well as the longing for military life was natural with me. However
this may be, the desire to join the ranks of the boys in
blue, and do battle for the integrity of the Union,
under the old Flag of Freedom was simply irrepres-
sible. Whenever a company, or squad, or detachment
of soldiers, was about to leave town for the front, my
anxiety, young as I was, to gird on the sword and
march to the scene of battle, could not be extinguished.
What were the arts of civil life to me, when my country
was in peril, from the hand of confederate traitors.

Often would I quit the store, and go home to plead
with my father for the privilege of enlisting in defense
of my country; and as often would he repel my plea,
and convert my hope into discouragement, by the can-
did and truthful statement, prompted as it was by a
father's tenderness for his first born, that I was too
young to bear the hardships and privations of a soldier's
life. Again, and again would I return to my vocation

in town, sick at heart and almost in controversy with Heaven, because I had not been born sooner, or because the war for the Union could not be postponed for a few years, so as to give me a man's assured prerogative to decide for myself the grave issue between my parents and their son.

Meanwhile, I was not wholly inactive, in regard to military discipline. Along with Mr. Walker, who was quick in comprehending the drill, we filled our hours of recreation, when the mood was strongest upon us, in going through the manual of arms; and, months before the period at which the Greenville newsboy became a boy in blue, I was quite proficient in some of the more difficult exercises performed by the educated soldier. After a little time, my desire to enlist became almost insupportable. I went home for a time, and in the course of a few weeks after this, my employer, to whom I was strongly attached, went into the service, leaving me to all the anguish of spirit, which comes from hope deferred!

DEATH OF MR. WALKER.

Months again sped away, and the news at last came to us that Mr. Walker had been severely, if not fatally, wounded, and was about to return home. This intelligence proved to be true. He came back among us once more to gladen our sight with his familiar presence, but sadly altered in appearance. Though still young the elasticity of his form was gone; yet in some partial degree his health was temporarily recruited.

At this time, he took to the altar a young lady to whom he had plighted his troth before he went to the war, and his numerous friends who esteemed him for his solid virtues, and loved him for the kindliness and attractiveness of his manners, began to entertain the hope that many years of happiness were yet in reserve for him and his beloved wife. This hope was destined to be disappointed. The wound which he had received in the service of his country was beyond the skill of the most scientific surgeon, and after lingering awhile longer among us, enduring pain with the patience and fortitude of a true soldier of the republic, this excellent friend of mine, whose memory is prized as a precious legacy, passed away from the conflicts of earth to the repose of the grave. His widow did not long survive him.

> When this frail body shall have done with earth,
>   And this heart shall be free from care;
> When my spirit shall enter the other world,
>   Oh, say shall I know thee there.
>
> When the last hours of life close round,
>   And death's summons cometh to me,
> Will God send an angel messenger down—
>   Shall I know the bright spirit as THEE?
>
> Rest weary heart, rest patiently and wait
>   Till thy happiness cometh to thee,
> Thou'lt meet and thou'lt know when thou gainest that shore
>   Which opes to eternity.

CHAPTER II.

AN ANXIOUS YEAR.

We pass out from the city's feverish hum
To find refreshment in the silent woods.

N. P. Willis.

But 'tis not thus—and 'tis not here—
Such thoughts would shake my soul—nor now—
Where glory decks the hero's bier,
Or binds his brow.

Byron.

INTEMPERANCE AND GAMING—MY UNREST AT HOME—MY TRIP EAST—TOBACCO AND REFORM—TRIP TO OHIO—RESOLVE TO ENLIST.

INTEMPERANCE.

BEFORE proceeding with the march of events in their regular order I must pause here to speak of a subject of the highest possible importance, especially to my young readers. If any part of my experience can be employed as a warning to deter others from imitating a bad example I am perfectly willing to make the proper recital, no matter how deeply I may deplore the events which it becomes necessary for me to record. In producing this volume my object is to accomplish good, and I am well aware that there are passages in my career which, while they bring remorse to me as they are recalled, may, nevertheless, be instrumental in saving some poor misguided being from indulging in vices, the effect of which are hurtful and indeed pernicious to the souls and bodies of men.

Not long after taking up my abode in Greenville I had occasion one day to pass through a certain portion of the town, on some unimportant errand. A little distance in advance of me I saw a long narrow building of unique structure, and, as far as my knowledge extended, its character was profoundly mysterious. It may be that I noticed the sign above the door, on which were inscribed the words, "Ten-pin Alley." If I did so, the words themselves gave me no definite information; for whatever the business was which was carried on in the building it was unknown to my limited experience. Inspired by curiosity I passed through the door and took a view of the interior. Several persons were there busily engaged in rolling large balls along alleys, which traversed the entire apartment. Settees, for the accommodation of patrons and visitors, were posted along the wall, on one of which I seated myself to take a deliberate survey of the scene in progress. Having satisfied my curiosity, for the time, I departed. The next day found me there again. On this occasion, when some gentleman had the good fortune to knock down the pins, I was invited to set them up. Being a novice in the business I answered that I did not know how. The proprietor kindly proffered to show me how this feat was performed, and after a little time, I learned the art to perfection.

Part of the next two days was consumed in the same thoughtless manner. It was on the fourth day, I believe, after my entrance into the Bowling Alley that I was induced to take something to drink. Before, when liquor was called for by the contestants in the games, I took candy for my share, rejecting the beverage that was offered. On this day, however, there were tormentors present who plagued me for my boyish love of candy, and challenged me to drink with them. I weakly yielded to the temptation. A small quantity of liquor was poured out for me into a diminutive glass, and I drank it. Its effect was immediate and very pleasant; and from that day forward I was in the habit of drinking every time I visited the place. At last I became so used to the familiar beverage, that, when I wished to imbibe, I would not permit the bartender to measure out the amount of liquor I was to take, but assumed that high privilege myself, fearing perhaps, that he would economize to a greater extent than my increasing appetite for stimulating drink would warrant.

Several days after my induction into the mysteries of ten-pins, I met a boy at the alley, of nearly my own age, who invited me to play a game with him. At that time I had but little confidence in my ability in this direction, and beside this, I had no money with me. Under the circumstances, I deemed it prudent to decline the invitation; but the boy was importunate, and at length I yielded. The result was as I had anticipated. I was beaten, and the proprietor gave me credit for the drinks. Next day I met the same boy at the same place, and another invitation to play grew out of this meeting. After considerable hesitation on my part, as I feared the consequences of a second defeat, I finally consented, as usual. This time victory perched upon my banner, and my competitor was compelled to pay the charges. I began now to take a deeper interest in the game than ever before, and vastly too much of my time was occupied in acquiring proficiency in it. Ultimately, my dexterity in rolling the balls was the subject of much compliment in gaming circles. Once I had the honor of entering the lists against an expert from New York; and on another occasion, I was pitted against a star player from England. Out from both of these contests I came victorious. My fellow townsmen, who took part in such games, were always sanguine of success when I was chosen on their side.

Inspired with a boys' vanity, my success seemed to warrant me in the belief that in other games besides the one in which I had borne so conspicuous a part, I would be equally fortunate; but in this I was sadly mistaken. Repeated trials at cards developed the fact that I had no chance for success while playing against professionals; and the effort to master the science of billiards which I frequently made, resulted in no better fortune. The minute confession I have made in these paragraphs of my increasing fondness for alcoholic drinks, after the first perilous glass was taken, will operate, I trust, as a salutary warning to all my young

readers; and as gambling is essentially allied to drinking, I hope that the recital I have given in reference
to my deep passion for a game which not only con-
sumes precious time and squanders money, but often
leads its poor victim to moral shipwreck, ruin and
death, will also do good. In retrospecting this melancholy portion of my life, I cannot be too thankful that
the poor boy, who, in his thoughtlessness and inexperience once trod the verge of a great moral disaster to
himself, was, in after time, saved from the snares that
beset his pathway, and his feet were transferred from
the places of danger to that Rock which constitutes
the only sure foundation.

MY UNREST AT HOME

After I left town my mind was so embarrassed that
home had no charms for me. As one pleadeth for his
life, so I plead to go to the army. But my father was
unyielding. So like Noah's dove, seeking rest but
finding none, I engaged in the various duties of domes-
tic farm life; but this was unsuited to my restless
nature. I could not be contented. I loved activity—
something new and thrilling.

MY TRIP EAST.

Noting the condition of my mind, which now
amounted to agony, my father gave me permission to
quit my monotonous life on the farm, and take a trip
East. As a matter of economy in my mode of travel,
I hired out to a Mr. Nisby, who was about to take a

drove of sheep to the eastern market. Any one who knows what the life of a drover is, understands the fact that it is full of perils and moral quicksands. In this sense, it was peculiarly hazardous at the period of which I am writing. On account of the war, society was in an inflammable condition, and the moral restraints which are so useful in peace times, were driven away. The hotels along our route were commonly crowded with excited men; and the temptation to drink of the poisonous cup was repeated on every hand, with a fascination and power which I did not attempt to repel or control. It is no wonder, therefore, that the habit which began in the Bowling Alley in Greenville, suffered no abatement in my wanderings eastward.

Late in June, 1863, I took this trip; I was much delighted with it. I passed through a richly fertilized country. The fields were waving with golden grain, the trees were loaded with fruit, and all nature seemed to rejoice. I gazed on the hills and saw hundreds of cattle grazing on them.

As I passed through the valley, my mind was everywhere regaled with the enchanting scenes of nature. The redolent flowers, the rich herbage, the green shrubbery, and majestic trees, all sharing alike the bounties of nature, and expanding and basking in the resplendent rays of the meridian sun, impressed my mind with the goodness of God.

The rural village, cozily nestled among the trees; the enterprising town, with its busy throng hastening to and from their daily toil; the city, with its grandeur, its richly furnished palaces, and templed churches whose spires seemed to reach the clouds, were subjects of much interest to me.

The Fourth of July, that glorious day of Independence, I spent at Philipsburg. This village is situated at the foot of the Allegheny Mountains. The scenery from this place is imposing. The rugged mountain peaks, clothed in living green, whose tops tower one above the other until they are lost in the ether blue of heaven, are on one hand, while on the other a winding river glides rapidly away.

The next place that arrested my attention was Penn's Valley. This is the grandest and most picturesque portion of land through which I had passed. The generosity of the inhabitants is unequaled. They welcome a stranger as a friend, and treat him as a brother. My entire journey was full of pleasant and interesting scenes.

At this time Lee was invading Pennsylvania, and the country was submerged in the wildest excitement. Business was suspended, and men were responding to the immediate call for troops. You who have felt the symptoms of war-fever can imagine my feelings at this epoch.

On the 3d of July, when we were within a few miles of Phillipsburg, heavy cannonading from the field of Gettysburg was distinctly heard. The reader will remember that this was the third, and the final, day of the greatest battle of the war. It was fought in a free State, and it was intended by the Confederate General to be the first of a series of Rebel victories in the North; and during the night which preceded the glorious Fourth, his demoralized army, crushed into fragments by the assaults of Freedom's hosts, fled away, as a gory remnant, from the scene of carnage. From that time forth the overthrow of the rebellion was a question simply of time. It was already in the last stage of collapse. To have participated in the crowning engagement at Gettysburg would have been glory indeed; but, if I was denied that privilege, I was compensated by hearing the thunderous voice of war, as it came down from those sanguinary hills, on which the fate of the great insurrection was decided.

TOBACCO CHEWING AND REFORM.

My Eastern trip gave me ample apportunity to indulge in another vice, which had been contracted some little time before—I refer to tobacco chewing. My father, whose freedom from the habit gave him authority to speak, had often expostulated with me, but without effect. My passion for the weed was progressive in character, like the one which referred to stimulating drinks. In other words, it increased very rapidly. In my capacity as drover, it took full possession of me; and my friends would not have regarded me in a normal or healthy condition, if they had not found me in the full tide of expectoration, with my cheeks inflated by the passionable weed. Although a little out of the regular order, in point of chronology, I will conclude in this chapter what I have to say on this subject, hoping that others who have been victimized by the nauseous practice, may be warned and benefited by my experience.

The habit with me grew so enormously, that on returning from my Eastern trip it was my custom to consume half a dollar's worth of tobacco in a week. This wholesale consumption, for a boy who had not tarried long enough in Jericho to develop a manly beard, did not embrace the habit of smoking, for up to that time this latter accomplishment had not been learned. I was sensible all the while I was doing injury both to my health and to my morals; and, aside from this, I was exciting the displeasure of my parents. But still I went on, rolling the sweet morsel in my mouth, and postponing indefinitely the day of reformation.

One Saturday afternoon, late in the year 1863, I laid in a supply of tobacco for the coming week, paying the customary fee therefor, fifty cents. That night I remained awake very late. Next morning in passing out from the breakfast table, I was observed to take a chew. This was an uncommon thing for me to do in my father's house, in spite of the fact that the habit exercised such a dominant influence over me. My father expressed a very strong wish that I would quit the vile weed. A sudden inspiration seized me, I saw my chance, and immediately took advantage of it. I had reached that age of incipient manhood, when the boy, for a variety of reasons, has a passion for fine clothes. I turned to my father, and propounded to him this simple question:

"What will you give me, sir, if I quit chewing."

"I will give you most anything in reason," was the fatherly response.

"Will you give me a suit of clothes?" I asked.

"Yes," was the laconic answer.

I knew that my father was in earnest and so was I. The quid in my mouth was ejected with a gesture of contempt. My resolution was formed, and I knew it would be held sacred in the future. In matters of trifling moment compared to this, when changes of base were decided, my perseverance in reform was rather doubtful; but, a resolution of the character I had just made, involving results immeasurably superior to the suit of garments that had been promised, would be faithfully kept to the end. And so it has been thus far. From that day to this tobacco chewing has not been in the list of my habits, nor will it be to the end of life. My father was even better than his word, for the clothes he gave me, as a reward for patient continuance in well-doing, were better than I expected, and were all that I could have desired.

To pursue this subject further before dismissing it, it is proper to state, that when I entered the army, as detailed in another place, I found that smoking was almost universal among my comrades. For a chewer, or one who has been such, to gravitate into a smoker, is to pass through a very easy transition. Amid such surroundings as the army afforded, it was far more difficult to resist temptation than it would have been in civil life. The conventional restraints of home society were not there, and the reader will not be surprised when he hears that I was, in time, transformed into a common smoker; but the promise I gave to my father, which referred to chewing only, was strictly observed.

In the army, and out of it, I remained a smoker until New Years day. 1871, when, at Monroe, Iowa, I abandoned the habit forever. On that day I was surrounded with peculiar temptations to continue the bad practice. Every one seemed to enjoy his cigar or his pipe, yet in the midst of this smoking mania I threw away my cigar and vowed never to tolerate in myself the vice again. When I stopped chewing, years before at home, I sold for ten cents my last instalment of tobacco, which had cost me, the day previous, five times as much, and thus removed myself from its pernicious influence; and years after, I bade adieu to the kindred vice of smoking. Any honest and intelligent user of tobacco must concede that either of these habits injures the digestive organs and enfeebles the common energies of the system. It often produces dyspepsia; sometimes terminates in neuralgia. It engenders a host of bodily evils, and besides this, it is the strongest ally of drunkenness, as it begets a taste for alcoholic stimulants. I am an avowed enemy of tobacco, in all the forms in which this narcotic drug may present itself; and glad am I that my system, and my Christian morals, have been purged forever from its gross im-

purities. My dear reader, if one or the other, or both
of the vices about which I have been writing, are clinging to you, I beseech you to throw them off, before
your very manhood shall have been crushed out by
their malign power!

TRIP TO OHIO.

I must now return to the regular course of events.
My journey, during the summer of 1863, was, as here-
tofore intimated, an expedient to withdraw my mind
from the settled gloom, which was caused by an ungratified longing to go into the service. It is true that
the change of scene induced by travel gave me some
relief, but this was temporary; and when I reached
home once more and found that so many of my old
friends had already gone to the front, leaving a melancholy vacancy behind, the war fever, which had never
been conquered, burned again in my heart with renewed power. A young friend of mine who had just
enlisted was about to visit his relatives in Ohio before
proceeding to the army, and my father, seeing my
distress of mind and being anxious to relieve it, yet
unwilling for me to go to the war, gave me permission
to accompany my friend in his journey.

On this trip I had an opportunity to see much fine
scenery, which was distributed through wealthy and
populous sections. We met with a kind welcome
everywhere, and our stay was deferred beyond the
time at which we had designed to return. On the
return trip, while we were yet within a few miles of

home, we happened to be present in a little musical assemblage, where I had the happiness to meet my sister. I was pained to learn that, during my absence, the report was circulated that I had enlisted and gone off to the army. This was afflicting news to the family; but, when my father heard it, he seemed to recede from the strong position he had all along taken with me in regard to the war question. He stated to the family, as my sister informed me, that he had ex-hausted every plea, and every argument in his power, to induce me to remain at home, and now, if I were still resolved to go, he would take no further steps in oppo-sition. Although this language did not give me the full consent I desired, yet it filled me with joy. I accepted it as a tacit permission, at least, to use my own discretion in the premises. In a burst of patri-otism, I then and there dedicated myself to the service of my imperiled country, feeling a willingness, if need be, to die in so sacred a cause.

RESOLVE TO ENLIST.

I went home with a happy heart, only to be dis-heartened by the unwillingness of my friends to have me go. They tried to discourage me in every way, telling me my constitution was too delicate to endure the duties that would be required of me; but this was of no avail. I assured them that I would come back; and, with an anxious heart, I counted the weary hours that necessarily intervened before I could have an opportunity of enlisting.

4

Ah! little did I think these would be the last hours
I would spend in the then unbroken family circle—the
last advice I would receive from the lips of a kind
mother, or else these hours would have been far too
short! I little thought that happy circle was soon to
lose its guiding star, and the dear face that always
welcomed me with a smile would greet me at the gateway no more. Oh, these sad partings! Little do we
think when we give the parting hand that we shall
meet no more until we meet on the echoless shore of
eternity!

CHAPTER III.

LIFE'S TURNING POINT.

Who can be loyal and neutral
At the same time? No man.
Shakspeare.

We fight for our liberty, our country and its free institutions.

Talk with Recruiting Officer—Incidents of Enlistment
—My Mother's Bible—At Home—Strange Presentiments
—Final Departure—The Gallant Thirteen—From
Pittsburg to Camp Copeland—Roundheads and French
Furloughs—Incidents in Camp—Last Ordeal.

TALK WITH RECRUITING OFFICER.

I HAVE now brought up this record of personal events
to the most momentous period of my life—the most
momentous, because the incidents I am about to relate
were of a character to change the whole course and
fashion of my subsequent history—I refer, of course, to
my enlistment.

Monday morning, Feb. 29, 1864, I left home for
Greenville, designing while there to institute some
means to get into the service. Before starting I mentioned the purpose of my visit to town to the family,

no member of which entertained a thought that this would be a decisive day to me, in regard to my ultimate enlistment. In previous chapters the reader has been made acquainted with the persistent and systematic opposition with which my desire to go into the army was confronted from first to last by my friends at home. Entreaty, arguments and parental authority had been used. My extreme youthfulness was a crowning argument employed on all occasions, and my father never gave up the contest until he saw that by maintaining his position to keep me at home, he would not only interfere with my plain conviction of duty, but would possibly embitter my whole future life.

While at Greenville, on that eventful Monday, I met a recruiting officer of my acquaintance, of whom I asked this question:

"Do you think, sir, I would pass an examination if I were to enlist?"

"I don't know," was the answer.

I then said to him: "I want to enlist, and if you will put me through, I will go."

To make the subject understood I will here state that the office of the Provost Marshal for our district was at Meadville, twenty-six miles by rail from Greenville. I had no money wherewith to pay expenses. After a little reflection the officer expressed a belief that I would pass, and kindly proposed to take me to Meadville, and also have me sent home again if I failed to go through the ordeal of examination.

INCIDENTS OF ENLISTMENT.

On the same day we took the cars for Meadville, at which place I was enrolled a few hours later. It was in the afternoon of the second day after my arrival, that I was called upon to pass through the first ordeal in presence of the examining surgeon, Dr. Baskin. Many others had preceeded me in this examination; and some of these, as they came out of the surgeon's office, I closely interrogated in regard to the tests that were applied. I soon discovered that unless the applicant weighed 110 pounds, he would, in all probability be rejected.

Several times, during those memorable days of trial and apprehension, I repaired to places where scales were to be found, to see how nearly my weight would correspond with the government standard. Each trial of this kind resulted in the conviction, that unless strategy were summoned to my aid I would return home rejected, and sadly dissappointed. At last my name was called, and with many misgivings I appeared in the presence of the surgeon. There were some points on which I passed very well. I remember that in measuring my chest, and in noting the power of my lungs in respiration which increased the girth of the chest from 28 to 34 inches, he said I would never die of consumption. After running and leaping about the room for a time, to give proof of personal activity, the critical and doubtful part of the trial came, the part, indeed, which had, by way of anticipation, shaken me with a feeling of uncertainty and dread. The doctor invited me to take my place on the platform of the scales to ascertain my weight. The proper peas were adjusted, indicating 110 pounds. Whatever my apprehensions may have been, I suppressed all outward display of feeling, and bringing into requision all the address and moral courage I possessed, I leaped, rather than stepped upon the platform, expecting to see the beam rebound under the quick pressure. To my dismay no such event occured. The beam remained immovably in its place. I had, however, taken the precaution at the proper time, to regard the surgeon with an expression, so full of anxiety to carry myself successfully through the examination, that, as I stood on the scales, in a state of terrible suspense, he authorized an assistant to record my weight at 110 pounds.

Thus far I had gained a decided victory, but another sharp ordeal awaited me. Along with a number of other applicants, I was ushered into the room of the provost marshal, Capt. Derickson. Among the new recruits in the marshal's office, there were three who, although smaller than their companions, were all larger than myself. Apparently conscious of their bodily inferiority, these three volunteers placed themselves at the foot of the column, to await the verdict of the marshal. I felt sure that if I joined them my cause was hopelessly lost. Inspired by a sudden resolution, I stepped boldly between two applicants who, though not greatly taller than myself, were sure, in my opinion, to pass muster with the officer. If an observer had been at the rear of the column he would have noticed, perhaps, that in giving a fictitious stature to my person, the heels of my boots were elevated perceptibly from the floor. The three boys to whom I have referred were promptly dismissed and sent home. Glancing along the column, as it remained, the Captain fixed, for a moment, his penetrating eye on me. Unabashed by this official inspection, I reciprocated by directing my gaze on him, in such a determined manner that it seemed to baffle his scrutiny. Immediately afterward, all the recruits in line, including myself, were invited to hold up our hands while the oath was administered. The reader need not be told that my hand went up with remarkable quickness on that occasion. Thus was I sworn into service, on the first day of March, 1864.

MY MOTHER'S BIBLE.

After my induction into the service I received a permit to return home for a couple of days. This brief interval of time was occupied in visiting friends, and in making preparation for my departure. An incident which occurred on my way home will never perish from my memory. Just about half way between Greenville and my father's residence I saw my mother approaching along the road. It was her custom to ride when visiting town, but at this time she was walking. As she came near me, I saw in her face the traces of mental suffering; tears were trickling down her cheeks. When she saw me a smile of glad recognition lighted up her features. I was anxious to know the cause which had induced her, in her lapsed state of health, to undergo the fatigue of walking to town.

"I am going there," said she, with an accent of motherly tenderness which I shall never forget, " to purchase a Bible for you, my son, that it may be your guide and counsellor, in camp and on the march, when you are far away from home."

She had already learned that I was an enlisted soldier, and with a mother's anxiety, she was executing her plans for my comfort, and especially for my religious training, when away from under the parental roof.

" I am glad to know, mother," said I, taking out a volume and showing it to her with pride, " that I have stolen a march on you in this matter. Knowing that you desired it, and believing, also, it would be of great benefit to me, I bought a copy of the Bible to-day in Greenville. Here it is, mother."

A flood of conscious joy seemed to overspread her countenance. Her heart was full of unutterable happiness, and every feature seemed to reflect it. I make the honest confession here that I purchased the book. not so much to benefit myself, as to give comfort and satisfaction to my mother. Readers of this work have examined it so far with but little attention if they have concluded that the obligations of Christianity possessed any great influence with me at this time. Such was not the case. True, I had been surrounded with religious advantages of no common order. My parents were both devotedly pious; and their example and their admonitions were such as would naturally flow from such a source; yet the thoughtlessness and waywardness of my disposition, combined with the recklessness which commonly attaches to the young, had too often withdrawn my mind from the contemplation of religious subjects. Still, young and thoughtless as I was, the expression of joy in my mother's face when her eye fell upon the inspired volume in my hands thrilled me to the very depths of my being; and were I to live to the age of the oldest patriarch. that meeting with my dear mother and the circumstances connected with it, will live and bloom in fadeless remembrance.

AT HOME.

The two days allotted to me on furlough were busy ones indeed. My blanket, haversack and canteen were made to display my name, or the initials thereof. A variety of delicacies, such as a mother only knows how to prepare, were stored away for my future use; and the other members of the family vied with each other in showing me those delicate and affectionate attentions which give strength and grace to the sacred bond of relationship. How quickly the hours flew by on golden wings, never to return. It may be that now and then a feeling of regret for the farewells of the morrow would flit vaguely through my mind, giving me a sense of uneasiness and unrest, but a moment later the compensation would come in the thought that I had given myself as a free offering to my country, and that my highest happiness as well as my most sacred duty would be associated with its defense, so long as armed traitors were seeking to destroy it.

STRANGE PRESENTIMENTS.

At length the day came, and the hour, in which I was destined to move out from the charmed circle at home, leaving a vacant place at the table and around the family altar. It was an impressive day to me, the incidents of which are inscribed on the tablet of memory, never to be effaced! I took the parting hand with friends that day, whom I was never to see again; but as I parted with them. no premonition came to me that before I should return from the gory field of war they would be removed to the shadowy realm of the grave. There were two, however, my mother and my old employer, Mr. Walker, whose hands, as they grasped mine, with an endearing and lingering pressure, thrilled me with a strange and indescribable feeling, such as I had never felt before. If I failed, at the time, to attach any special importance to this magnetic or spiritual sensation, I had occasion to recall it afterward, with the liveliest emotion, when, amid strange and hostile scenes, far away from the home of my childhood, the news came to me that my patron and my mother had passed away from the tribulations of earth. I knew, then, that the electric thrill which, months before, I experienced at the moment of parting, was a presentiment that the farewell then spoken was final and irreversible, so far as earth is concerned, and that no reunion would follow until the light of eternity would break on that hallowed scene.

FINAL DEPARTURE.

Early in March, after my first furlough expired, I reported at the provost marshal's office in Meadville, and the following day we took the cars for Pittsburgh, via Greenville.

The train was heavily laden with "boys in blue," and, as we came into Greenville, the station was crowded with men, women and children. As the sun burst forth and cast her resplendent rays upon this scene, and while the band was filling the air with sweet music, the train slowly moved on. One thought of home, one thought of its loved associations, one glance at the place where my happy boyhood was spent, and all faded from my view.

As the velocity of the train increased peals of laughter were ringing in all parts of the car; but, alas! of that merry band many are now sleeping with the silent, silent dead. "Rest, noble heroes, in your graves unknown; from toil and trouble ye are free."

As we passed the crowded stations loyal hearts would cheer us as the defenders of peace and liberty.

THE GALLANT THIRTEEN.

For some reason, and it may be a superstitious one, the number thirteen has often been regarded as ill-omened and unfortunate. From the immediate community of which I had been a member, there were thirteen of us who enlisted in the service. Whatever may have been the feelings of the others in reference to their ultimate return to their friends, I may here say for myself, that I had the strongest conviction, from first to last, that I would be among the survivors; and, when friends would dissuade me from enlistment by predicting for me a cruel death, I laughed at their fears and spoke lightly of their prophecies.

The melancholy confession, however, must be made, that whatever good fortune was in store for any of us, there were but four of the original number who survived the war, and but one (Cassius Fell) who came home unwounded. The names of the four are as follows: Cassius Fell, Horace Granger, A. D. Homer, and myself. The nine to whom war was fatal were: Abner Woods, E. W. Keck, Simon Smith, Samuel Smith, Harvey Smith, Israel Gongeware, G. A. Blank, Thomas Shaner, and John Vanderpool. Three only of the thirteen were not members of my company, viz: E. W. Keck, and Simon and Harvey Smith. In point of time Mr. Keck was the first to enlist. Three of the nine who perished, as will be seen by the names, were brothers. Such, in part at least, is the history of this little band of soldiers, with whom I was identified, through weary months of peril and privation, in the Army of the Potomac.

FROM PITTSBURGH TO CAMP COPELAND.

At length we reached Pittsburgh. Here everything was in motion. Everywhere were to be seen groups and squads of soldiers; for they were pouring into this general rendezvous from every direction. After wading through the crowded streets, we reached the "Soldier's Rest," where we rested for the night, and, in the morning, took the train for Braddock, and marched from there to

CAMP COPELAND.

This camp is eleven miles from Pittsburg, situated on an eminent bluff, and from this elevation you have a commanding view of the surrounding country. On either side stretches forth the iron rail, over which the lightning trains pass with impetuous velocity, while to the southwest flows the waters of the Monongahela. I passed weary hours watching the locomotive as it sped along, or watching the steamboats quietly making their way up and down the river.

Reader, we will now take a view of the interior of the camp. As you enter, to the right is the headquarters building, with the nation's flag proudly floating over it. Beyond this, the medical depot, the book store, and the sutler's shop. The attraction of this last named place was so great that a crowd was constantly congregated there, purchasing pies, cakes and other eatables. It was suspected that these articles were not genuine, but composed of inferior and adulterated substances—in short, that they were " drugged." In this way a larger percentage was made than if the articles had been made of genuine material. A remonstrance was sent in against the sutlers. Accordingly, an investigation was made by four physicians of Pittsburgh, who pronounced their pies, cakes and so forth. drugged. The hospital showed the effects of this nefarious practice.

To the left and oposite the headquarters were field tents, and beyond this three lines of barracks. In the rear of these were vaious buildings—artists' rooms, cook houses, guard-house, invalid barracks, offices, etc. These were the prominent features of Camp Copeland.

ROUNDHEADS AND FRENCH FURLOUGHS.

In March, 1864, the 100th Regiment Pennsylvania Volunteers, known as the "Roundheads," returning from veteran furlough, pitched tents and encamped for several days alongside of our camp, and, as the guard had no authority to prevent them from passing in and out at leisure, this afforded the inmates of our camp a splendid opportunity to take "French furloughs," which they were not slow in doing; for many availed themselves of this opportunity by placing the figures "100" on their caps. They could thus pass the guard unsuspected and unmolested.

But it was no wonder many were tired of this camp, for it was completely flooded with mud and filth of every description. The very air seemed thickened with noxious vapors, which arose from the stench of decomposing matter.

Reader, this is not an overdrawn picture, but every feature is colored with the pencil of truth.

INCIDENTS IN CAMP.

At the time of which I am writing Camp Copeland contained between two thousand and three thousand persons distributed around miscellaneously. Some were officers, many others were new recruits like myself, waiting for the final disposition that was to be made of them. The guards who were taken from the Invalid Corps established their cordon around the entire encampment; but, situated as they were, a rod apart, they were unable, as intimated above, to restrain the boys from frequent escapes. It was an easy matter, as my own experience will testify, to conceal myself, in the dusky twilight, on one side of a wagon, while the unsuspecting guard was on the other. In this manner I made my way out several times, without detection; but some of the soldiers were not so fortunate. The punishments for this offense, and for others of a graver character, were prompt and severe.

There were four kinds of dicipline administered to the boys, when found guilty. For the more common violations of military law, imprisonment in the guard house, was the usual penalty. The barrel punishment was somewhat novel and exciting, and not at all agreeable to the victim. A brief description of this form of correction may be deemed necessary to its proper understanding. The entire head of an empty barrel is taken out, while from the other end the central piece only is removed, leaving quite an orifice. The barrel then is placed down over the culpit so that his head will project from the central opening, which has been mentioned. In this way the arms of the poor fellow are pressed rigidly against his sides, while at the other extremity his power of locomotion is greatly embarrased on account of the compulsory shortness of his strides. Accoutred in this style the culpit is compelled to walk around, exciting the laughter and ridicule of all who witness the strange spectacle. On other occasions the guilty party is forced to shoulder a heavy piece of. timber; and thus freighted he is made to keep step with the guard, often for hours without intermission, while sweltering in the heat of the sun. The thumb punishment embraces all that is fearful, inhuman and horrible. A small cord of extreme tenacity, is tied tightly around each thumb, while the other end is fastened to a strong spike, which is driven into the exterior wall of the guard house, some distance above the head of the delinquent. In some cases the victim is compelled to stand on tiptoe. In this unnatural attitude, the strain on his thumbs and arms, as well as on his whole bodily organism, is intense and exquisitely painful.

It happened one day that a recruit, who had enlisted for the Roundheads and was here waiting to be sent to his regiment, was found guilty of some misdemeanor, and the thumb punishment was applied. While the poor fellow was suffering the tortures of the inquisition, a sympathizing soldier, belonging to the Roundheads, clandestinely cut him down and hurried him off in the direction of his regiment, which was encamped on the other part of the bluffs. An immediate excitement in the camp was the result. Hundreds of enlisted men, whose sympathies were actively with the victim, and against the abuses of tyranny, followed the two in a tumultuous throng. Observing that the crowd were forcing their way, in contempt of authority, past the guards, the officers hastened to obstruct their course; but the mutiny was in full tide, bearing down all opposition. One gentleman, with shoulder-strap attachments, who was taking a prominent part in quieting the riot, was struck several times by his assailants. At last, when all other means had failed, the order was given, and a volley of musketry was fired into the advancing throng.

Unaware, at the moment, that the guns had been loaded with blank cartridges, the boys thus fired on were seized with a sudden panic, and turning round in consternation fled in every possible direction. The scene that ensued was simply indescribable. For half a minute, or less, nothing was seen but an undefined mass of human forms rushing, wriggling and quivering, in every attitude of distress and confusion that could be assumed. Scores of the men fell sprawling in the execrable mud that abounded in the camp, and before they had time to rise, dripping with filth, many others, somewhat less unfortunate, tumbled in layers upon their prostrate bodies.

Some time elapsed before order was restored in camp, and when this desirable condition was established, it was discovered that the victim of arbitrary punishment and his friend had escaped to the 100th

5

regiment. A formal demand was made by our officers for their return, but it was peremptorily refused. Official communications on the subject passed backward and forward between the opposing camps, and at length the mutual hostility became so intense that the Roundheads sent their mortal defiance and drew up in order of battle. Ultimately, however, better counsels prevailed, and order again reigned in Warsaw.

It was not all recreation at Camp Copeland. We had our regular periods for drill, and a part of each Monday was occupied in submitting our military quarters to general inspection. Meantime, much suffering and disease were experienced. From exposure and from eating poisonous food, and from the measles, also, which broke out among us, the deaths some days reached as high as seventy-five. This was terrible mortality, in view of the comparatively small number of persons from whom the victims were taken.

A festive scene was always presented when the mail was in process of distribution. A soldier can appreciate better, perhaps, than any other man, the value of news from home. When it was understood that the mail had arrived, the boys would instantly mass themselves at the appointed place, and as each name was called that was found in the address of some letter, the liveliest excitement followed. Sometimes, the welcome missive, as it fell from the hands of the official, would pass from hand to hand for many yards, over a sea of upturned faces, until it reached the person to whom it was directed. Soldiers have very vivid imaginations, and on occasions of this kind, when a very large letter, as was often the case, was finding its way overhead to its destination, it was cheered in its progress by a salutation like the following:

"There comes a blanket from home, and the next one I see is a regular feather bed."

My bunk-mates in this camp were Cassius Fell, G. A. Blank and Samuel Smith, of whom mention has been made elsewhere. Blank was afterward killed in the battle of the Wilderness, and Smith was reported missing in another engagement.

PASSING THE LAST ORDEAL.

On the 22d day of March, I was to appear in presence of the paymaster, to receive the first month's pay, in connection with the first installment of government bounty, amounting in all to seventy-three dollars. After having passed the first ordeal with the Examiner, and the second also with the Provost Marshal, I concluded that this third one would amount to a form simply, and that my entrance into the army was, therefore, an assured fact.

Just before going in, I had a little conversation with an acquaintance by the name of Leach, who had failed to pass this final examination, and who was now awaiting his discharge in order to be sent home. Having been under eighteen years of age, he sought to supply this deficiency by resorting to falsehood; but his fiction had not been matured properly, and on being asked by the Pay Master to give the date of his birth, he hesitated and blundered, until his falsehood was thoroughly exposed, and his rejection was an inevitable consequence. The fate of my friend, when reported to me, put me upon my guard. In order to win, I found it would be necessary to call myself eighteen years of age, although the truth would not have supported any such declaration; and in anticipation of questions similar to those which had ruined the cause of young Leach, I had prepared in my own mind a series of answers which would save me from hesitation, and make one fiction coincide with another. I was resolved, however, that if the Pay Master required me to make these false statements under oath, I would back down as gracefully as I could, and go home quietly, without the sin of perjury on my soul. As the event shows, I got along with this delicate matter much better than I expected.

On entering the Pay Master's presence, I confess that a feeling of trepidation and even alarm made me fairly tremble. Were all my efforts to find a place in the army of the Republic to be neutralized by this last tribunal, before which I was now arraigned? The first question was direct and searching:

"Mr. Sallada, how old are you?"

"Eighteen," was the brief and cool answer. That was enough, and that was all, except that before I left I received a large amount of greenbacks; and then I went away rejoicing.

On the 24th of the same month a large number of

us convened near the railroad, waiting for the cars to transport us to our final destination. While there, a man of very gentlemanly appearance came on the scene, bringing with him a large assortment of watches and cheap jewelry. The boys were flush with money, and felt rich. The desire to make purchases proved to be an epidemic, and in less than a quarter of an hour the stock of the cunning trader was largely diminished. It was discovered afterward that the watches and jewels were a pitiful cheat, and that the boys had been duped by an itinerant scoundrel. So much for experience.

CHAPTER IV.

ARMY INCIDENTS.

Hark, borne upon the Southern breeze
Are whispers breathed above the trees:
Be of good cheer, your cause belongs
To him who can avenge your wrongs;
Leave it to Him, our Lord.

ENROUTE TO WASHINGTON—GOING TO REGIMENT—OLD REBEL CAMP—ROUND OF DUTIES—RECREATION IN CAMP—REMOVAL AND PROMOTION—MARCH TO CHANCELLORSVILLE—BATTLE OF THE WILDERNESS—IN THE REBEL LINES—HONEY ADVENTURE—CHARGED BY REBEL CAVALRY.

ENROUTE TO WASHINGTON.

THE close of the last chapter left us at Camp Copeland on the 24th day of March, 1864, waiting for the cars which were to take us to the seat of war. The regiment in which I had enlisted, and to which I was now about to be transferred, was the 57th Pennsylvania Veteran Volunteers, 2nd Brigade, 3d Division, 2nd Army Corps, commanded by Gen'l Hancock. I was to become a member of Company B., of this regiment. So far in my desire to enlist I had triumphed over all opposition at home; and afterward, I had in order to gain my point, encountered grave and severe trials, which, if the object to be obtained had been less important, would have filled me with discouragement, and driven me finally from my purpose. If, on this particular day my heart was swelling with a feeling of pride, as a result of the personal victories I thus far had achieved, I am satisfied that the indulgent reader will pardon me.

In passing through Harrisburg, on our way to the regiment, we received a patriotic welcome from the citizens; and this was the case at all the places through which we passed. On all hands the loyal people were glad to do honor to their country's defenders. At last we reached Washington, where we stopped for the night at the Soldiers' Rest. Next day we marched to the Capitol, where I had the happiness to see, for the first time, many of the dignitaries of our country. Among these were President Lincoln, Secretaries Stanton, Chase and Seward. Besides these there were other high government officials, including senators and representatives and foreign ministers. By these, and by many of the common citizens, we were greeted with demonstrations of respect, and even of enthusiasm.

Sometime before the war my political sentiments, if a youth of twelve or thirteen can be supposed to entertain such sentiments, were of the Democratic school. On this subject, as well as on others, it was natural for me to inherit my father's opinions; and such was the case. In 1856 I was an ardent friend of Buchanan, the Democratic candidate for President, although I was but ten years of age at the time; but at the close of his administration, when, either from cowardice or treason, he was yielding up the government and the liberties of the people into the hands of their implacable foes, my eyes were opened, young as I was, and I became as zealous upon the other side as I had formerly been in my Democratic convictions. I had learned to love the character of President Lincoln, and as I looked upon his homely, though noble countenance, I was more than ever impressed with the belief that, like Washington before him, he was indeed the father of his country.

GOING TO REGIMENT.

We then marched down to the wharf, got aboard the transports, and after a short voyage landed in Alexandria. Here we met with a warm reception (or rather our greenbacks did) by the female pie and cake peddlers, who swarmed about us, almost compelling us to purchase their eatables. We then marched to the Soldier's Rest, and the next day marched to the Arsenal and received our arms and equipments, then returned to the Soldier's Rest. The next day we marched to Convalescent Camp, and from there took the train for Brandy Station, Va., and a few hours' march from Brandy Station brought us to the regiment.

It was on the 29th of March that I reached my company. The first thing in order was the erection of a tent, and in this work I was assisted by my companions, Blank and Fell. We labored assiduously for three days before the work was completed. We then enjoyed a refreshing repose for one night within the limits of our new home, anticipating many more enjoyments of the same kind before leaving the scene of so much toil, but on the fourth morning we were ordered to vacate our new premises and march with the regiment to another location.

OLD REBEL CAMP.

On the 2d day of April we arrived at an old rebel camp, where we took up our quarters. Here we were in the very citadel of war, for on all sides of us, stretching away for many miles, the tents belonging to the Army of the Potomac dotted the earth. Here, within this vast area of country, was marshaled the most formidable array of soldiers that had ever marched to victory on this continent. It was an inspiring thought to me, that this grand body of men had not been called to the field to fight for a despotism or to elevate a tyrant to power, but to defend the integrity of the old Union against the Slaveholder's Rebellion.

The camp we were now occupying had been abandoned some time before by the retreating rebels. It was laid out somewhat imperfectly and irregularly, still it answered very well the purpose to which we devoted it. The large log chapel connected·with it was quite a feature, for, besides the religious services which were conducted within its walls by our chaplain. it was the scene of social and literary entertainments, which helped us to pass away the otherwise monotonous hours. In the absence of the "girls whom we had left behind," and in memory of home scenes never to be forgotten, we, that is the young soldiers, would frequently gather about the door of the chapel after the adjournment of meeting, and while some of us would personate the absent ladies, the others, as gallant beaux, would step up to them and do the honors of the occasion, by offering them their arms, to escort them home. Sometimes, as it is among scenes away from war, the ladies, or those who purported to be such, would start back with a contemptuous toss of their heads, and repulse every gentlemanly attention. It is certain that one of the worst elements of military life, is the withdrawal of the common soldier from the society of the other sex. It is not strange, therefore, that while suffering from this privation, the boys should improvise such sports as would most forcibly remind them of the associations of home.

ROUND OF DUTIES.

The routine of daily duty, during these times, was severe, and often very tedious, embracing a whole day. To give the uninitiated reader some idea of the grave responsibilities which devolve upon the private soldier, I will here present the daily order of service for several days, commencing with April 12th. On that day there was corps dress parade, continuing all day. On the following day we had corps review in the forenoon, and in the afternoon battalion drill and brigade dress parade. It was on that day I saw Generals Meade and Hancock, the former being in command of the army. Next day battalion drill, and the next pickets relieved. April 19th, division review in the forenoon, and in the afternoon battalion drill and brigade dress parade, at which Generals Kearney and Ward, and Hays of our regiment, were present. On the 15th, some days before this, 10th corps picket relieved. April 21st, target shooting, brigade drill, and dress parade. April 22d was a great day, for we had corps review, with Generals Grant and Ward to inspect us.

Thus it will be perceived, that the common, every-day life of a soldier, is crowded with toil, hardship and rigid discipline. Novices, who think that going to war is an easy pastime, are indulging a sad mistake, as thousands have found it, to their cost.

RECREATIONS IN CAMP.

In another place I have spoken of the religious services held in the chapel, which included preaching and prayer meetings. We also devoted time here to the cultivation of our musical powers; besides these, we had lectures, patriotic meetings and concerts, all of which tended to lift us above the dead level of military existence.

We had a diversity of sports and recreations; in fact, our ingenuity was taxed to devise means for relaxation and enjoyment. We had a large ball, composed of rubber, from which we extracted much sport and merriment; with it we played the game of football. It caused a vast amount of fun when some luckless fellow, full of earnestness, would launch forth his foot to kick the ball, but before his foot, though it went straight for the mark, could reach the desired object, the ball would be kicked away by feet more active than his own and he would measure his length on the ground, to the infinite amusement of the spectators. He found that kicking into vacancy, with all his might, was attended with disaster, like the recoil of a gun when it is overcharged. It is apt to kick back and do injury. The merry laughs which often resulted from our rubber ball exercises, were loud enough to startle the natives.

Those of us who were posted in the game of ten-pin. and I was among the number, as the reader knows, were anxious to invent some substitute for it. At length we discovered a plan that would work. A destructive implement of war, called a spherical case shell, weighing about twelve pounds, would answer for the required ball. Dangerous as they were, a number of these were employed for the purpose. Alleys of the rudest formation were made, and in a short time we were up to our eyes in this new play, drawing from it an immense amount of interest and good humor. We knew that a very slight cause might explode one of these engines of death with which we were playing so carelessly, but lives were cheap in the army, and the fear of danger, or sudden death, was too seldom in our thoughts, and we went on

with the exciting diversion regardless of consequences.
On a certain occasion, one of these ten-pin shells,
filled with elements of destruction, resented the violence with which it was handled, by bursting, suddenly and awfully, to the horror of all who saw it. A
quick, sulphurous flame shot from it, mingled with
that appalling sound which is the signal of its disrup-
tion; and then flying bullets, and fragments of the
parting shell, hurtled through the air, carrying dismay
to every heart. It was singular, indeed, under the circumstances, that none of us were injured by this
unexpected explosion, but it taught us the danger of
playing with these deadly instruments. It has been
my opinion since then, that spherical case shells are
not good ten-pin balls.

REMOVAL AND PROMOTION.

On the 26th of April, our regiment vacated the
rebel camp, which we had occupied as winter quarters.
We now pitched our tents in an open field. On the
29th I was detailed on the field staff as Orderly. I
also carried the regimental mail, and had the post
besides of Regimental Marker. The duties of this last
position required me to stand at one extremity of the
regiment, holding a marker, or small flag, corresponding with another flag, held by some other person at
the other end of the line. By this means the officers
were enabled to keep their line perfect.

MARCH TO CHANCELLORSVILLE.

On the third of May we struck our tents and prepared to march, and at half-past eleven at night we took up our line of march. We marched all that night and the following day, and at night encamped on the battle ground of Chancellorsville. About nine o'clock at night I was sent with explicit orders to have the camp fires extinguished immediately, as the enemy was reported to be in our vicinity. The next morning I was satisfying my curiosity by examining and comparing the differently shaped skulls as they lay strewn over the old battle ground of Chancellorsville.

BATTLE OF THE WILDERNESS.

On the fifth of May, and about twelve o'clock, the two great armies came in contact with each other, and the battle raged furiously. About two o'clock our corps, under the command of Major General Winfield S. Hancock, was ordered to form and attack with Getty's division. At first the attack of Hancock and Getty was successful, but Mott's division of Hancock's corps was overpowered and gave way, thus forming a temporary breach in our line. Then my brigade, of Birney's division, rushed in to repair the broken line, commanded by Brigadier General Alexander H. Hayes, who was shot dead while leading us. We sustained no greater loss that day than Hayes; he was a bold and intrepid officer, and Coppee, in his Life and Campaigns of General Grant, says:

"He was frank, quick and energetic, the model of a commander."

We loved him because he not only commanded us, but led us. Thus ended the career of our noble commander. During the afternoon my Colonel, P. Sides, was wounded in the arm. He requested me to go with him to the general hospital and take care of him. I declined, for I did not want to go; I wanted to stay with my regiment. Early in the afternoon my bunk mate, G. A. Blank, was killed, and as I thought of the lifeless form who, in the vigor and prime of youth gave his life for his country, I thought of the many happy hours we had spent together in the school-room and in each other's society at home.

One more buried
  Beneath the sod,
One more standing
  Before his God.

We should not weep
  That he has gone;
With us 'tis night,
  With him 'tis morn!

Night coming on closed the carnage of the day. The next morning the battle was renewed with fresh vigor. Volley after volley, and cheer after cheer rent the air as the surging tide of war swept on.

But, reader, I do not propose writing a history or giving minutely the details of the battles through which I passed, only presenting the most illustrative incidents that I witnessed.

IN THE REBEL LINES.

On the eighth day of May, while the regiment was on a forced march, I went forth in pursuit of water, the want of which was oppressing me. Being ignorant in regard to the face of the country, I had not gone far before the discovery was made that I was within the rebel lines. This was a new experience, and although my love of adventure was in those days a dominant feeling, I cannot say that this one was altogether delightful. As secretly and as speedily as possible I retired to cover in a swamp near by, on which grew a dense thicket of laurel. While concealed here, I was surprised by the presence of another Union soldier, who had for the same reason that influenced me, sought refuge in this hiding place. Though we were utter strangers, it did not take us long after the first surprise was over to become thoroughly acquainted with each other. The bond now between us was very strong, for we were companions in a common peril, and what was safety to one promised to be the salvation of the other.

The afternoon was well advanced when we found ourselves involved in this fearful danger. We freely consulted together in reference to plans of escape. On all sides we were environed by active and watchful enemies, and any attempt to leave our retreat by daylight would be disastrous. My companion seemed to be very hopeless in regard to our chances of escape, and intimated that it would be the most prudent course to surrender, and thus throw ourselves upon the mercy of our foes. I could not take this view of the subject, for the war had been in progress long enough to develop the natural brutality of the Confederates toward their prisoners. I had heard horrible things concerning the prison hells of the South, and I was in no hurry to transfer myself to any of these places. If I went there, it would not be a voluntary act.

My plan was to wait in our place of concealment until after nightfall, when, as the sky would be moonless, we would emerge from the thicket, and proceed on our hands and knees between the vidette posts of the enemy, myself in advance all the while. If halted on our perilous way by the sharp question of "who goes there?" we would instantly rise and respond "friends in gray."

We would then accept whatever chances were left to us in so dread an alternative. My friend had many misgivings as to the feasibility of this plan, but finally acceded to it, hoping for the best.

While we were yet consulting in low tones so as not to be overheard by any casual listener, a rebel general and his staff were seen riding past, only a few hundred yards away. A sharp shooter from our position could easily have taken him down, but we had no arms, and in any case such a course would have been rash and suicidal. To say that we were startled at this unexpected sight would hardly be an exaggeration.

My heart smote with violence as I crouched closely among the bushes, glaring out like an animal at bay upon the passing cavalcade. Having reached a point a little distance beyond us they halted for a moment, and then one of the officer's aids was seen to separate from the main body, and move off on a different road from that on which the officer and those with him were proceeding. When this danger was passed and our minds were liberated from the strain to which they had been subjected, we resumed our consultations, and having finished it waited for the protecting mantle of darkness to cover us.

It was a splendid night for an adventure like ours, where the utmost secresy was required. There was neither moon nor stars, for the sky was draped in mourning. Masses of clouds swept over it's face, giving the color of blackness to all earthly objects.

Emerging from our place of concealment, we cautiously took our way in the darkness, never pausing until we supposed ourselves in the immediate vicinity of the rebel picket lines. I was in the lead, and retained this perilous position to the last. Before dropping to our hands and knees I suggested to my friend the vital importance of guarding all our movements with scrupulous care. An awkward stumble or the mere breaking of a dry stick under our weight would probably prove fatal to our enterprise, bringing swift punishment down upon our heads. Now came the thrilling part of our adventure. On we groped in thick darkness, our hearts palpitating the while with suspense and excitement. I do not know how far we had progressed on this uncertain and dangerous course when the very thing happened to me against which I had an hour before impressibly warned my companion; by some dreadful mischance for which I cannot account my hand pressed a decayed stick with such force as to produce a quick, crackling sound loud enough to be heard some distance away, and in the same instant the report of a gun fell upon my ear with sudden and appalling distinctness. We stopped short, and the perspiration stood in clammy drops on my forehead. It was a moment of real agony, for I was certain that the accidental noise I had caused had betrayed us to the enemy. I was almost in the act of springing to my feet to answer the summons of the picket in the best way of which I was capable, when another report off to the left held me in breathless suspense. Soon a recurrence of shots, some of which were off to the right and others to the left, proved to me that the Union and rebel pickets were engaged in firing at each other. What a blessed relief we realized when the truth flashed upon us. The reports from the right were, as I naturally inferred, from the Union lines, and those on the left were from the rebels. This very circumstance made me comprehend for the first time our true position in reference to both armies. Instead of approaching the rebel pickets as we believed, we had been groping in the rear of their lines, and moving parallel with them. Thus corrected in our course we turned sharply off to the left, and moved off into the darkness, still groping on hands and knees. All at once the dead silence which reigned around was broken by a sharp click near at hand, followed by the exclamation: "Halt! Who goes there?"

Believing that I was still in the confederate lines, I sprang to my feet, intending to say: "Friends in Gray." I did not, however, say what I had intended; but in the confusion and terror of the moment, aided perhaps, by my spontaneous loyalty, I exclaimed: "Friends in true blue!"

The deed was done, and I could not now recall it; but I had done without knowing it, the best thing that could have been done under the circumstances. I was not long in perceiving, dark as it was, that we had been halted by Union pickets; and it only remained for us to identify ourselves to escape from any suspicions that might attach to a couple of midnight adventurers. The corporal of the guard was sent for, by whom we were escorted to headquarters, where we gave satisfactory evidence of our identity, and were released.

I afterward learned that the danger we were in of being shot that night by Union pickets was greatly increased by the fact that the strictest orders had been given them to shoot down, remorselessly, every moving object in their vicinity. Some little time before a a vigorous rebel, ensconced in a hog skin, had approached our line, on all fours, in the obscurity of the night. Having been taken for a respectable swine, engaged in his professional pursuits, he was permitted to come within a few feet of the picket, and then hurling himself with all his power on that astonished gentleman, he succeeded in disarming and holding him until a number of confederates, secreted in the background came up, on being signaled, and carried off their victim in triumph. On that night half a dozen or more of our pickets were relieved in this original way before the ingenious trick was discovered. It was this circumstance which induced the officer commanding to issue the strict order to which I have referred.

HONEY ADVENTURE.

From headquarters I went to the Division Hospital near by. I had not as yet rejoined my regiment. Near the hospital I fell in with three others who, like myself, were in immediate need of rations. We concluded to start out together on a foraging expedition. Not long after starting we came to a rebel farm house, which was, at the time, occupied by an old man and woman, and three girls.

As was customary in such cases, we asked for something to eat. The answer was that the farmer's stores had just been cleaned out by the Union cavalry; and as a consequence, there was nothing to bestow upon us, for love or money. Observing a number of beehives near the house, and believing that the possession of these hives afforded the only chance of relief to our empty stomachs, one of the boys, a little more reckless, perhaps, than the others, snatched up one of the desired articles, and ran away with it at the top of his speed. Noting this maneuver, the rest of the foraging

party, myself along with them, went in swift pursuit;
and overtaking our predatory friend in advance, assisted him on his way by relieving him of his load.

Alternately carrying the rich prize we finally reached
a place of safety, when, pausing in our rapid flight we
began to help ourselves to large quantities of the
honey. Our stomachs being empty, the sacharine
substance soon began to develop symptoms of terrible
nausea. Perhaps, in all the army of the Potomac,
there was not on that day, a sicker set of fellows than
ourselves. If we had taken doses of lobelia, or tartar
emetic, the result would not have been more trying to
our nerves. We lay around for a while groaning in
concert, anathematizing the rebel honey until the atmosphere was fairly blue with our maledictions. At
length, forlorn and sick and uttering groans by the
way, which were audible for some distance, we stag-
gered back, in a state of complete demoralization, to
the Division Hospital, where our systems were righted
up by medical assistance. On this excursion we discovered that honey is not the best thing in the world
to alleviate the pangs of hunger.

CHARGED BY REBEL CAVALRY.

Next morning, after my wasted energies had been
recruited by medicine, but not by food, I started with
another party of foragers in search, again, of provisions. We were four in number, two of the company
being brothers. Sometime after we left camp a farm-
house attracted our attention, and to it we proceeded

without hesitation. Arriving there we found that the occupants were two elderly people, of opposite sexes, and two girls, possibly their daughters. Before reaching the house I noticed that it stood in an open space skirted on two sides by timber, one body of which stood in the direction of the hospital from which we had come.

Describing our situation and enquiring, as usual, for something to eat, the tenants of the house answered as we had been answered the day before. The inevitable cavalry had been scouring the country carrying devastation into every hamlet and neighborhood. While some of us were conversing with the farmer, one of the brothers, who had been prowling around the house with an eye to the main chance, had succeeded in capturing a chicken, of the rooster variety, which he brought to us in great triumph. While holding the prize before us, the family became very much depressed on account of the liberty that had been taken with their poultry, and to make the occasion more interesting the girls went off into a paroxysm of tears, begging us to respect the rights of property, and show mercy to them in their destitute condition. Hungry as I was my pity was at once excited; and one of the brothers joined with me in the desire to leave the poor people unmolested. The captor of the chicken however, was obdurate, expressing his determination to carry off the spoils, no matter who might oppose him.

A fierce quarrel ensued between the brothers, followed by a pugilistic encounter of no insignificant character. In the confusion of this unexpected fight the captive rooster regained his freedom, and hopped away crowing with delight. His great joy was shared by the girls, who, seeing the turn which affairs were taking, dried their pretty eyes at once and clapped their hands in exultation. Up to this point I had commiserated the situation of the family, prefering to go hungry myself rather than take away property from them which they so much needed; but being incensed at their ungracious joy on account of the liberation of the chicken, my pity gave way to disgust, and I joined my comrades in pursuing the fugitive rooster.

Eager in the chase, I was just turning a corner of the house, when on looking up for a moment I saw a party of rebel cavalry bearing down with speed toward us, and only a few hundred yards from us. I suddenly forgot all about the chicken, and turned to flee. I have already stated that there was a skirt of forest on that side of the house which looked toward the hospital, and as the coast was clear in that direction I made for cover with as much agility, perhaps, as I had ever before exhibited in my life. In the excitement I was separated from my companions, and never saw them again. I presume that they escaped as well as myself, but of this I cannot speak positively.

Down came the flying troop, yelling with the full volume of their lungs; and at the exact moment in which I plunged into a friendly thicket of undergrowth my enemies were but a few yards behind. This was one of the narrowest escapes of my military experience; but I only escaped from one difficulty to encounter another, for the brambles in this friendly thicket tore my clothes and mutilated my flesh until I was hardly recognizable by my nearest friend. This circumstance, however, proved my security from the enemy, for mounted as they were they could not follow me on my thorny pilgrimage. Ultimately, when I found my regiment, I had suffered for two days without anything to eat except the honey to which I have referred and two ears of corn which happened to fall in my way.

CHAPTER V.

THRILLING CAMPAIGN.

RESULTS OF SIX DAY'S FIGHTING—CHARGE AT SPOTSYLVANIA—AGAINST THE WELDON RAILROAD—TEMPORARY REST—INCIDENTS AMUSING AND OTHERWISE—DESCRIPTION OF THE COUNTRY—RECONNOISANCE—SPRINGING OF THE MINE—BRANDY MELON—BOTH EYES TORN OUT—CAPTURED, ROBBED AND RECAPTURED.

RESULTS OF SIX DAY'S FIGHTING.

MAY 11.—Since the battle of the Wilderness, May 5, to this date we have had six days of very hard fighting; have lost in that time about 35,000 men; the enemy's loss must have been greater than ours; we have taken over 5,000 prisoners and forty cannon, while they have taken but few men from us; the result to this time was much in our favor. It was upon this day that Gen. Grant sent that memorable dispatch to the Secretary of War, "I propose to fight it out on this line, if it takes all summer."

CHARGE AT SPOTSYLVANIA.

On the morning of the 12th, that memorable day, our corps formed in two lines; we moved silently and unseen toward the enemy's works, until we crossed the rugged space that intervened. Then with terrific charge and volleys of cheers we reached the enemy's works, surprised and captured Edward Johnston and his entire division; also two other brigades under the command of Gen. Geo. H. Stuart. This was the most successful charge on record; we captured between three and four thousand prisoners and about thirty guns. When Hancock heard that these generals were captured, he ordered them to be brought before him. Offering his hand to Johnson that general was so affected that he said he preferred death to captivity. He then offered his hand to Stuart, with whom he had been previously acquainted, and said: "How are you Stuart?" to which that officer impertinently replied: "I am General Stuart of the Confederate army and under present circumstances decline to take your hand." Hancock cooly replied: "And under any other circumstances, General, I should not have offered it." Hancock's pencil dispatch to Grant, within an hour after the column of attack had been formed, was these words: "I have captured from thirty to forty guns; I have finished Johnson, and am now going into Early." At noon it began to rain, but there was not an entire lull in the battle; the fifth corps only leaving a weak line of skirmishers, was moved to the left, as it was found that the enemy was continually massing his troops in that direction. Neither general was deceived for a moment, and our attempts to turn the enemy's right, at once met by the rebel commander, was not successful. Charges and counter-charges were made until night fall, and the carnage was terrific. When at length night put an end to it the armies had fought for fourteen hours, and the losses on either side numbered *about ten thousand.*

To give the reader some idea of how our time was occupied during this memorable campaign, I will here introduce a few weeks as a sample from my daily journal.

MAY 13.—We are driving rebels all day, but cannot get in gun shot of them; they move off lively.

MAY 14.—It rained to-day; we still kept following the enemy; had a small fight in the evening; rations run short.

MAY 15.—Still raining; our troops are still following up the enemy; we are very scarce of rations.

MAY 16.—Not much fighting to-day; in afternoon some pretty sharp firing.

MAY 17.—Quiet on the battle field, except firing on the picket line; think the Johnies are leaving.

MAY 18.—In the morning there were two heavy charges; our artillery kept up fire; to-night we lay down to sleep; in half an hour we were aroused and marched three miles, then lay down again, but were soon roused up.

MAY 19.—To-day we rested; pitched our tents; were all very tired; in the evening the enemy got in our rear and began to capture our train, but we soon drove them back.

MAY 20.—This morning we took two thousand prisoners; marched three miles, then halted until twelve o'clock that night; marched rest of night; read three chapters in my Bible.

MAY 21.—Marched all day; crossed the Matapony river; passed through Millford station and Bowling Green; the troops are very tired.

MAY 22.—Marched two miles through woods, then built breastworks and stayed all night; got a good rest; it is very warm.

MAY 23.—Crossed the North Anna river; marched hard all day; the rebs are shelling us, but we hold them back; there was very hard fighting; we routed the enemy.

MAY 24.—Terrific cannonading, and sharp skirmishing kept up all day; our division crossed the North Anna towards evening; rained very hard all night.

MAY 25.—Moved to-night a little; no fighting except the pickets kept up sharp fire; another hard rain; we are out of provisions; the boys are all hungry.

MAY 26.—Rained all forenoon; we lay behind breastworks all day; at night moved to the outside line of works and lay three hours, then marched the remainder of the night; re-crossed the North Anna.

MAY. 27.—Started at noon; marched until two o'clock next morning, then lay down and rested until daylight.

MAY 28.—Marched until noon; stopped an hour for dinner, then marched on; crossed the Pamunky River on pontoon bridges; after another march of two and one-half miles pitched tents for the night; very tired.

MAY 29.—Moved out about noon; marched until three o'clock; stopped and built breastworks until evening; soon as had those completed moved on and built others; we are now within ten miles of Richmond.

MAY 30.—In the morning built breastworks; heavy cannonading in the afternoon; the enemy made an unsuccessful charge on our left.

MAY 31.—There has been heavy cannonading all day, and sharp firing between the skirmish lines; about nine o'clock in the evening we moved three-quarters of a mile and built breastworks, then marched to the front and stayed until two o'clock in morning; then back to fourth line of breastworks; stayed until morning.

JUNE 1.—Moved out from the breastworks to the front; stayed until ten o'clock; marched remainder of night; skirmish lines kept up heavy fire; enemy charged on us but we drove them back.

JUNE 2.—Marched until eleven o'clock; stopped until two o'clock, then marched to front and pitched tents; stayed all night; rained afternoon and all night.

JUNE 3.—Moving; stopped one hour for breakfast; marched until eleven o'clock; stopped until four o'clock, then marched to front; fifth corps made a charge and repulsed the enemy.

JUNE 4.—Were in a woods near Gains' Hill all day; had a good rest; evening marched to front; rained again; the rebs shelled us.

JUNE 5.—Laid behind the breastworks near Mechan-

icsville until five o'clock, then moved out by left flank
on front line in sight of the Johnies.

KILLED BY A SHELL.

One day while lying in my tent I was aroused by a
terrible noise near by. I hastened to the spot from
whence the noise came, and there learned that a shell
had exploded, killing one young man and wounding
three others. It seems one of the boys had found
a small percussion cap shell; five or six of them were
examining it when one of them accidently let it fall;
striking on the cap it exploded with the above fatal result. The comrade that was killed belonged to a regiment in the fifth corps; his time of service having expired he had come to take leave of his friends in our
division before going home. This shocking affair
seemed doubly sad as after having endured the hardships and perils of a three years term of service, and
being filled with joyous expectations of soon meeting
with the loved ones at home, to be thus suddenly cut
down when he had least reason to expect. "But such
is war."

June 6.—Lay behind front line of breast works to-
day at Beaver Dam; some of the boys traded coffee to
the gray coats for tobacco.

June 7.—Still at same place getting rested; drew
four days rations.

June 8.—To-day lay still; everything quiet until
three o'clock; the batteries fired sharp for a while;
drew beans and apples.

At a certain point on our picket line several of our pickets were killed or murdered in a very mysterious manner. These casualties always occurred either in the evening or morning twilight. At length two pickets instead of one were stationed at the place, to discover, if possible, the cause of the trouble. The result was that one of these unfortunate men was killed and the other wounded, yet no discovery of the mysterious and dastardly perpetrator was made. At last one of our captains, with half a dozen men, volunteered to hunt down the desperado, who had made that part of our picket line a terror. The party concealed themselves in the underbrush; and very early in the morning an explosion was heard, coming from the forks of a large elm tree, which stood in front of a house, about a hundred yards away from the place where our men were concealed. The captain and his men rushed to the tree, when on looking up, they saw an old gray-haired civilian, of the Confederate school, seated on a board which had been ingeniously placed at the forks of the elm, so that in his murderous work he had not been perceived by the pickets. His wife came out from the house and begged that her husband might be permitted to come down in safety. The only response of the captain to this entreaty was a peremptory order to his men to fire. They did so, and the body of the old man, perforated by balls, shot through the air to the earth!

"There is your husband!" said the captain, and he and his men retired from the melancholy scene.

June 9.—Still at the same place; very heavy cannonading in afternoon for an hour or two; I was detailed as doctor's orderly.

June 10.—To-day everything quiet along line; twelve confederates came in to-day, they don't like fighting.

June 11.—Resting; all quiet along line; drew five days rations.

June 12.—Last night at nine o'clock packed up; marched all night with four days rations.

June 13.—Marched hard all day; staid all night in cornfield within two miles of James River; built breastworks.

June 14.—To-day marched two miles to river; crossed, marched up river one and one half miles; stopped for night.

June 15.—At eleven o'clock this morning started; marched until two; stopped one hour for dinner; marched until night; stopped for supper, then marched all night.

June 16.—About twelve o'clock arrived in rifle pits which some colored troops had taken; staid until four o'clock, when we advanced and opened a fight which lasted all night; we were relieved at 11 o'clock.

June 17.—At twelve o'clock we marched to front line of breastworks; we strengthened the works and had a sharp skirmish. Enemy lay fifty rods from us.

June 18.—Made a charge before Petersburgh, within one and one half miles of city; we were relieved at four o'clock; sharp skirmishing.

June 19.—This morn we lay behind third line of works; the sharp shooters pick the men off as fast as they stick up their heads; we have four mortars here, and they do good work.

June 20.—To-day we are on front line; sharp skirmishing all day; were relieved by ninth corps; after dark moved to rear and staid all night.

AGAINST THE WELDON R. R.

June 21.—This morning our corps and the sixth moved out rapidly across the Norfolk R. R., and then accross the Jerusalem plank road to where the fifth corps was already extended; the great objects of this movement was to extend our lines to the Weldon R. R.; one source of immediate supply both to Petersburgh and Richmond, but the enemy were as anxious to hold it as we were to capture it, and met our troops in such forces at Davis' Farm, between the two roads, as to compel them to retire for a short distance.

On Wednesday, June 22, this movement against the Weldon road was resumed by the second and sixth corps, the sixth on the left; but by some misunderstanding the corps waiting for each other, the attack was too long delayed; and when moving independently of each other a gap was formed between the sixth, which had not completed its line, and Barlows division of the second. Into this that skillful General, A. P. Hill, threw a division of his corps, rolling up Barlows division, which exposed our (Birney's) now Motts. Our regiment had just completed their breastworks and were sitting down to rest when Joe Smith cried out: "Oh, God, there comes the rebs." I arose up to look around, and saw the boys all running. I supposed they were going to get their arms, which had been stacked a little distance in our rear. The bullets were flying so fast that I crowded up close to the breastworks; on looking around again, I found the boys had all left and the rebels coming up in our rear, and mowing the thick underbrush with their bullets like they would with a scythe, and yelling like demons to us to surrender. My first thought was I would have to surrender, the second thought flashed upon me NEVER; acting upon this second thought, I picked up my budget and struck for the timber, which was very swampy. I came to a brush fence having a small pathway on either side of which stood a large tree; just as I passed the tree a rebel came running along the opposite side of the fence, and came around the tree from one side just as I came from the other. We were both surprised, he immediately called to me to surrender, but being in considerable of a hurry I did not stop. The Johny, vexed at my lack of courtesy, stuck out his gun and fired at me without taking aim, being so very close I suppose he thought it would be impossible to miss me, but he did; at every step I exspected to be shot. This was the only time I relinquished the idea I had always entertained of returning home safe; but in a few minutes I reached the second line of our works, which we were able to maintain. This was a terrible adventure, and the closest call I had yet had.

JUNE 23.—Were relieved this morning from the front; we lay still until night; heavy firing on our right; we took the railroad.

JUNE 24.—Were relieved in morning; moved to rear and put up breastworks; lay here all day and night expecting to move.

JUNE 25.—Still laying at same place; very warm and dusty; all quiet on picket line; hear some cannonading on our right.

JUNE 26.—Still at same place, very hot; hot enough to fry eggs on a stone in the sun, but we havn't got the eggs; was to church, heard a good sermon.

JUNE 27.—Raining; heavy cannonading to our right; gun boats playing with the enemy.

JUNE 28.—Moved out front, put up strong breastworks; our's (the second) is the flanking corps, the switch engine for the Potomac army.

JUNE 30.—*Very hot;* policeing around tents, washing and sleeping; drew soft bread to-day.

JULY 2.—Inspection to-day; got fresh tomatoes and onions from sanitary commission.

NEUTRAL CORN FIELD.

There was a corn field between the Union and Confederate lines at a certain point before Petersburgh, a little to the left of Cemetery Hill. The opposing pickets of the two great confronting armies would in spite of all occasionally creep into that field for a friendly chat or for a game of cards, or would swap papers for papers, tobacco for coffee, or jack knives, hard tack or sugar for corn cake. Two of them were playing a game of cards one day with Abe Lincoln and Jeff Davis as imaginary stakes; the Lincolnite lost. "There," says the winner, "Old Abe belongs to me." "Well, I'll send him over by the Petersburgh Express." The express was a very large mortar on a car built expressly for it, and every morning and evening it would run up around the bluff near the fort line on the City Point R. R., and throw a monstrous shell into Petersburg.

TEMPORARY REST.

It was now manifest that after two months of continuous fighting of the most desperate character, and now that we had reached a point where the siege of a stronghold must take the place of battles in the field, there must be a brief period for rest and re-organization. Our losses had been between sixty and seventy thousand, and although corresponding re-enforcements had reached Grant, the losses could not be repaired by the raw troops sent to the army. We had lost six hundred officers killed, more than two thousand wounded, and three hundred and fifty missing; those could not be immediately replaced. Thus far I participated in all the fighting and marching to which my command was subjected; made many narrow escapes of my life; was never excused from duty, but always enjoyed that invaluable blessing, good health, and that too without thinking God preserved my life; depreciating His loving kindness, and resisting the advice of a fond mother, for her letters were always sermons to me. I read my Bible because I promised my mother at parting that I would. But I never allowed my mind to inhale the sweet passages of that precious book. My mind was absorbed in the pleasures and excitements of the world, indulging in what leads the mind from Christian piety. But I was in the army with all kinds of people, and being very young, was more easily influenced to indulge in wicked habits. I will relate a little incident that happened under my observation: One Sabbath while strolling through the different regiments, my attention was attracted by a concourse of soldiers quietly seated on the ground. In their midst stood a chaplain expounding the word of God. Toward evening as I was returning to my regiment I passed the colonel's quarters; attracted by a little confusion, I glanced in; there in the middle of the tent sat three officers and the chaplain whom I had heard preaching in the forenoon, all busily engaged at card playing, and a roll of money lying on the table in their midst.

Sunday, July 3.—Drew full suit of clothes; ninth corps kept up firing their mortars.

Monday, July 4.—To-day visited the fifth and ninth corps; while passing a regiment of fifth corps issuing rations, my attention was attracted to a cracker box of different size, shape and color than any I had ever seen; it had been captured from the rebs, and bore this peculiar inscription, "B. C. 603," the figures being beneath the initials. While we were speculating upon the probable meaning of this peculiar brand, various interpretations were surmised, but all rejected, until one individual who was then in the act of attempting to masticate a piece, declared it was plain enough, "couldn't be misunderstood." "Why, how so?" was the query. "Oh," he replied, "that is the date when the crackers were made—six hundred and three years before Christ." (603 B. C.) A general roar followed, and we proclaimed *him* the hero of the occasion. While passing the ninth corps, in front of which the opposing lines were in full view and hailing distance of each other, a Confederate jumped upon the breastworks, flourished a large flask of whisky, and cried out, "Yanks, come over and drink the Fourth of July with us." Five others made their appearance, one having a violin. An amusing little dance was indulged in for our benefit. A Confed. who was concealed in a little dug out under the top of a fallen tree was very annoying and destructive to our picket line. "G," an experienced artilleryman, said he could silence that fellow, and placing a little mortar into position, on a second trial dropped a shell into the dug out from which so many fatal bullets had come; there was *no* more trouble from that point. Every evening the mortars opened up fire, and continued for several hours after dark; they presented the grandest specimen of fireworks I ever witnessed; and for hours I sat and watched the shells from opposing batteries with their long tails of fire passing to and fro, some bursting low and others high in the air; this artillery practice was kept up until after the springing of the mine.

JULY 11.—Tore down breastworks and packed up to move.

JULY 14.—Laying within ten miles of City Point, Va.; in evening went out on fatigue; worked hard all night tearing down Johnie rifle-pits; drew whisky.

JULY 15.—Regiment went out on fatigue, tearing down captured forts.

JULY 17.—Moved camp fifty rods; put up good quarters. A lot of brush lying around camp took fire, in which some shells were deposited; the bursting of the same gave us a scare and made it lively for us a while.

JULY 23.—Moved camp; now on the flank; occupy rifle-pits joining the fort.

DESCRIPTION OF THE COUNTRY.

By this time we had passed through a great many large and beautiful plantations, but the country looked desolate; fences were down, and fields of corn and wheat, mostly ready for the sickle, were destroyed by the armies. In some places, fine and costly buildings were defaced and demolished, and nothing but a row of negro huts remained to mark the place that had once been the home of wealth and luxury. I say some were thus, while others remained in their grandeur. The inhabitants consisted of old men, women and children, for the young and middle-aged men were in the Confederate army, fighting to destroy that government to which they now call for protection. I conversed freely with a great many on the condition of the country; most of them expressed an anxious desire for peace, but the F. F. V.'s were inimical. Rich in this world's goods, they were, generally speaking, haughty and overbearing; while the poorer class, or "clay-eaters," were very ignorant and used very uncouth language. A lady of Ohio, in describing a southern clay-eater, says "they don't look like a fresh dead man, but like one that had been dead a long time." It seems they do not appreciate the free school system, for I saw but two school houses during the whole time I was in the army. Why is it that they do not appreciate the value of free schools, or do they not know the value of education? Think of a race of human beings in this enlightened country, and having it in their power, depreciating that which is to their interest and the first essential duty of life.

RECONNOISANCE.

On the 26th of July we took up the line of march; crossed the Appomattox river at Point of Rocks. It will be remembered this is the place where Pocahontas rescued Captain John Smith, which the reader has no doubt found recorded in the history of the United States. The residents showed me a tree under which they said the scene had transpired. It was a large tree, probably four feet in diameter, with large massive boughs. It stands alone, and is on a gradual ascent from the river. Beneath its boughs is a spring of pure crystal water. The river banks at the place are lined with large brown rocks, which makes the place picturesque. We crossed the James at Deep Bottom and reconnoitered in the direction of Fort Hamilton, and on the night of the 28th our division recrossed the river, and on a forced march reached Petersburg. We took the front line of works.

SPRINGING OF THE MINE.

On the 25th of June, Col. Pleasants took his regiment, forty-eighth Pa., and commenced to dig a tunnel under the enemy's fort; the tunnel was some twenty feet below the surface, and at its extremity under the fort there were two lateral galleries, one extending thirty-eight feet to the right, the other thirty-seven feet to the left under the enemy's redoubt; in these galleries were eight magazines of powder placed. about four tons in all. on the morning of July 30. At half past three the fuse was lit; owing to some defect it did not go off as expected, when Lieutenant Jacob Douty and Sergeant Harry Reese, two brave men volunteered to go in and relight the fuse. Again, at ten minutes before five, the insidious flame travels to its destined goal. A quiver, which becomes an earthquake—tremor—and then with a tremendous burst a conical mountain rises in the air streaked and seamed with lightning flashes. The vast mass is momentarily poised. and as it thus hangs in air discloses timber planking, earth, bodies and limbs of men, and even one or two of the sixteen guns in the work. It is known that the work was occupied by portions of the seventeenth and eighteenth and twenty-second South Carolina regiments, under Col. Fleming. Except the guard the garrison was asleep. One instant of wakening and then the crushing death. And then from every gun, great and small, that can be brought to bear, we pour in such thunderstorms of artillery as have rarely been witnessed or heard in America.

BRANDY MELON.

Our suttlers were not allowed to keep or sell intoxicating liquors to the boys. But they would resort to different methods to evade the law and accommodate us. At one time they sold small cans labelled "Clingstone Peaches" for $1.25 each—they contained two or three peaches and the rest brandy. When detected in this they would plug water melons and fill them with brandy and sell the melon out at from 25 to 50 cents a slice. Once we treated an old German to a slice telling him it was a new variety of melon. So delighted was he with the flavor of it that he at once purchased of the sutler four seeds, paying $2 each for them, saying: "I'ch will sent does seets hame, und ven does vor's ish ober I'ch vill moch von forchune owet or dem vatermelons." /

Another German who came out with the hundred day men, near the close of the war, and who had not seen any fighting, was determined to take two small cannon balls home with him, saying he wanted dem for his poys, und to remember de vor py."

BOTH EYES TORN OUT—CAPTURED, ROBBED AND RECAPTURED.

On the 12th of August we again took up our line of march and it was rumored that we were going to Maryland, as Lee was in the vicinity of Washington. We accordingly marched to City Point, where we took transports and started in the direction of Washington. This was to mislead the rebels, for we did not go a great ways until the lights were extinguished, and our fleet turned right about and went in the opposite direction, passed City Point, and in the morning landed at Deep Bottom. We advanced on the rebel lines slowly and steadily, driving them back until within seven miles of Richmond, where I was wounded. I had been back to the rear and was going to the front; on my way I stopped in a house. As I entered the lady of the house poured a shower of oaths on me, telling what ill treatment they had received at the hands of the Yankees, and how they had inhumanly murdered women and children. I quietly seated myself, and after she was through, asked her how she knew this. She said it was in the Richmond papers. I asked her if on the other hand it said anything about their raids through the North. She said "No, they never did that, and never was guilty of such inhuman deeds." She said we Yankees were getting into a trap, if we only knew it; to which I replied that if her head was longer than Gen. Grant's she had better take the field. She then said she wished none of us would ever cross the river alive, and that I would get killed. I said:

"Madam, that is a pretty hard wish, I never wished bad luck to any one." "I know it is pretty hard." she replied, "but it is hard for you'n's to come down here and fight we'n's." I replied, "The next time behave yourselves," and left the house. This was my last interview with the women of the South, and she was the most bitter one with whom I had ever conversed.

I mounted my steed and rode rapidly to the front; after going some distance I came into a heavy timber; here I met Gen. Birney, formerly commander of my division, a noble officer, and part of his staff; these were the last Union soldiers I ever saw. After I passed them I turned into a small by-road; soon came to an obstruction formed by slashing timber across the road; this was done to impede the progress of our advancing line. I worked around this, but soon came to another, and a little farther on a third one, which was more formidable; in order to get around I was compelled to go quite a distance in the timber. The moment I reached the road again, a squad of rebels rose up and fired into me, wounding my beast in the neck and dislocating the horn of my saddle. Then a giant-like rebel rose up and called to me to surrender. I instantly took hold of the rein close by the bit and wheeled about, and as my eye left him he was raising his gun to his face, after which he fired, and I was the victim of the charge. The ball entered the lower margin of my left temple between the eye and ear, passed through my head, cut off the bridge of my nose, and came out through my right eye; where it entered it cut the lower portion of

NOTE. — A cut was intended for this page. The author received word on going to press that it would be impossible to furnish it.

my temple loose from my cheek, splitting my left
cheek in three different places, and my right in two
different places. It was supposed by the surgeons that
the charge was buck and ball; the ball passed through
my head and the buck glanced over my eyebrow,
mashing it considerably. I was most horribly man-
gled, and three days elapsed before I received proper
attention. After I fell I instantly arose, and having
the sight of my left eye the first object that met my
gaze was my horse rapidly retracing his steps. I
started after him, running three or four steps, which
brought me to a little embankment on the side of the
road. I jumped it, and in so doing the blood ran into
my left eye, totally blinding me; but I kept on until
I ran against a tree. I sat down beside it and put my
arms around it to keep from falling over. As yet I
had not realized any very aching pain. My head was
completely benumbed, and my clothes were being sat-
urated with blood. A rebel now came up, and the
following colloquy ensued: "O, here is one of our
boys. Don't you want to go to the hospital?" to
which I replied, "Yes, sir, if I can get there." He
said he would go and get a stretcher and some one to
help bear me off the field, requesting me in the meantime to let him take my things, as some one might
rob me while he was gone. I replied that they were
not of much value, and that I guessed I could take
care of them myself. He at once proceeded to rob
me. I had on a very fine military vest with gold
plated buttons that had been presented me the day

before by our division surgeon; this he took off me and appropriated to himself, then rifled my pockets. My great anxiety was to get into our lines. With the blood pouring out both sides of my head, to all appearance I could live but a short time; I could not expect any attention from my captors, and in all probability would be left alone in this forest to die. At this juncture a part of a brigade of colored troops who were relieved and was on a road a little to my right moving toward the rear; hearing this firing and comprehending the situation, they immediately without orders charged the enemy and re-captured me. The reb who robbed me was captured, and my things recovered, which I gave to the brave man who captured the reb. Meantime my horse had made good his escape. I had ridden through a gap which had occurred in our lines, and had come upon a squad of rebels who were taking advantage of this gap. It seems that the second corps in forming did not make connection with the tenth corps which lay on the left, and this occasioned the gap into which I rode. After I had been re-captured one of the charging party came to me and said in the exact words of the rebel: "Oh, here is one of our boys." By this time I was growing weak from the loss of blood, and was reiterating "if I could only get into our lines, if I could only get into our lines." They then took me to the rear, and by the time I reached the division hospital at Deep Bottom, on the bank of the James, my head was swollen to such an extent that I could not speak.

8

CHAPTER VI.

SUFFERING AND SORROW.

On the Stretcher—Taken to Carver Hospital—Surgical
Attention—Progress of my case—Miss Whetton—The
Death of my Mother.

ON THE STRETCHER.

This most terrible misfortune, involving the total
and permanent loss of sight, occurred about half past
10 o'clock on the morning of August 15th, and but a
short time afterward I was transported from the place
at which the catastrophe took place, and was left on a
stretcher in front of the Division Hospital. The
weather was warm, even sultry, and I lay for hours
exposed to the fervid rays of the sun. The dust on the
highway was more than a foot thick, spreading itself
everywhere and collecting in my undressed wound,
causing great irritation. It is difficult to imagine a
more desolate and melancholy spectacle than my condition presented that day. My features were so dis-
figured by the rebel shot; they were beginning to swell,
and dust and blood mingling together in a horrible

mass, gave me, I know, a revolting appearance. Through all the harsh experiences of those hours passed on the stretcher sweltering in the heat of an August sun, I believe that my consciousness did not leave me for an instant. At times, comprehending the awful nature of the wounds I had received, I expressed a desire for some one to shoot me and thus put me out of my misery. The hospital before which I was lying and into which I was not permitted to enter, was already crowded with sufferers, and what made the matter worse, as I afterward learned, some of the surgeons in attendance were too drunk to discharge, with any sort of decency, their professional duties. The 2d New York Regiment had been decimated in the recent engagement, and many of its members were now in the hospital. From the first my case was considered hopeless. There was but one opinion expressed by surgeons as well as others who surveyed me in my forlorn condition, and that was I was mortally wounded, and my days and even my hours were numbered!

A benevolent chaplain, whose name I would be glad to record here if I knew it, saw me several times during the day in passing to and fro on his errands of mercy. His christian sympathies were excited, and, in spite of the universal belief that I could survive but a few hours at most, he resolved to do what he could to have me taken to Washington and placed under proper surgical care. Full of kindly feeling for the unfortunate boy, he went to the transferring surgeon, under whose authority the wounded men were conveyed to the General Hospital at Washington, and besought him to have me taken aboard of the transport which was to leave for the Federal Capitol at 4 o'clock that afternoon. The surgeon had seen me before this interview, and his opinion in reference to the hopelessness of my case was that of all others. He said:

"That boy is mortally wounded; he cannot possibly live longer than a few hours. The boat will be crowded, and what is the use of giving to a person who is practically dead, a place on the boat which ought to be occupied by soldiers to whom we can be of some advantage. Your request, sir, must be denied; the boy cannot go."

The chaplain went away disheartened. He believed, with others, that I had but a very brief time to live; but, as he passed by me again and again in the course of the day, his emotions were profoundly painful. He thought of the mother far away who was waiting and watching, perhaps in vain, for the return of her son from the tented field, and as his feelings increased in poignancy he went again to the transferring surgeon and begged him, with all the eloquence of warm entreaty, to send me to Washington, but the only concession that was made by the surgeon, was the statement that if I survived until nine o'clock next morning the request of my friend would be granted. A concession such as this was cruelty to me, and the chaplain knew it. The hours which would necessarily intervene between the time of this and the time when the transport would start next day, would prove fatal to me unless I were removed to some more comfortable place and carefully and skillfully attended. Incited to renewed action by this thought, the chaplain, as a last alternative and a perilous one to himself, for he was transcending his official duties, went to the captain of the transport and besought him to take me on board. If this act of the chaplain, in disobedience of the surgeon's authority had been reported at headquarters, he would have been punished and possibly dismissed from his place; but he was imitating the kindness of the good Samaritan no matter what would be the consequences, and so pleadingly did he cling to the captain that the privilege was granted to him to bring me on board. Overjoyed at this favor the good chaplain hastened to the stretcher, and then, having obtained help from others, he took me on board the transport State of Maine.

TAKEN TO CARVER HOSPITAL.

Thus through the kindness of a christian friend, I was conveyed to the boat; and at midnight, August 17th, I was admitted as an inmate of Carver Hospital, Washington City. It will be perceived that from the date of my wound to the date of my arrival at Washington, more than three days and three nights elapsed, during which, as my death was expected every hour, I received no surgical attention whatever; and now as I recall, as far as I am able, the incidents of those terrible days, I am impressed with a feeling of wonder, as

well as of gratitude, that I am still living to record
these fearful events. Before leaving this subject, an
explanatory word, in reference to the good chaplain, is
necessary. Of his good offices to me I was not aware
at the time; for if I was not in a state of delirium, I
was, at least, in a condition in which a person is not
supposed to have any adequate knowledge of his surroundings. Months afterward the chaplain happened
to meet me in one of the streets of the capitol; and
notwithstanding the great change, for the better, which
had occurred in my personal appearance, he thought
he knew me, and on accosting me he discovered he was
right. From him I learned the facts which are detailed in the preceding paragraphs. It is a source of
sharp regret to me, that, here, before leaving this good
samaritan, I cannot present his name; but his memory,
nameless though he is to me, is enbalmed in my heart,
to remain there, imperishable as the mind that en-
shrines it. While many of our army chaplains were
doing more harm than good, often bringing reproach
to the cause they profess to serve, it stimulates my
faith in christianity, to bring back the incidents connected with my removal from the stretcher to the comforts of a federal hospital.

CARVER HOSPITAL.

This hospital is situated on 14th street, and joins
Columbia College. It comprises some thirty acres of
ground, which is about twice as long as wide. On
every side, except the street, are wards standing to-

wards the center, and one row across the center. Across each ward is a covered walk, which adds very much to its excellency and convenience. Head quarters dispensary and diet kitchen are in the center; also a three story water tank, and an operating room—the dread of soldiers. A little south of the head quarters is the cook-house and dining hall, which has two tables and will accomodate about four hundred persons. North of headquarters is the band room. The grounds are laid off in beautiful beds, highly decorated with flowers of almost every kind, which perfume the air with their sweet odor. The little weekly paper, *Reveille*, together with the splendid library, all added to make Carver the coveted resting place of many a wounded and worn out soldier. In fact Carver stood second to no hospital in Washington.

SURGICAL ATTENTION.

From the nature of the wound I had received, my case, from the first, attracted general attention, especially among medical students and professional men. There are few, if any, instances on record, in which men have recovered, where the conditions, in respect to the wound, were identical with mine. My case has been thought almost phenominal in the history of surgery.

After my arrival at Washington, I had a dim perception that several physicians approached the bed on which I was lying, and examined me with great curiosity. Believing me to be unconscious, they expressed their professional opinions with much freedom. I heard them say:

"Poor fellow, he is past all help! He is done with his campaigning forever."

I mention this circumstance to show that my recovery was regarded by men of high standing as utterly hopeless from the start. My death was expected to take place at any time; it could not possibly be deferred many hours longer. It was a good thing for me, as the result will show, that I was placed under the special care of Dr. Wynants, a venerable and excellent surgeon, to whose skill I was, under Heaven, indebted for my final restoration to health.

Next morning the operation of probing the wound was performed. This ordeal was keenly painful, for, before the entire operation was concluded, a piece of silk was drawn three times through the wound, each time enlarged to meet the demands of the occasion. My sensations while passing through this treatment were those of unmixed agony. The needle was too short for the purpose for which it was required, making it necessary for the operator to introduce, to a slight extent, his finger into the wound, thus pushing the instrument along its course. Fragments of bones were in this manner disturbed, and the irritation caused in this way was a most torturing experience.

It was not only my good fortune to be treated by a skillful and conscientious surgeon, but to be attended, likewise, by a faithful and devoted nurse, James Buckley, of Brattleboro, Vermont, whose kind offices contributed greatly to my eventual recovery. The name of our hospital surgeon was O. A. Judson, who ranked as major. The Surgeon-General, whose name was Barnes, favored me with a visit. Indeed, there was no end to such favors from medical men. There were physicians from New York, Pittsburgh, Philadelphia, and other points, who heard of my singular case, and who traveled all the way from their homes to gratify their professional interest.

PROGRESS OF MY CASE.

As Dr. Wynants informed me afterward, he came to my bed morning after morning during the first weeks of my sojourn in the hospital, and at each visit he expected to find me either dead or in the last stage of dissolution. To his surprise, however, as he returned day after day to his accustomed place of observation, he found me alive, with my system still striving hard to obtain the mastery over death. He possessed a wide range of surgical reading and experience, but in this case of mine there were features of novelty even to him. When a month passed away and my constitution was still bearing up bravely against pain and death, he began to indulge a faint glimmer of hope, and resolved from that moment to employ all means known to medical science to prolong my existence and bring me back to health. His professional pride was aroused, and he was conscious that if he cured me he would achieve a marvelous victory in a case which was regarded by common consent as beyond the reach of surgery.

During the first month, and it was possibly longer than this, the only sense left to me which enjoyed any great degree of perfection, was that of hearing. Next to this in vigor was the sense of feeling, but this was in a manner benumbed, for it was less sensitive than it would have been if I had realized ordinary health. The senses of smell and taste were both paralyzed, and sight was gone forever! Never again was I to be permitted to look out, as I had been wont to do, on the familiar scenes of nature; never again would I look on the green earth, or the blue sky, glittering with its retinue of suns and stars; and never again would I have the unspeakable privilege of looking into the faces of those home relatives who were dearest to me in life. I cannot say that these thoughts, or any others which may have been logically connected with them, occupied a place in my mind during those long, dull, and monotonous weeks, which seemed to "drag, like a woundeed snake, their slow length along." It would be difficult to analyze the state of my mind while I was lying there waiting, without any special consciousness and yet without any delirium, the developments of the future. Except at intervals, I did not suffer very great pain, and as the wound began to heal in a healthy manner I had rare opportunities for reflection; but for a long time, as I lay in a sort of apathy, or rather in a condition of animal enjoyment, the grave thoughts of death, the judgment scene, and eternity, seemed not to demand any fixed attention. This part of my life comes back to me with a kind of vagueness, like a dream, which, in spite of its general impressiveness, is but half remembered.

MISS WHETTEN.

One of my best friends in those hospital days, was Miss Harriet D. Whetten, of New York. She had inherited an estate worth half a million dollars; but, when the war broke out, instead of enjoying her large patrimony, in the pomps and vanities of fashionable life, she went to the hospitals and even to the battle fields of the great civil war, devoting herself in kind ministrations to the service of our sick and wounded soldiers. Her arduous duties impaired her health, and she was compelled, against her will, to return home; but as soon as her health was in a measure restored, and her business matters, which had suffered in her absence, were adjusted, she resumed her old place in the hospitals. Glad am I that I met this lady. She provided for my wants, and saw that I was kept comfortable. After I was able to sit up, she visited me daily, often two and three times a day, and each time read and explained a portion of the Bible, and talked to me of the goodness of God. She seemed to take an interest in my spiritual welfare, and to her the inmates of Carver Hospital owe a debt of gratitude which they can never repay.

THE DEATH OF MY MOTHER.

I come now to speak of an event which cast an additional gloom over my life, the death of my mother.

One day shortly after the disastrous one in which I was wounded, my parents stopped in Greenville, at the store of S. P. Johnson, while on their way to visit my uncle's family, at Shakelyville. about ten miles distant. My mother remained in the store while my father hastened to the post office to get his mail. He returned, a little while after, with two letters, observing, at the same time, to my mother, that these letters which he had not as yet opened, contained news, he believed from the seat of war. Sometime before a false report of my death had been communicated to my friends at home; but this report had been denied. When my mother saw the letters, and knew that they were from the army, she was overjoyed at the thought of receiving intelligence from me.

"Don't be too fast," said my father to her, kindly, as he noticed her delight; "these letters may contain sad news, and it is well for us to be prepared for it. We will soon know the best or the worst."

Having said this he opened one of the letters, and to his dismay, read the announcement sent by some well-meaning friend, that I was mortally wounded, and that if my friends expected to see me alive, they must hasten with all speed to Washington. I need not dwell on the effect which this melancholy announcement had upon my parents. It was a bitter, gloomy day to them, and my mother seemed utterly broken in spirit. Relief, in a measure, came to her when the other letter, which was from Miss Whetten, was read. It contained the information that I was badly wounded; but this was accompanied by the statement that I was in good hands and was receiving every possible attention, both in respect to nursing and medical treatment. This letter had a tendency to allay the excitement from which my parents were suffering; but, at the least, the news just received was very sad. Instead of pursuing their way as intended, my parents returned to their home. At the gate my mother was met by my brothers and sisters; and as soon as they saw the evident signs of grief in her face, they inferred the truth. A sad scene was that which presented itself when the different members of the family were grouped at the gateway, their minds wandering far away to a bed in a hospital, on which a wounded soldier was, possibly at that very moment, breathing his last. How many scenes like this were reproduced in the minds of northern homes, by the war for the Union? This was but one among multiplied thousands; but taken alone as an isolated instance, it was sad enough to photograph itself forever, on the memory of those who shared in this great affliction.

It was a journey by rail of several hundred miles from Greenville to Washington, and the state of the country was such that traveling, especially for a lady, was not the pleasantest occupation in the world. It was decided that my mother should visit me as soon as preparation could be made for starting. At last everything was in readiness for her proposed trip, and my father went to Greenville to purchase a railroad ticket. While there he received a letter from Washington stating that it would not be advisable for any of my relatives or friends to visit me, as my condition was so critical that the surgeons would not allow even an old acquaintance to speak to me, as they feared that the least emotion, excitement or worry might snap the slender cord on which my life hung. Thus the last opportunity to pass an hour or a moment in company with my beloved mother was past forever.

On the third day of December, between three and four months after I was taken to the hospital, my mother died without seeing her absent son. When the sad news reached me, it brought back to my mind the old parting scene with the greatest vividness; and in the light of the mournful bereavement which had just shadowed my life, I was able to interpret aright the strange presentiment I experienced when my hand lingered in hers for the last time. It was pleasant to know that her last days were soothed and comforted by encouraging letters from Miss Whetten, who, from time to time all through those weary months of waiting and watching, apprised the family of the certain progress of my cure, and of the great kindness of my many friends at Washington. It was pleasant to think of these things, as I often did, when removed so far from the home circle.

I was getting along remarkably well, when the sad tidings of my mother's death arrived. This was almost more than I could bear. I immediately sent for Miss Whetten, who came, and with tears of sympathy in her eyes and words of condolence, tried to soothe the pain of my aching heart.　I thought of the loved one who had gone and left me to finish my journey alone.

"A lesson sad, but fraught with good—
　A tearful one, but strength'ning food,
　　Thou gavest me.
　We learn that dust returns to dust—
　Anew in God we put our trust,
　　And bow the knee.

"She sleeps in peace—yes, sweetly sleeps,
　　Her sorrows all are o'er.
　With her the storms of life are past—
　　She's found the heavenly shore."

CHAPTER VII.

LIFE IN WASHINGTON.

Incidents in Hospital.—Home Furlough—My Sister—Hospital Scenes—Abraham Lincoln—The Museum—Secretary Stanton—Visiting my Regiment—Insolence of a Lieutenant—A glance at the Capitol—View of the Navy Yard—Grand Review.

INCIDENTS IN HOSPITAL.

The closing incidents of the last chapter disturbed, in some degree, the order of time in my narrative, and I will now go back to relate some things which occurred in the hospital before the date of my mother's death. The reader is already informed that my wound had begun to heal, and after the first month and a half of treatment, my convalescence was well established. My cure went on rapidly. Just before the advent of cold weather, a soldier whose place was near me was pronounced to be suffering from gangrene in a wounded limb. At this period I was familiar enough with wounds in general to know that if gangrene were to introduce itself into the wound I had received the whole college of surgeons would not be able to save me. It so happened that the assistant nurse on one occasion carelessly employed the same sponge and basin for me which he had used in dressing the wound of the gangrenous patient. On learning this I became alarmed, and shortly afterward I was removed from my quarters in number 32 to 27. My new place was much more warm and comfortable for the season than the one I had vacated. Here for several days I was troubled with my new apprehensions in regard to gangrene, and as I took a severe cold, consequent upon removal, my uneasiness was intensified. The pain in one of my eyelids helped to confirm me in the false idea I was entertaining in reference to my wound. It was not long, however, before my imaginary fears were put to rest.

Some time before my mother's death, a physician, Dr. Brown, whose residence was at Clarksville, but a few miles away from Greenville, paid me a visit. He very kindly proposed to take me home with him. At first, weak as I was, I was very strongly prompted to go, but remarked to my friend that I could not take this step unless my doctor consented. Earnestly as I wished to go, I could not think of doing so if it in any wise would retard my recovery. The opinion of Dr. Wynants was unfavorable and the contemplated trip was therefore abandoned. Thus the last chance to see my mother was lost.

9

HOME FURLOUGH.

January 12th, 1865, I started home on a sixty days' furlough, accompanied by Luke Hubbard, a musician, who was detailed as my guide on the route. I was kindly met and warmly received by my friends and associates, and enjoyed myself while in their society. On the 26th of March I returned to Washington and was welcomed back to Carver Hospital by my soldier friends, in whose company I had enjoyed many happy hours.

MY SISTER.

I pause here in my narrative to pay merited tribute to a member of our family, whose name has not hitherto been mentioned, my sister Lizzie. At the period of my mother's death this good sister of mine was but fourteen years of age. Young as she was, the sad event which had just occurred introduced her to new and heavy responsibilities. The other children at home were all younger than she, and on this account as well as on that of special fitness for the position, she was called on to take the place made vacant by death. In this new sphere of effort and accountability she acquitted herself nobly, not only as a faithful friend and ally of our father, but as a patient and judicious elder sister to the others. For four years, and until my father married again, she discharged the duties devolving upon her with unswerving fidelity.

Pursuing the history of my sister a little farther, it is proper to say that, years after, she became an inmate of my family, remaining with us until her marriage with A. W. Davis, a merchant of Prairie City, Iowa, a noble man, and they now have a pleasant and happy home.

HOSPITAL SCENES.

My furlough expired on the 12th day of March, but in consequence of a flood which damaged the railroads and made travel impracticable for days, I did not reach the city until the 26th, fourteen days behind time. The tardiness of my arrival was made the subject of many jokes on the part of my friends at the hospital. One of them jestingly said: "You will be shot as a deserter." Another of my companions replied, that "if I was to be shot for a breach of rules in remaining at home too long it would not do to use a minnie rifle with which to take my life, for the rebels had already tried that without effect, and if it was to be done at all in any effectual way a battery of artillery must be called out, for nothing short of this will stop his wind."

On my return to Washington, my reception from friends and casual visitors was very flattering. The highest men, as well as women, of Washington society, seemed to take a pleasure in calling upon the sick and wounded soldiers. On two occasions Mrs. Lincoln, on her round of visitations, came to see me.

As my strength was returning, privileges were accorded to me which were not usual. Cap. McCollum. of the Guard, kindly gave me a daily pass under which I was free to visit Congress, or any other place of public interest, in the federal capital. My companions, among the convalescent soldiers, each one of whom could obtain only a weekly pass, were very anxious to act as my guide, for this would enlarge their privileges. Each morning when I was about to start there was a friendly, but very exciting competition among them, as to which one of them should be my escort. The value attached to the office of guide was enhanced by the fact that at restaurants and hotels and places of amusement, a blind soldier was the recipient of many kindnesses, which cost him nothing, and which were shared alike by his friend.

My nurse in number 27, was George Roby, of Roby's Corner, N. H. He was a pleasant and kind hearted man, devoted to his vocation and very popular with the boys. The pranks of which we were guilty, at his expense, were numberless; and yet, as the victim of our practical jokes, he never complained, but joined at once in the mirth that was caused. One day I took hold of a chair, the entire back of which was gone, and thrust a thumb into one of the large holes on the side. Lifting the chair, with my thumb in this position, I began to groan in apparent anguish, calling out at the same time to George to help me out of the difficulty. Believing that my thumb was actually imprisoned, and as a consequence I was suffering great pain, the kind nurse went to work in good faith to liberate me. He tried several methods, but from the way in which I manipulated the chair, his efforts were all in vain. At length, in sheer dispair of bringing about my freedom in any other way, he took a hatchet, and chopped the chair to pieces. He never comprehended the joke, until, at the conclusion of his thankless toil, he was greeted by a round of immoderate guffaws from my companions who were witnesses of the amusing scene.

On another occasion I placed some hard, dry currants, which could not well be used for any good purpose, on the sheet of Mr. Roby's bed, and besides this I arranged his bedstead in such a manner as to make it fall if too great a pressure were put upon it. At regulation time George blew out his light and clambered unsuspiciously into his place of repose. Immediately the contact of those horrible currants with his feet and limbs made him exercise himself in a sort of spasmodic way, which resulted in bringing his bed with a loud crash to the floor. Of course we all sympathized with him in this catastrophe, and to this day George does not know, perhaps, what made his bed fall so easily.

While we were thus diverting ourselves as the days went by there were other scenes often in progress, the sadness of which would arrest us in our merriment, and bring the unbidden tear to our eyes. A poor mother who had received word that her son was lying wounded in the hospital and was anxious to see her hastened with all eagerness to be present during his sufferings. There was a world of anxiety and love depicted in her face as she asked to be shown to the place where her son lay. I leave the reader to imagine, for I cannot describe it, the feelings of that devoted mother when the intelligence fell upon her heart that her idolized son was already dead, and his body removed from the hospital. Such heart-rending scenes in those days often occurred.

A little trick with cards prevailed among the boys by which in some mysterious way known only to experts the age of a person could be told with great accuracy. I became proficient in this trick, and one day while on the street cars I met a grave United States senator, in whose presence, being invited to do so, I exhibited my skill in this acquirement with cards. He looked on with much interest, remarking at length that if he had possession of the cards till Monday he would find out the secret for himself.

"If you do," said I, somewhat saucily, "don't tell anybody."

"I won't," replied the senator, in such a literal, matter-of-fact way, that its very drollness was irresistible. A general laugh from the ladies and gentlemen present ensued. I loaned the cards to the senator, and on the day designated he returned them with the statement that he could not see into them.

ABRAHAM LINCOLN.

The high estimation in which President Lincoln was held by the soldiers of the Republic is too well known to need comment here. I shared in a very large degree this universal feeling, and on Tuesday evening, April 11, 1865, just three days before his death, I had the honor of hearing the last public speech of his life. It was delivered in front of the White House, to a large concourse of citizens and soldiers who came to do honor to the President, and to celebrate the final victories of the war. I append here the opening paragraph of this last address, as it refers to the achievements of the soldier.

"We meet this evening not in sorrow, but in gladness of heart. The evacuation of Petersburgh and Richmond, by the insurgent army give hope of a speedy peace whose joyous expression cannot be restrained. In the midst of this, however, He from whom all blessings flow must not be forgotten, nor must those whose harder part gives us the cause of rejoicing be overlooked. Their honors must not be parceled out with others. I myself was near the front and had the high pleasure of transmitting much of the good news to you, but no part of the honor for plan or operation is mine. To Gen. Grant, his skillful officers and brave men, all belongs. The gallant navy stood ready, but was not in reach to take active part," etc.

Just one week from the date of this address the body of the late President lay in state at the White House and many of us visited it, and two days later it was placed in the rotunda of the Capitol. I went there on that day and mourned with a bereaved people. The popular excitement at Washington caused by his death has had no parallel in our history, and that man rashly threw away his life who, in those days, spoke

disrespectfully of the dead.   Several instances occurred
in which rebels or rebel-sympathizers were killed out-
right in the city because of their intemperate language
in reference to our lost leader.

THE MUSEUM.

The Medical Director took a lively interest in my
case from the first; he frequently sent his adjutant or
orderly to inquire how my wound was progressing.
When I was able to walk around and enjoy the sights
and scenes of the great Legislative Metropolis, he had
the goodness to send for me.   I repaired at once to
his office and was received by him with marked attention and kindness.   He conducted me through the U.
S. Medical Museum, showing me, with pains-taking
patience, many wonderful curiosities which were there
on exhibition.   Fragments of the human frame, and
entire skeletons, were strewn about in melancholy pro-
fusion.   Among other relics he showed me the skull
of a soldier who had fallen in the earlier part of the
war.   A spent ball, which yet possessed force enough
to do injury, had struck him behind the eye, in the
exact place in which I had been shot myself.   The ball
did not penetrate far, and in comparison with my
wound it was, to all human appearance, less dangerous
and deadly.   Yet, superficial as this hurt was, no one
believed that the soldier had any sort of show for his
life; but despite this strong belief he did not die until
the nineteenth day after the accident.   The natural
inference from all this was, as the medical director in-

formed me, that my case was, perhaps, the most remarkable on record, taking into consideration the
grave character of my wound and my ultimate recovery.

SECRETARY STANTON.

One day I had occasion, in company with my friend,
Matthew Nolan, to visit the office of the Secretary of
War, to obtain an order for a suit of clothes to replace
those I had lost when wounded. Mr. Stanton received
me with considerate kindness. This was my first interview with him, but he had often seen me before as
I was passing along the streets. His great heart was
filled with sympathy for the common soldier.

It matters not to my purpose how the conversation
detailed below originated. Suffice it to say, that in
the course of this interview the subject of passes was
canvassed. I showed him mine from Capt. McCullom,
on which, in apparent astonishment, he asked:

"Do you need a pass?"

I answered him: "According to the rules and regu-
lations of our hospital we are required to have a
pass."

The Secretary then rejoined:

"Is it possible that they require a pass from you?
Well, you will not be required to show a pass here-
after. You can go wherever you please, subject to no
restrictions of this kind."

I remarked to him that this was a great privilege.

"Yes," he promptly replied, "a greater privilege

than Gen. Grant enjoys in the field." He went on to say afterward: "I see that the citizens manifest much sympathy for you, and that it affords you great pleasure to enjoy your liberty to go where you please, and I here detail this friend of yours as your guide and orderly while you are in the service."

I thanked the Secretary very warmly, after which he presented me with an order on Capt. Tomlinson, head-quarters clothing store, for the clothes I needed. Here, before closing this paragraph, it is a fitting tribute to a worthy friend to say that Sergeant Matthew Nolan was not only a guide and a companion but an amanuensis and reader as well, helping me to keep up a correspondence of large proportions.

VISITING MY REGIMENT.

About this time the victorious armies of the United States were encamped in the vicinity of Washington. I desired to visit my regiment which was then stationed at Arlington, some miles distant. In visiting places in the city, a pass from Captain McCullom was necessary; but when the boys wished to go beyond the city limits, they were obliged to obtain a pass from the Provost Marshal.

Next morning after my interview with Mr. Stanton, I went, more as a matter of form than anything else, to ask the guard to pass me. The result was, that I was obliged to go from the guard to the captain himself, who was busy at the time, and not in his usual good humor.

"Mr. Sallada," said he, "you don't want a pass to-day. You have been getting one every day."

I then informed him of my late interview with the Secretary of War, and the result of it.

Said the captain: "If you have a pass from Mr. Stanton, show it and go your way."

To show this pass, was the very thing I could not do; for the authority I had received from the secretary was simply verbal, and nothing more. Taking advantage of this circumstance, the captain said, rather pettishly:

"Secretary Stanton don't run this hospital."

I left the captain resolved in my mind to settle this matter as speedily as possible. Along with my guide, I went to the rear of one of the wards, where, finding a place in a high board fence most easily scaled, we managed, with some difficulty, to clamber over it without being observed. We then repaired to the war office, where we apprised Mr. Stanton of the trouble we had experienced. Having heard us attentively, the secretary remarked with feeling:

"Some of our contract doctors in these hospitals, put on more style than the brigadier generals in the field."

He then dispatched a messenger for Captain McCullom; and after we were dismissed, and while on our way back to the hospital we met the messenger along with the captain, proceeding to the war office. It is needless to say I had no more trouble with the hospital guard.

INSOLENCE OF A LIEUTENANT.

Under this authority from Mr. Stanton it was not necessary for me to apply to the Provost Marshal, for a pass to visit the regiment, but as my guide would probably need such assistance, we went to the Marshal's place of business, and secured the required papers for both of us. We then started for the regiment. In proceeding to the river we were compelled to run the gauntlet of three guards, stationed a little distance apart from each other. First, there was a corporal, next came a sergeant, and lastly a lieutenant. We passed all three without me being required to show my papers. Having crossed the river in a boat, we found three guards of corresponding ranks on the opposite side. These we passed in the same way, without any challenge. Proceeding onward to the regiment, I spent two happy days with the boys, enjoying their society, and hearing them recount their thrilling stories of camp and field life.

On our return to the city the boat on which we recrossed the Potomac was crowded with ladies and gentlemen. Among the latter were officers of the highest rank, some of whom favored me with sympathetic attention. I happened to be pretty well dressed at the time; and to add to my appearance, I wore a belt given to me by one of Sheridan's scouts, during my visit. It was formerly worn by a Union major-general, and was captured from him by a rebel brigadier, from whom it was recaptured by the scout, and presented to me.

The three guards whom we passed before re-crossing the river did not challenge me. Approaching the lieutenant on the Washington side, we were about to proceed past him when he promptly demanded my papers.

"You don't want a pass from me, do you?" I inquired, fumbling in my pocket as though in search of that document.

"Yes, I do," he replied, in a very surly tone, "and what is more, I intend to have it."

A crowd was gathering around us, among whom were some of the officers from the boat, and several ladies were there likewise. Incited by this circumstance, as well as others, I reasoned the case with the lieutenant to the best of my ability. I resolved not to present my pass. Argument, however, was lost on him. He grew more and more angry and vociferous, ending at last in downright brutality, so far, at least, as his offensive manners were concerned. Here I cut him short by saying: "I see, sir, that you have never been at the front, where there is danger as well as glory. Your conduct proves this to me, for if you had ever been at the front and had shared in the dangers and privations of a soldier you could not have the heart to treat an unfortunate comrade in this way."

These remarks hit him hard, and he squirmed, for there were certain passages in his past career which they seemed to unearth, but of which I was then ignorant. Stubborn and dogged to the last, he threw himself angrily on his dignity, exclaiming at the same time " do you know who I am, sir?"

"No, sir, I don't, and what is more I don't care," I replied, with all the emphasis I could summon to my aid.

Drawing himself up with a show of vast military pride and haughtiness, he rejoined "I am a lieutenant sir."

"Well," said I, "catching at the first repartee which suggested itself, "is a lieutenant above a captain?"

My answer was wholly inadvertent, given on the spur of the moment, but somehow or other it had the effect to disconcert the lieutenant and bring out a roar of laughter at his expense from all the bystanders. Even the ladies who happened to be present could not repress their mirth. Thus repulsed, my antagonist retired from the contest, and we proceeded on our way masters of the situation. Whether my major general's belt or my coat with gold plated buttons had anything to do in backing up my last chance shot, I leave the reader to determine.

It is a fitting close to this episode to say that it was reported by some one in the Washington *Chronicle,* and it was discovered afterward that this lieutenant had belonged to an eastern regiment. Some time before I met him he was severely injured in the ankle while he was involved in a midnight brawl. So this was the cause of his admission into the Invalid Corps. It was true he had never been to the front.

A GLANCE AT THE CAPITOL.

This structure covers four acres of ground. The dome is two hundred and fifty feet high. On top of this is the Goddess of Liberty, which is eleven feet high. As you ascend the east steps you immediately emerge into the rotunda, which is the interior of the dome. This is round and surrounded by gorgeous paintings, such as the Discovery of the Mississippi River, Landscapes, and Perry's Victory on Lake Erie, which I count the most splendid of all. This picture cost the Government twenty-five thousand dollars. Over the west door is a portrait of General Grant, the hero of the war. North of the west door is a marble statue beautifully illustrating the death of Tecumseh. The north door leads to the floor of the Senate, and the south one to the floor of the House. The yard, of about four acres, is beautifully shaded and filled with seats. In front of the Capitol is a large basin of water filled with various kinds of fish. This basin is carved out of stone and is probably over sixty feet in circumference.

VIEW OF THE NAVY YARD.

Here we find some eighty acres enclosed by a high brick wall. The main entrance is armed by two ancient brass pieces, one on either side, and captured in 1804. At the dock we find a man-of-war carrying ten guns, nine inch calibre. Next is a Monitor, the Montauck, that has passed through many a fiery ordeal. Her sides are covered by five and deck by four plates of iron, one inch thick. Her turret is round and covered with eleven plates of iron, one inch thick. This immense amount of iron is dented in places. One place it is bulged in four inches by the shots it received, while her sides are jammed five inches, most of the plates giving slightly instead of breaking. In this castle are two guns. The largest is four feet through at the breech and eighteen feet long. It weighs over twenty-one tons, and throws a fifteen inch shell with thirty-five pounds of powder, or solid shot weighing four hundred and thirty pounds with seventy pounds of powder. I witnessed the effect of one of these solid shots on a target of ten inches of iron and four of wood, and one more shot would have pierced this huge body of iron and wood. In the practice battery there were a great many curious guns. The most beautiful of all was a piece captured in 1793; also another called Whitworth, which threw a slug-shot eleven inches long seven inches into solid iron. The largest shell on exhibition there was twenty inches through or five feet around, thrown by a mortar as wide as long, and weighs about nine tons; when charged it is nearly full to the muzzle. One may read of all this and have good powers of comprehension, but never will they have an idea half extravagant enough until they have themselves seen these things.

GRAND REVIEW.

The two great armies under Meade and Sherman were now at Washington, preparing for the great review. Stages or stands were erected near the White House, on Pennsylvania Avenue. At length, all being in readiness, the review commenced May 22d, 1865, and lasted two days. Stand number two was occupied by the President, Foreign Ministers, Generals Grant, Meade, Sherman, and a number of other generals and high officials of our land. I received a complimentary ticket to stand number three, next the President's stand. The weather on this occasion was beautiful, and the scene was imposing, as the columns of Boys in Blue marched by, while the bands swelled the air with notes of thrilling music.

> " 'Twere worth ten years of peaceful life
>   One glance at that array."

CHAPTER VIII.

IN PHILADELPHIA.

My Contest with Red Tape—The Hat Cord—Trick with
Cards—My Manufacture—Discharge and Commission—
The Brave old 57th.

MY CONTEST WITH RED TAPE.

In the spring of 1865, after I had been an inmate
of the Washington Hospital for several months, the
thought suggested itself to me to secure the removal
of my quarters to McClellan Hospital, Philadelphia.
As a general thing my time had been spent very hap-
pily, but there were two circumstances which seemed
to demand, or at least to justify, this contemplated
change. The condition of my left eye was such as to
inspire me with some hope that, under the treatment
of a skillful occulist, the sight of that eye might be
restored. Hearing of Satterlee's Eye Infirmary, I
deemed it advisable to visit that institution. Besides
this, there was in the city of Philadelphia one of the
finest asylums in the country for the education of the
blind. The reader will now see what inducements I

had to secure this removal. It may as well be stated here as elsewhere, that the fond hope I indulged in reference to the partial recovery of sight was altogether delusive. Nothing short of a miracle like those which were performed by the Savior while on earth, could raise my dead eyes to life.

Having decided upon the change just referred to, I determined to take with me my Orderly Sargeant, Nolan. He had been with me so long, and his services had become so invaluable in many respects, that to lose him would have been a calamity indeed. The first thing in order was to send to headquarters my application to be transferred, and the next thing was to wait as patiently as possible the arrival of the necessary papers. Each morning at nine o'clock was the time set apart to transmit all such documents into the hands of the parties for whom they were made out. My application had been on file several days, long enough in all conscience for the transfer to reach me through official channels. Every morning I posted myself at the proper place, but as days passed and my name was not called out, as I had every reason to expect it would be, I finally became disgusted and determined to bring the matter to a definite and speedy issue.

I secured an interview with the officers of the hospital, consisting of the captain and the two surgeons, one of the hospital and the other of my ward. I inquired of them if my transfer had come from the Medical Director. The answer was that it had not.

I soon saw by the questions they began to present to me that there was something wrong. One of the surgeons wanted to know who was to be my guide and companion during my stay in Philadelphia. My answer was not at all satisfactory. They concurred in the declaration that Sergeant Nolan's services in the hospital were too indispensable to permit them to let him go. So far as my own transfer was concerned, provided I would take some one else as guide they interposed no objections, but on this point I was unwilling to yield. My trip to Philadelphia would have been robbed of more than half its interest in the absence of my inseparable companion. Finding at length that these officers would not be moved from their purpose by any common argument, I left them for that time, resolved, however, to renew the contest at an early opportunity.

I went over to the office of the Medical Director a week later, where I discovered what I had believed to be true all along, that the transfer was made out but a short time after my application had been sent in. It had been forwarded to the M. D. for his signature, and it was at that very time, as I had cause to know, sleeping the sleep of death in the Circumlocution Office at the hospital. Such was red tape in those days, backed up as it was by prejudice, and a disposition to oppress the private soldier. Indignant at the way I had been treated, I returned to the hospital and renewed my inquiries in regard to the official papers. Here I was repulsed again by the declaration that if

I went at all to Philadelphia I must go without Sergeant Nolan. They were ready to hand over my papers, but as to my friend, he should not accompany me. The captain said that as Nolan was the only non-commissioned officer of his company doing duty in the hospital, and as he was very serviceable in keeping books and other official records, his place could not be supplied. The ward surgeon was equally tenacious in holding on to Nolan. He said that as a nurse he could find no substitute for my friend, and the other surgeon flatly declared that the sergeant should not go. Thus, I was in direct collision with the authorities, and rash as it may seem, I was as obstinate as my superiors, asserting that as Nolan knew better than any one else how to contribute to my comfort and happiness, I would have him as my companion. This hot controversy came at length to a close, and I went away determined to appeal to the last and highest tribunal to which I could go.

Next morning I proceeded with my guide to the War Office, where, meeting Mr. Stanton, I expressed to him my desire to go to Philadelphia, and stated that I wished the sergeant to go with me, but this last wish was denied. It did not take the good Secretary long to decide in this case. His remarks to me on a former occasion when I applied to him for his generous interposition in my behalf, revealed the fact that he was a true and earnest friend of the soldier. He not only comprehended the routine of duties and humiliations through which I had been called to pass, but he seemed to penetrate the very thoughts of my heart, stimulating me with words of cheer, and sympathizing with my condition, as no other high functionary has done from first to last.

On hearing my case, the Secretary said, in his pointed way:

"You shall have the sergeant. Come here on the day after tomorrow and your papers will be made out."

The intervening day was the one which had been set apart, by proclamation, as a day of National Thanksgiving for our victories on land and sea. Next morning we returned to the war office and found our order of transfer made out ready to be signed by the adjutant-general and medical director. Afterward, when the order was signed by these officers, I was informed that it must yet receive the signature of the hospital surgeon. I disliked very much to go back again and beard the lions in their den, and therefore went after office hours, depositing the order with the clerk, in the absence of his superior. As soon as he saw the document, the clerk, who was really my friend, said:

"What have you been doing? You'll catch it."

Next day the triumvirate sent for me. They were now excited by anger, and repeated their resolution to keep the sergeant with them. Referring to the order from the war office, the terms of which were very direct and explicit, embracing both Nolan and myself in its grant of privileges, I asked them if they were able to get over that? Finally the hospital surgeon, who was terribly incensed as well as the others, because I had appealed to the Secretary, declared most emphatically that he ran that hospital and would not sign any order that took Nolan away.

"All right," said I, and departed. I went away resolved to apply again to the Secretary of War, but while I was making some necessary preparations before starting the surgeon's clerk came down to invite me to return, as he had been authorized to do so by his superior. I declined to go and he went away, returning a short time afterward with the transfer, signed in the proper manner. I accepted it, and thus this contest terminated.

To show the reader that I was not prompted, in this long struggle with power, by a boy's vanity and egotism, permit me to say that the full sympathy and co-operation of all my comrades in the ranks, throughout this trying ordeal, were mine; and they were mine because these comrades had often been trampled on, in the most ruthless way, by "contract" tyrants who had never been at the front, and who for that very reason did not know, or what is more did not care, how they treated the common soldier.

At the close of our last interview with the Secretary of War, he took my companion aside and spoke to him in the most feeling manner in reference to the great confidence I reposed in him, exhorting him to continue his worthy efforts to make my unfortunate life as pleasant as possible. Mr. Stanton knew how strong my attachment was to my friend and he it was, as the reader knows, who had detailed the sergeant as my orderly some weeks before.

All things were now in readiness, and early in June, 1865, we transferred our theatre of operations to McClellan Hospital, in the city of Brotherly Love. Not long afterward we were changed to Mower U. S. Hospital, in the same city. This is a beautiful and convenient building. We had a large and neat chapel with a library and reading room attached to it. In this chapel we had Bible-class twice a day. In the forenoon we were instructed in the Old Testament by Miss Biddle, and in the afternoon in the New Testament by Mrs. Talbot. We had religious services twice on Sabbath, and very often during the week. Here the chaplain and others became deeply interested in me and desired that I should become a christian. Among the rest was Miss Biddle, who would have me call very often at her room, and would spend an hour or more in exhortation and prayer. But I was inflexible, resisting her entreaties.

The ward in which we were placed contained sixty-five persons, not one of whom professed religion. It is no wonder that, with surroundings such as these, my heart was inclined to continue in rebellion against Divine goodness and mercy.

"He that covereth his sins shall not prosper, but whoso confesseth and forsaketh them shall have mercy."

THE HAT CORD.

I will relate a little episode in hospital life which caused much feeling at the time, and which I think is worthy of publication. Every Sabbath morning the members of our ward (and the same routine applied to other wards) were commanded to organize themselves into two lines, so as to be prepared to receive the visit of the inspecting surgeon. While this ceremony was in progress it was usual for our hats to lie on the foot of our beds. One Sunday the surgeon made his appearance supported by his escort, consisting of the corporal of the guard and ward master. My unpretending hat was ornamented by a military cord, which had been given me by an officer of my acquaintance. It was a fine one, it is true, but there was nothing in it which ought to have offended the sight of any one.

On the occasion to which I have alluded the surgeon came in with his usual pomposity. Observing my hat with its attachment he said angrily to my friend:

"Is that your hat, sergeant?"

"No; it is Mr. Sallada's," was the reply.

"I want you to take that cord off!" thundered the doctor, in a tone of imperial authority.

Instead of obeying him I persisted in keeping it to its place, and during the following week I sewed it so tightly to the hat that it could not be pulled away without destructive consequences. The next Sunday he presented himself, sporting his flaming epaulettes, for he drew the pay of lieutenant, and the shoulder-straps were used to publish that fact to an admiring world. Again his eye fell upon the obnoxious cord and again his wrath was kindled. In a paroxysm of fury he grasped the hat, and tearing away the cord with violence, he put it in his pocket and carried it off with him. The hat was seriously damaged, several holes being left in it.

From that moment the doctor became a very unpopular man in the hospital. His next inspection in our ward was attended by scenes which must have burned themselves in his memory. From all parts of the room in systematic succession would come the ominous questions: "Who stole the hat cord?" "Who stole the blind soldier's hat cord?"

When the irate doctor would turn in one direction to discover the aggressor who could thus contemn and mock his high authority, there was silence and airs of innocence in that part of the room, while in his rear the same dreadful questions would be repeated from half a dozen voices. Active as he was, the surgeon in performing his series of comic evolutions could not identify the offenders, and in sheer disgust and baffled rage he threatened to send the boys in a mass to the guard-house.

A few days later this contract surgeon in company with a lady was passing in a buggy along that part of the street which traversed the hospital. Quite a number of us were seated near by, and as the doctor came in sight enjoying the pleasure and the dignity of his excursion, he was suddenly assailed by a volley of questions like those which had fired his proud heart a few days before: " Who stole that hat cord?"

This was too much for him. Whipping up the horse, he rapidly passed beyond the line of our irritating fire never to trouble us again. When the next Sabbath came he was not our inspector, nor was he such ever afterward.

TRICK WITH CARDS.

A vein of mischief in my composition, or rather a disposition to while away the monotonous time led me frequently to improvise plans for our common amusement. I have spoken of one trick with cards; I am now to speak of another: I would propose to a stranger or to any other novice in the trick that he might select any card in the pack I was holding, and I could indicate the card without failure every time. This seemed to be so impossible of performance, especially in view of my blindness, that I could have won hundreds of dollars if I had seen fit to gamble on the result. The secret of the mystery, however, was very simple. I had a confederate in this trick who would station himself in a convenient but not conspicuous place, and after the cards had been thoroughly shuffled, and when the novice had made his selection, I would pick off the cards one at a time, holding them in such a manner that my confederate could see them, as well as all other interested persons. Retaining an attitude of indifference, as though he knew nothing and cared nothing about the matter, my confederate would beguile his time by humming a favorite tune. When I came to the card which had been selected, and which was known to all parties except myself, my friend would change the tune to something else, showing by this circumstance that the right card was reached.

MY MANUFACTURES.

But my time was not always so badly employed as it was when I was attempting to deceive by some trick or artifice. Many hours were employed in manufacturing watch ·chains and rings, generally from gutta percha. In time I acquired great adroitness and proficiency in making these articles. Those of us who engaged in this kind of manufacture realized quite a revenue from it. The products of our handiwork commanded ready sale, for a good deal of popular interest centered in the fact that they were made by soldiers who had suffered in the service.

DISCHARGE AND COMMISSION.

I have stated in another connection that Philadelphia was honored with a first class asylum for the blind. On my first visit to this institution a copy of the book of Psalms in raised letters was handed to me. It was the first specimen of the kind I had ever met with, yet in spite of this fact I was able to read the title with great readiness. Mr. Chapman, a principal officer of the asylum, could hardly believe that I

was unacquainted with the strangely formed characters,
my sense of touch seemed to be so perfect. I applied
for admission into this institution, passed an examination and was admitted. I designed to make instrumental music a specialty, as on my acquirements in
this branch of education I designed to depeud for
future support. All that now remained for me to do
was to apply for my discharge from the service. This
I did in due form, and about the same time my friend
Nolan started to Washington to secure his discharge
and be mustered out from his company in the Invalid
Corps stationed at that city.

My discharge came, but before its arrival the melancholy news came that he was dead, having lost his
life by some accident, the nature of which I never
fully learned. This was sad intelligence, for the sergeant had been endeared to me by close and fraternal
intimacy. It was his intention after receiving his
discharge to return and accompany me on a brief trip
home, preparatory to my entrance into the asylum;
his death was a sore bereavement to me.

Before closing this chapter I will briefly advert to
another circumstance which engrossed my attention
for a time. While at Washington I had a conversation one day with Mr. Abbot, of the Sanitary Commission, in the course of which reference was made to
the events which took place on the day in which my
wound was received. It was his opinion, and that of
others who were cognizant of the case, that I rendered
valuable service to my country on that day, contribut-

ing to turn the tide of battle in our favor. He stated that a commission should be given me by which I would be placed on the retired list with the rank of captain. He would gladly assume, he said, the task of making out the papers, and he was satisfied that success would crown the effort. Col. Hardy of the war office was another friend who interested himself in this matter. I did not ask for any such testimonial, but was glad that I had such strong friends at the capital.

About the time I decided to become an inmate of the asylum I received a letter from Mr. Abbot, enclosing the last paper I was to sign in furtherance of the proposed commission; but strange as it may appear to the reader, I sent back the document unsigned, declining respectfully the honor. I had an idea that the commission, if secured, would compel me to go every two months to be mustered for pay at Harrisburgh. involving me in large expenses as I would be forced to take a guide. Viewing the subject from my inexperienced standpoint, and being delighted at the thought of acquiring an education, I declined the commission. Mr. Abbot wrote to me expressing surprise and grief at the decision I had made; but whatever may have been duty in this matter, I acted according to my best convictions at the time.

THE BRAVE OLD FIFTY-SEVENTH.

As this is the close of my military career I will conclude the chapter by giving a short history of my regiment, which was organized at Harrisburg, Pa., September 18, 1861. Term of service, three years. Re-enlisted as a veteran organization December 31, 1863, at Brandy Station, Va., and was commanded by the following officers:

COLONELS.—Wm. Maxwell, Mercer, Pa., attorney-at-law, now in Greenville, Pa.; Chas. T. Campbell, Franklin, Pa., promoted to Brigadier General; Peter Sides, Philadelphia, from Captain Company A to Lieut. Colonel, to Colonel; George Zinn, appointed Brev. Brigadier General; Geo. W. Perkins, Bradford, Pa., from Adjutant to Captain of Company B, to Lieut. Colonel, to Brev. Colonel, a noble officer, for whom I will ever cherish the kindest and tenderest regards.

LIEUT. COLONELS.—E. W. Woods, Mercer, Pa.; T. S. Strohecker, Venango, Pa., from Captain Company I; Wm. B. Neeper, Alleghany, Pa., from Adjutant to Captain of Company C, to Major, to Lieut. Colonel; L. D. Bumpus, Venango, Pa., from Captain of Company I, a fine man and good officer.

MAJORS.—J. Culp, Bradford, Pa., killed at Fair Oaks in 1862; S. C. Simonton, now a justice of the peace in Clarksville, Pa., from Captain of Company B, a brave, good man, filling both civil and military offices very acceptably; Samuel Bryan, Lycoming, Pa.

ADJUTANTS.—Clark M. Lyons, Susquehanna, Pa., died from wounds received in action; James D. Moore, Mercer, Pa., to Captain of Company I; R. J.

McMillan, Mercer, Pa.; Thomas E. Merchant, Philadelphia, Pa.

QUARTERMASTERS. --Horace Williston, Israel Garrettson, Mercer, Pa.; John H. Rodgers, Mercer, Pa.; John W. Parke, Mercer, Pa.

SURGEONS.--John W. Lyman, Clinton, Pa.; H. G. Kritzman, Franklin, Pa.

ASSISTANT SURGEONS.-- A. W. Fisher, Northumberland, Pa.; Thomas Downs, Philadelphia, Pa.; J. R. Cassell, Bucks Co., Pa.; William Jack, Indiana, Pa.

CHAPLAIN.—Wm. T. McAdam, Mercer, Pa.

Our regiment participated in thirty-three general engagements besides minor battles and skirmishes, and was mustered out of service June 29, 1865, near Washington, D. C. As noble and brave a band of officers and soldiers as ever wore the blue.

CHAPTER IX.

—

CIVIL LIFE.

At Home—Contest with a Swindler—Engaged in Book Business—Stung by a Locust—Nearly a Tragedy—Memorable Introduction—Swimming the Alleghany — Home and Home Work—Religious Experience.

AT HOME.

In the latter part of September, 1865, I left Philadelphia and returned home, designing, as intimated before, to enter the asylum, after a brief visit among my old friends. This return to the old haunts and to the old associations of home constituted a happy era in my life. I was treated everywhere with cordial kindness, and I shared largely in all the parties of pleasure which were organized among my young friends. We had spelling and singing parties, and, in brief, nothing was lacking to make my sojourn preeminently pleasant. So far as our sports and festivities were concerned I was admitted to an equal participation in them, and at no time did my companions seek to impress me with a feeling of inequality on

11

account of my blindness. In all exercises, whether athletic or intellectual, I resolved to play my part. never standing back because I was deprived of one important sense. In other words, I was determined to accept nothing from sympathy or loyal gratitude which could be earned by actual meritorious service, and in thinking upon this subject now I am surprised that my acquaintances, in those days, seemed to vie with each other in keeping in the background all present consciousness of my misfortune.

CONTEST WITH A SWINDLER.

In the following December I received a visit from a fellow soldier, named Swartzwelder, with whom I had become acquainted in the hospital. He was from Pittsburg. My stay at home being protracted by one cause or another, I began to feel inclined to engage in some temporary business. About the first of February, 1866, a man named George Tate came to our house to sell the recipe for the manufacture of Roorbach's Chemical Compound Soap. He was quite a prominent member of the United Brethren Church, at a place some miles distant. He made a loud profession of religion, and was regarded as a sort of semi-official preacher, assuming the functions of the sacred office when the regular minister happened to be absent. It was on Wednesday that this man made his appearance; after dinner he began to talk business in a very voluble way. He proposed, for fifty dollars, to sell me the right for the township in which we were residing.

He declared he had entered it Monday afternoon of that week, and the little canvassing he had done over this territory was confined to less than two days. As to his standing in his own community, he was willing, he said, to supply us with all needed references. Fully believing the man's statements, I proposed at last to give him $45 for the township right. The proposition was accepted, and I borrowed the money from the bank, as my partner in the venture, Mr. Swartzwelder, was not able at the time to furnish his proportion of the expense. The kind of soap in which this investment was made was manufactured from simple ingredients, without the agency of ashes, or ley or grease. Thus, simple in composition, and quickly and easily made, the soap was of excellent quality. On going to work, we soon discovered that Mr. Tate had nearly canvassed the entire township before the right was sold to us; in fact, we were the victims of a very mean and dishonorable swindle. Some of the bonds our neighbors had given him, which bound them not to reveal the nature of the recipes they had purchased, were three weeks old at the time we bought the territory. This was proof enough of the swindle; but we went to work as cheerfully as possible, and, in spite of the obstructions in our way, realized quite a profit in the course of the next few weeks.

If I had not forgotten the above circumstance, I had at least permitted it to pass without serious notice, when, some months later, I chanced to be at the residence of Mr. Phillips, a large coal-land proprietor, and

a very worthy christian gentleman, who lived some
miles away. While conversing with him, he informed
me that George Tate, who then lived near him, had
often made his boasts of over-reaching a blind soldier
near Greenville, in the matter of certain soap recipes.
Mr. Phillips concluded his information by asking if I
was not the dupe of this swindle? I satisfied him on
this point; and, after tarrying for the night, went my
way, reflecting on the meanness of an arch scoundrel,
who had not only perpetrated a wretched swindle, but
had followed it up by publicly glorying in his own
shame. My indignation knew no bounds, and I was
determined to spare no pains in exposing him to sum-
mary and speedy justice. To do this would be a real
service, I thought, to society.

On my return home, I immediately wrote to Mr.
Tate, telling him what I had heard, and respectfully
demanding restitution. His answer was couched in
the most insolent and offensive terms; throwing off all
hypocritical disguise, he refused to refund a cent, and
dared me to do my worst. He told me to crack my
whip and go ahead; he was ready for me. Incensed
by this indecent display of bad temper and dishonesty,
I took the letter to Mr. Hamlin, an attorney, and a
good friend of mine, at Greenville. I made him fully
acquainted with the nature of the swindle, and all
succeeding circumstances connected with it. Having
heard me through, he resolved to do what he could to
punish the swindler; he wrote a letter to that individual, which brought him to his senses. Tate hastened

at once to town, and secured an interview with my lawyer, in the course of which he was informed that, unless he paid back the forty-five dollars which he had obtained by fraud, suit would be promptly instituted against him, and the whole case would be ventilated in court, to the ruin of his reputation for honesty and fair dealing. He was alarmed, and begged to have the privilege of compromising the affair, on the payment of a less sum, however, than was demanded. He pleaded poverty, and spoke of some recent misfortune by which he had been crippled; stating, in conclusion, that it was impossible for him to pay the entire sum. On this point Mr. Hamlin was inexorable; he would not move a hair's breadth from his first proposition. He demanded $45 for his client, and nothing short of this amount would satisfy the obligation.

In his extremity, Tate employed the professional services of a lawyer named McDowel, who would not have touched the case if his own reputation had been above that of a common blackleg and pettifogger. This lawyer, small as he was in his profession, soon discovered that nothing could be gained for his client, except by compromise; for, if the case went to court, scores of witnesses, summoned in my behalf from our township, would prove the fact of the swindle; and, besides this, the letters Mr. Tate had written to my lawyer and myself were so contradictory and self-convicting that they operated in a very damaging way against their writer. McDowel undertook the case; but, instead of appealing to Mr. Hamlin for a mitiga-

tion of the demand, he would waylay me when I was
visiting town, and depict the annoyances and uncer-
tainties, as well as the expense of going to law, winding up with the common-place declaration that it
would be much better for that little affair between
Tate and myself to be compromised. At last, after
referring him many times to my lawyer, and putting
him off in various ways, I consented to take fifteen
dollars and let the matter rest in oblivion. The haste
with which the lawyer transferred the money to my
keeping was somewhat surprising. He was overjoyed
to obtain such good terms; and, so far as my knowledge extends, George Tate has never, from that day to
this, boasted of his prowess in swindling a blind
soldier.

ENGAGE IN BOOK BUSINESS.

In company with Al. Swartzwelder I went early in
March to Pittsburgh, where we engaged with Ashur
Ellis, general agent for W. J. Holland, publisher,
Springfield, Mass., to solicit orders for a fine new
work entitled "Grant and his Campaigns." In
starting on this new enterprise we were advised by
Mr. Ellis to go into the country, as it would offer us,
in our inexperience, better facilities for success in canvassing than the city. A practical canvasser, he said,
had just made a failure of it in Pittsburgh.

I listened to this advice, but as I had formed a
number of agreeable acquaintances in the city, some
of whom would doubtless serve me in my business

relations, I concluded to remain where I was, hoping to compensate by zeal and energy for my want of experience. My success justified me in this decision, for the very first day I took in seven orders, and from that time forward my success was assured, going beyond my most sanguine expectations.

In May I returned home, and on the 22d of that month I went with my brother John to Clarion county, Pa., to visit the family of Samuel Shaner, father of. my old comrade, who died in the service. I designed also, while there, to canvass for the sale of books.

Before I took this trip I wrote to Mr. Chapman, of the Philadelphia Asylum, informing him of my engagement in new pursuits and of my intention to remain in them. Whether right or wrong, I thankfully declined the advantages which the institution proffered. If I had gone to Philadelphia the whole course of my after life would have been changed, but whether for better or worse I cannot tell. I only know that I acted from the best light I had, and however smooth and pleasant my life's highway through Philadelphia may have been, I cannot now regret the decision that was made.

STUNG BY A LOCUST.

My first visit to Clarion county was characterized by an event which nearly cost me my life. I was stopping temporarily with the family of an estimable lady, known as Mother Shakely. Her son John was to me a congenial spirit, full of life and fun, and the daugthers of the house were sufficiently attractive to make my stay there quite pleasant. Brother John and myself had been doing a fine business in piling up orders for "Grant and his Campaigns," and our business prospects were anything but gloomy. At the time of which I am writing the locusts were making their periodical appearance in vast numbers. In some sections the forests were desolated as though a tremendous frost had spread its blight and devastation all around; in other places, thousands of these repellant creatures seemed to emerge into the hard highways from subterranean cavities, literally massing themselves in the roads, to be crushed by heavy wheels or trampled by the hoof of passing animals. The sting of the locust is thought to be as fatal to human life as the bite of a timber rattlesnake. Just before this visit to the family of Mrs. Shakely two children and one young lady, all of them living in that part of the country, were stung by these insects, and death in each case was the result.

One morning I went with Miss Ada Shakely into the garden to help her pick currants. While there I felt something on my neck which seemed to require attention. Quickly putting my hand to the place, my fingers pressed a living object; and at the moment this pressure was applied a sharp prickling pain convinced me that I was stung. The fact is that I had been victimized by a locust. When the truth was discovered I went to the house, believing that if some specific or antidote could not speedily be found my days on earth were numbered. In a little time a sense of terrible giddiness seized me; and a deadly sickness pervaded my system. It was well for me that mother Shakely was familiar with a great many vegetable nostrums, the virtues of which were beyond question. Without showing any needless alarm she went deliberately to work, applying her specifics with readiness and skill. I remember that, among other things, onions were used; and when the poultice of these vegetables was withdrawn from the wound it was noticed that the onions so used had turned black, showing the malignant character of the sting. The remedies of mother Shakely along with the hospitable nursing I received, saved my life; but I had made a narrow escape. If the venomous sting had been inserted a little nearer the great vein of the neck, so as to give the poison a little better opportunity to mingle with the circulation, no earthly remedies could have saved me from sudden death.

NEARLY A TRAGEDY.

While we were at work in Clarion county, many happy hours were spent at the home of Samuel Shaner, of whom mention has been made in this chapter. The tie that bound me to this interesting family was very strong; for one of its members belonged to that band of thirteen, with whom I had been identified in the war for the Union, and of whom there were now but few survivors. Thomas Shaner was not one of these survivors; his place was vacant in the family circle.

Here in this pleasant home I was engaged one day in some sportive amusement with Addison Shaner, who, like myself, was young and full of jovial good humor. I remember in recalling the incident, that I seated myself on Addison's knee, and in this attitude, while under the influence of merry and prankish excitement, I took out a pistol which had but one chamber, and being certain that it had no load in it, I playfully placed the muzzle against his forehead, directly between his eyes. The weapon was cocked and I pulled the trigger; to my surprise the hammer did not fall. This was an uncommon circumstance with this pistol, and I pulled again at the trigger, employing more strength than before. The hammer was still immovable. I then took the pistol down from the dangerous range to which it had been leveled, and without saying a word to any one, I went aside to examine into its condition. On investigation I found, to my astonishment and horror, that it was loaded. Some person had, unknown to me, deposited a deadly cartridge in the chamber, and if the hammer had fallen, in obedience to forcible and repeated pressure, the brains of my young friend would have bespattered the floor, and a scene of terror would have been the consequence. To this day neither Addison himself, nor any other member of the family knows that the pistol was charged. Terrified and dismayed, as I certainly was, I had enough discretion remaining to keep the secret to myself; I was unwilling to let my friends know the extent of my foolish carelessness.

MEMORABLE INTRODUCTION.

As in other places to which my wandering steps had tended, I became acquainted with many warm friends in Clarion county. I was prosperous in business, and much genial sunshine was thrown into my life. It was here I met my destiny, for it was here and about this time too I met for the first time Miss Florence McGinnis, who subsequently became my wife. This first meeting with her was attended by a feeling singular in itself, and very important in its results. I will not call it, as a novelist would, love at first sight, but I will say that the sensation I experienced as I took her hand on this first introduction was of a character to impress me with the conviction that her destiny and mine were from that moment linked together. I did not know at the time that this feeling was reciprocal; I learned that fact afterward.

SWIMMING THE ALLEGHENY.

In describing so many narrow escapes from death which were experienced in my young days, it is reasonable for the reader to infer that I was not only fearless of physical danger, but really careless and reckless of consequences. To some extent this inference is just. I was ambitious to a fault, and in all feats of activity or daring I would not permit the loss of one sense to restrain me from taking a full hand with my young companions. On one occasion a number of us were enjoying the delightful exercise of swimming in the Allegheny. Though the river was quite wide at

the point where we were engaged in this lively recrea
tion, I swam across it. Returning toward the other
shore I heard the sound of an advancing steamer near
at hand. The impulse seized me to approach the boat
as nearly as possible without incurring any great personal risk. I was alone in this special enterprise, and
my companions remained near the shore as witnesses
of my exploit. I was precipitated into the vortex of
water in the rear that was caused by the passage of
the vessel, and the side-long sweep of the rudder. I
heard exclamations from persons on board and from
my friends at a distance who were conscious of my
perilous situation. I was an active and expert swim-
mer, but it required all my skill in the art and all my
power of resistance and endurance to keep from being
drawn under by the engulfing waves; I managed,
however, to keep afloat in the swirl and recoil of the
waters, and in a little while I passed beyond the point
of danger and was saved once more. It must be confessed that in the crisis of this peril I believed I would
be swept under the boat and lost, but at no time did
self-possession desert me. I calculated all the chances,
knowing well that I had brought on myself this danger, and must depend upon my own resources for
deliverance.

HOME AND HOME WORK.

The summer of 1866 had made its advent when we
again returned home, fully satisfied with our recent
canvassing labor. The farmers were about to com-

mence their annual toils in the harvest fields, and remarking that every one else was at work, I felt that
time with me would pass monotonously unless I took
up some congenial occupation. Beside this, I did not
wish to be regarded as differing in any respect from
the masses of my fellow beings. They wrought with
their hands, and why should not I? In spite of the
protest of many friends I went to work, assisting my
father in all the routine of harvest labor. I made a
full hand in binding wheat, and in loading and unload-
ing hay and grain. In addition to this I mowed and
raked hay, made rails and assisted in building fence,
and wound up the campaign of bodily exercise by
climbing tall chestnut trees and knocking the nuts
from their branches to be picked up from the ground
by my sister Allie, who accompanied me on these
excursions.

RELIGIOUS EXPERIENCE.

"If ye will not obey the voice of the Lord, but rebel against the
commandment of the Lord, then shall the hand of the Lord be
against you, as it was against your fathers."

"Rejoice, O young man, in thy youth, and let thy heart cheer
thee in the days of thy youth, and walk in the way of thy heart
and in the sight of thine eyes, but know thou for all these things
God will bring thee into judgment."

During my whole military life I had enjoyed the
very best of health. I had vowed to God, when suffering with my wound, that if He would restore and
preserve my life, I would devote myself unreservedly
to His service. My wound healed, and I was restored

to the bloom and vigor of life. But I forgot to pay my vow, and lived on in sin.

Reader, did it ever occur to you while enjoying the pleasures of sin and folly, that you had a soul to save, a hell to shun, and a heaven to win? Did you ever think that all you enjoyed came from God?

Everywhere I went I met with kind and warm-hearted friends; my joy and worldly pleasures were excessive; I had perfect success in business; I found in every form a friend, and yet I was inimical to God, who had endowed all these blessings on me. Ministers and christian people were advising and telling me it was my duty to become a christian; that my life had been miraculously spared; that I had a mission to fill.

In the fall of 1866, a protracted meeting was held in the vicinity of Greenville, by Rev. J. D. Domer, an able and efficient minister. My first impulse was not to attend the meeting, for fear I would be persuaded to become a christian. Then, my second thought was, there were my associates, and if they could resist the strivings of the spirit, I could; and so I attended the meeting. The sermons were powerful, and I felt as if they were personally directed to me. I then thought of what I had passed through; how often I had heard prayers at the family altar ascend to the throne in my behalf. They were earnest pleadings for my salvation. How many times I had seen the tears roll down the careworn face of a dear mother, and that mother now cold and silent in the grave. I thought of the vow I made when I, as it were, was snatched from the very jaws of death and restored to the bloom of life. How many sermons I had heard preached, how many exhortations and prayers, advice and entreaties from christian people. These I knew were all recorded against me. I felt that the last witness had given in his evidence against me. I was doomed and convicted, and only awaited the verdict. With these thoughts crowding my mind, I fell upon my knees and implored God to remove this burden of guilt, to wash away the many and long contracted sins, to disperse the dark clouds, and let His love rain down upon me in copious showers, and, like Saul, of Tarsus, said: " Lord, what wilt Thou have me to do?" Thus I wrestled with God till He blessed me.

What comfort, what consolation, and what inexpressible joy burst upon me at this moment! My heart was animated with the love, peace and happiness of Jesus Christ.

> "My God, I know that I must die,—
> My mortal life is passing hence;
> On earth I neither hope nor try
> To find a lasting residence.
> Then, teach me by Thy heavenly grace,
> With joy and peace my death to face."

CHAPTER X.

MOMENTOUS TRANSACTIONS.

Canvassing Again — A Cruel Suspicion — A Dangerous Slide—Mechanical Skill—Trip to Wisconsin—Mercantile Pursuits—Marriage.

CANVASSING AGAIN.

In January, 1867, I accepted an appointment as general agent for the sale of Hassas & Lubrecht's Maps and Charts. My duties were to constitute local agents as well as to effect personal sales. For a part of the time my cousin, John Fisher, was my partner, and afterward Fred. Umholtz shared in the venture. Good fortune crowned our efforts. In the following May I went on an excursion of business and pleasure to Clarion county again. Returning home, I obtained in June, from A. G. Campbell, of Berea, Ohio, a special agency for the sale of the American Practical Cyclopedia, a very large and comprehensive work, requiring much time and patience in the exhibition of its merits to purchasers. My partner in this enterprise was F. H. Umholtz, a gentleman of rare talent and acquisitions. This venture richly repaid us. In one village our success was so great that the number of copies we sold there was one more than the entire number of families. A stranger visiting the town took the extra copy.

A CRUEL SUSPICION.

While employed on this agency an occurrence took place one day which made me the victim of a cruel suspicion. It happened as we were entering a house my partner, who was not overheard by any one else, alluded to certain pictures or military charts which he saw hanging against the wall. I heard enough from him to know what the pictures were, for I had sold hundreds of them myself. One of them displayed Abraham Lincoln in the center, while around him were clustered, in artistic order, several of the dead generals of the civil war. The other one (for there were but two) represented Andrew Johnson in the center, with living generals grouped about him. Both charts were not only familiar to me, as I had handled them often, but I knew the place on the wall against which they were suspended. A little time after our entrance into the house I engaged in conversation with its owner. Looking straight at the pictures, as though seeing them, I began to comment on the massive brow of Gen. Sedgwick, and the bold martial bearing of Gen. Burnside, who was the finest horseman in the army. Having spoken in this way for a time and despatched the business that brought us there, we

12

took our leave. In passing out I did what I nearly always do on such occasions; being in the rear of my guide, my hand fell naturally on the knob of the door; pulling the door to I left the premises with my companion.

It is difficult for me to express my sense of outrage and humiliation, when on the next day I learned that I had been shamming, to excite popular sympathy and thereby multiply our sales. My apparent survey of the chart and my minute statements in regard to their relative positions and details, combined with the readiness with which I closed the door, had started the false and cruel report which was then in circulation. Even the man with whom I had been boarding for a month was influenced to believe in the truth of this groundless rumor. It was well for me that refutation of the most convincing character was near at hand. In cases where blindness is caused by disease of the optic nerve, the eye has a natural look except that the pupil is unduly enlarged; but in my case, when the glasses I wore were raised, the evidence of blindness, caused by a rebel bullet, was too manifest to be disputed. Thus this cruel suspicion was stopped in its course before any real mischief was done, except to annoy me for a while in the keenest manner.

Before this event took place I took great pains to do what I did in the most dexterous way of which I was capable. I knew that the loss of one sense must result in the greater discipline and efficiency of the others, and to help me farther, there were scores of little telegraphic signals employed by my partner and myself, and observed by no one else, by which many things came to my knowledge in what outsiders would call a very singular manner. After the painful event which has been narrated I tried for a brief time to be awkward and blundering in all my movements, but I soon became disgusted with this course and abandoned it. I had acquired a certain degree of dexterity in the different exercises in which I had played a part, and it was worse than folly to throw away the experience and teaching of years just because ignorance or envy had the power to fabricate false reports.

A DANGEROUS SLIDE.

In September, 1867, I paid another visit to Clarion county. On my return, which occurred the same fall, my father commenced the erection of a two story frame residence on his farm. The building progressed rapidly, and at the time the accident took place, which I am about to describe, the workmen had finished the roof on one side, and were just beginning on the other. The ladder was still on the finished side; and up this I clambered to take an observation. My friends had often warned me to keep away from places of peril, as my condition did not, in their judgment, warrant any such reckless temerity. Doubtless such warnings were very proper, and I ought to have been governed by them more frequently than I was; but being active and self-dependent, relying on my own resources with great confidence, I entertained the belief that I could go where any one else dared to venture.

The workman had left one cleat near the comb of the roof on the side on which I was ascending. This cleat, which formed a support for the feet, so that persons who were posted there would not slide down, was in a loose and dangerous condition. This I did not observe until it was too late to avoid the catastrophe. The moment my foot pressed, with considerable force, against this frail and imperfect support, all its fastenings gave way, and I began to slide, slowly but surely down the steeply inclined plane, which was formed by the roof. As soon as I felt myself sliding downward I began to use every means in my power, to retard or stop my descent, clinging as closely as possible to the roof. From the first I determined to raise no outcry for help. If I had done so relief would have come very speedily; for at that very moment friends were at work only a few feet from me, on the other side of the roof. I concluded that as I had involved myself in this fearful danger, and had done so, too, in the face of repeated and impressive warnings, I would rely upon myself alone for deliverance.

It is strange, however, that the thrilling struggle through which I was passing was not observed at all by witnesses. I could hear the men at their work close by, but I would not call on them for assistance. Sternly and silently, yet with palpitating heart I faced the great peril, resolving to save myself if the means of safety were within my power. As stated before my progress down the roof was very slow, and every inch of this gradual descent was attended by a sensation of thrilling and torturing suspense, impossible of description. I not only had friends on the house, but there were others on the ground, whose voices, raised in cheerful conversation, fell familiarly on my ears, as I was engaged in this terrible contest for life. They knew not of my danger.

Thoughts come quickly in a crisis like this. The ground on that side of the house, on which I seemed destined to fall, was covered with rocks and heavy pieces of timber; and near these was a pump, on which, if I fell, my life would be crushed out beyond all hope of restoration. From this great thought my mind reverted to the ladder, which stood against the house. If my foot would strike, by good fortune, against this support, I felt that I would yet be saved; but, how was I to know that any such good fortune would be the result? I was not able to see the course I was taking. I might come in contact with the ladder, but there was a fearful possibility of missing it, and thus losing the last chance to regain my footing. The moment came which was to decide my fate. I had done all I could to check my progress along this awful declivity. Instinctively I braced myself for the coming shock; and in that instant of supreme suspense, my foot touched the ladder. The sense of relief that followed this chance movement, was changed into renewed agony, when I felt that the upper part of the ladder was slipping along the eaves, under the slight pressure that was applied.   Certain it was that if this slipping were to proceed much farther the ladder would be precipitated to the earth, taking with it the last hope of rescue I could cherish.   It was at this period that my feeling of suspense was the greatest.   It was a moment indeed of absolute horror.   I was hanging over a dreadful abyss; and inch by inch the support to which I was clinging with desperate tenacity, was moving along the extremity of the roof.   It stopped at last, as it struck against some very slight projection among the shingles.   The instant I came to a halt in my thrilling journey, I managed, with effort, to take a knife from my pocket; and having opened it, I inserted the point of the blade in the roof, thus making myself secure in this position.   I was then master of the situation.   It did not take me long to adjust the ladder to its proper place.   I was safe.   This adventure was never known to my friends; I had my own motives for concealing it; but to this day a tingling sensation disturbs my nerves when I think of that frightful descent down the roof of my father's house.

The winter of 1867–8 was occupied in a variety of ways.   There were spellings, and singings, and religious meetings, and parties of pleasure.   Time passed very agreeably.   During that winter, I visited my relatives at Shakelyville.   In February, my father, who had been a widower for some years, was united in marriage to Lovina Rhinehart.   Anticipating an event of a similar kind in my own experience, I purchased for $500 a lot near my father's residence, containing five acres and embracing a house and fine orchard. This property I leased out for a time.

MECHANICAL SKILL.

About this time, or perhaps a little before, I began to try my skill at certain mechanical creations. Believing that I had some talent in this direction, I went vigorously to work, and made a bureau. To give the reader some idea of this product of my handicraft, I will state that it was two and a-half feet high and twenty-two inches wide. It was composed of alternate strips of black walnut and chestnut, the strips being two inches wide and glued together. Mechanics will readily perceive that a work like this, if it be done well, requires much artistic skill. The fronts of the drawers were made of walnut, while the surrounding finish was composed of chestnut. Persons who were invited to see it agreed with each other in pronouncing it handsome. In this connection it is perhaps proper to state that a writing desk, which I made, drew a premium of $4.00 at the Shenango Valley Fair.

TRIP TO WISCONSIN.

In April, 1868, I employed Wm. Stevenson, for $8 a month and expenses, to go with me to Wisconsin on a canvassing tour. I had obtained a general agency from the National Publishing Co., to sell Richardson's celebrated work, entitled "Beyond the Mississippi." Along with this, I sold copies of Beecher's "Norwood." Our destination, or at least the headquarters we established, were at the residence of Mr. Hoylands, a brother-in-law of Mr. Stevenson. The personal resemblance between Mr. Hoylands and Gen. Grant was too striking to escape attention. Miss Terza Hoylands, daughter of the gentleman with whom we were stopping, was a young lady of rare genius and cultivation. Some of her poetical contributions are real gems, flashing with the light of true poesy. My sojourn with this family was very delightful.

In the course of our excursions we had great business success at Monroe, Judea, and other places. We also visited Mineral Point and Darlington, where the extensive lead-mine region of Wisconsin opens its prosect before the gaze of the traveler.

MERCANTILE PURSUITS.

Returning in July to Greenville, I purchased there a confectionary store from Irvin Shade, taking my brother with me as an assistant. Sometime afterward I enlarged my stock of goods to a general assortment, embracing fruits and groceries. A good friend of mine, Wm. Waugh, largely benefitted me by his counsels and advice in regard to business. The purchase of my store was made August 1, 1868.

MY MARRIAGE.

My frequent visits to Clarion county foreshadowed an event which gives me infinite pleasure to record. Elsewhere my first introduction to Miss Florence

McGinnis is described. The more I became acquainted with her the deeper was my conviction that she was destined, in the order of a good and kind Providence, to become my wife. Whatever mistakes I may have made in reference to other subjects, I was sure that in regard to my contemplated marriage I had made a wise and happy choice. To be the wife of a man situated as I was, required certain elements of character which are not often found in society. Such elements, however, belonged to the one I chose, and I was about as happy a wooer as the state of Pennsylvania contained when the decisive "yes" was pronounced, and the day of our wedding was fixed.

On that day, bright and early, being the 11th of August, I arose from my bed, and in the hurry of preparation for our departure my garments were thrown into disorder, and I happened to put on my vest wrong side out. Seeing me in this condition my friends rallied me without stint, predicting that some accident would happen during the day to interfere with the proposed wedding in the evening. The ceremony was to be performed at Meadville, through which we were to pass in proceeding to Greenville. Seven miles of the route we had to traverse in a vehicle before reaching the station at which we were to take the cars.

There were four of us who started in a buggy for Emlenton station, viz: Charles Shaner, my sister Lizzie, Florence and I. We had gone about a mile on our way when to the surprise and mortification of the whole party an axle suddenly gave way, stopping us in our course. The prediction uttered that morning seemed to be on its way to fulfillment. but I was determined to carry out our common purpose in spite of the accident. I proposed that if Mr. Shaner would remain to take care of the team and our baggage, the two ladies and myself would proceed to the station on foot. A. general assent was given, and off we started in high spirits. The way was long, but we were equal to the emergency. Reaching an eminence overlooking the station, which was nearly half a mile away, we saw the train on which we were to go coming up to the depot. This sight accelerated our speed, causing us to perspire pretty freely. We arrived safely on time, but had barely seated ourselves in the cars when the train emerged from the station.

Mr. Shaner did not join us on this trip. At seven o'clock P. M. of that day we arrived at Meadville. An hour later we proceeded to the residence in that city of Rev. Mr. Craighead, a Presbyterian minister. by whom the marriage ceremony was duly performed.

August 24th we established our residence on Race street, Greenville. I actively pursued the mercantile business until November 1st when I disposed of the store to Henry James, who subsequently proved a defaulter, compelling me to suffer very serious losses.

In December, 1869, I put up a store building on the property which I had purchased near town, and on the 8th of January, 1870, commenced selling goods in this house. In April we received a visit from my brother-in-law, J. W. McGinnis, who was a musician of fine attainments. In time I built an addition to the store; meantime we were settled in our new home, which was known by the name of Diamond Hill.

In the multiplicity of other engagements, I undertook, about this time, to invent and make a Combination Bureau and Book Case. This was an elaborate piece of mechanism, comprising many difficult details. This work I completed, and I will not be considered vain if I state here that my invention was complimented in high terms by connoisseurs in cabinet work.

From the time at which I sold my store in Greenville until the period when I established myself in the variety store at Diamond Hill, I was engaged genererally in the book trade, reaping quite a harvest of profit in the business.

On the 6th day of November, 1869, our home in the country was gladdened by the advent of our first boy. He came to us as a precious gift from our Father in Heaven, cheering and blessing our hearts by his prattle and innocent presence.

In the fall of 1870 I was impressed with a desire to go west. In obedience to this desire I soon disposed of our property, and on the first day of November of the same year we bade adieu to the Keystone State and turned our faces toward the Great West.

CHAPTER XI.

LIFE IN THE WEST.

ARRIVE IN DES MOINES—SOCIETY IN MONROE—ENGAGE IN MERCHANDISING — BUILDING A 'HOUSE — GOING EAST—EMBARK IN THE MUSIC BUSINESS—ELECTED ALDÉRMAN—SAD TIDINGS.

ARRIVE IN DES MOINES.

AFTER a few days journeying through the states of Ohio, Indiana, Michigan and Illinois, we crossed the grand old Mississippi at Davenport into the beautiful state of Iowa with its broad prairies, stately groves of timber, and beautiful and enterprising cities and towns. We soon reached Des Moines, the capital of the state; here we found everything bustle and activity. I called on Percival & Hatton, gentlemanly, obliging and very extensive real estate agents. In conversation with them I soon learned that all branches of business was well represented here, and that a man with small means would stand no chance, but they advised me to go to some of the smaller towns. Next morning we went to Monroe, thirty-two miles southeast of Des Moines. This beautiful place is situated on the divide near the center of the state; seven miles from the Skunk, and eight from the Des Moines river, is surrounded by fine belts of timber and inexhaustible beds of coal and fine building rock; has about eighteen hundred inhabitants, two railroads, one weekly newspaper, six churches and a host of whole souled enterprising citizens, business men and people generally. I was so much pleased with the town and its generous hearted people, that I decided to locate accordingly, ordered my goods from Des Moines and purchased a house and lot. In January following I bought a grocery, boot and shoe store, of C. N. Hickox. In February I was elected member and president of the board of trustees of the Evangelical Church, which office I held for three consecutive years. February 21 our home was brightened by another little ray of sunshine, in the form of a tiny boy with hair and eyes like midnight. In March I sold my store to my brother, and engaged in the book business. In May I went to the southwestern part of the state, soliciting orders for the Franco Prussian War, and Family Bible, with good success. Returned home in July. Continued in book business until October, when I erected an addition containing four apartments to my house. I mention this because I laid out and framed the building—when it was raised it all went together without a single miscalculation.

Rev. Mr. Hertzog, a neighbor of mine used to watch me at work day after day, and had a great curiosity to see it raised, but when it was done he pronounced it very good. I laid the floors, sided, hung the doors, and in fact did all the work except a little help on the roof. I will state that while I enjoyed sight I had never seen a building laid out, much less worked on one. This addition being on two sides of the house, any mechanic will readily see was difficult. During the winter I built a fine combination bureau, secretary and glass front library handsomely finished, which to this day is pronounced a fine specimen of workmanship, even to those skilled in the art.

In the spring of 1872 my eldest sister, Lizzie, came west to live with us. Rev. A. C. Heckathorn, a rising young minister of the Evangelical Church, made our house his headquarters and we spent the summer in reading and improving property. In September I started with my family to visit our old homes. Spent the fall and winter very pleasantly among relatives and friends in the great coal and oil regions of Pennsylvania. Returned in March, 1873, and purchased an organ of J. P. Corliss of Des Moines, upon the following conditions: I paid him $50 down and gave my note for the balance, he giving me an agency to sell organs for him, the small commission which he would allow me on sales I made was to apply on my note. I went to work, and before my note became due I had made sales sufficient that my commission more than paid my note. I liked the business so well that I determined to continue in it. I therefore received an agency of W. W. Kimball & Geo. Woods & Co., of Chicago, carrying as many organs in stock as my small room would hold.

On locating in Monroe I had become a member of

the Evangelical Church; I was now elected super-intendent of our Sabbath School, and President of the S. S. Association. I have held and do at present hold official positions in religious, social and political organizations.

Kind readers, I do not mention this egotistically, but to demonstrate what an individual in my unfortunate condition *can* do if he has the *will*. I have met so very many, some of whose affliction is less grievous than mine, who have thrown themselves upon the charity of the public, and seem to think there is nothing they can do but sit down and bewail their misfortunes.

In July my brother John, who had been staying with us was married. During this summer I worked faithfully at my business with good success. In the fall of 1874 I purchased property of Mr. J. L. Scharf near the public square in order to get a better location for my business. After building an addition and otherwise improving I opened a general music store, keeping pianos, organs and all kinds of musical merchandise, and named my store "Monroe Music Emporium." In the spring of 1875 at the caucus for nominating municipal officers I was nominated alderman on the temperance ticket; this was done without my knowledge, and when informed of it next day was surprised to think that a person in my condition should be nominated for civil office. The temperance ticket was elected; the retiring officers were for license. When we entered upon our duties in March we had an empty treasury and found a debt of $112. Besides, the re-

tiring council had licensed the saloons three months
on our time, having received the money therefor.
The cry of the license portion of the community was
that the town could not be run without the license
revenue. We kept up and made crossings, sidewalks.
etc., beside some special improvements, and turned
the city over to our successors free of debt and saloons
and billiard halls, thus demonstrating that the government of our cities and towns need not be depend-
ent on whisky money, and that too without increasing
taxation.

SAD TIDINGS.

In September I received the sad intelligence that
my father was very sick. My sister immediately
started for home. A few hours after we received a
telegram that he was not expected to live. My brother
John and I followed on the next train. When we
reached Keokuk the eastern bound train which we
were to take had left just a few minutes before. We
had to wait until next train, and next morning we
came to a train laying in a ditch, some of the cars
literally smashed to splinters; that was the train we
just missed. Our anxiety to reach our sick father
was such that the moments we had to spend waiting
for the train seemed like torturous hours, but as we
looked upon this wreck it seemed that our delay was
Providential. It is useless to try to describe my feelings when I reached my old home where my boyhood's
happy days were spent and found my father very ill

with no hope of his recovery. This was the first time that all of our family had met together for five years, and sad as the occasion of this meeting was, it was a great comfort to my father to be surrounded by all of his children once more, and for the last time on earth. He suffered intensely, but patiently and resignedly, for over four weeks, when on the morning of October 9th, just as the light was breaking, with one loving, lingering look upon us all as we stood around his bed, he passed peacefully and calmly away and joined my mother and little sisters in the bright, beautiful land. My father led an unostentatious, earnest Christian life; he had not an enemy; to know him was to love him; he was a kind and just father; his house was ever open to the weary traveler and stranger.

Oh blessed is life when the warfare is ended,
  And the Comforter comes as the victor to save,
And the soul follows after its Master ascending
  Victorious forever o'er death and the grave.
And blessed was *he* when the summons was given,
  A friend and our father whose mission is done—
Who triumphed before the bright portals of Heaven,
  And spoke of the glories salvation had won;
Who left the glad witness—"Accepted I am,
  And on pinions elate
  I am sweeping the gate,
Upborne by the love of the Lamb."

We shall meet him no more in our unions forever,
  When the music of bells fills the air with delight—
When the sunshine of evening fades soft on the river,
  Or sets the gold stars of the diademed night.
  His spirit no longer on wings of elation

> Awaits the sweet seal of the heavenly kiss,
> But passed in its rapture the gates of salvation,
>   And now with the saints and the angels in bliss,
> He is safe by the throne of the mighty I AM—
>   On pinions elate
>   He has swept the bright gate,
> And is singing the blood of the Lamb.

A few days after my father's death my brother and I returned to our homes, and I set about adjusting my business which my unexpected absence had interfered with. Our Christmas and New Years present came to us on the 28th day of December, and was very highly appreciated, being our first and only daughter, a handsome, healthy little treasure.

In January, 1876, my youngest brother, George, came to be a part of our family, and in June sister Ray came. In July my youngest sister, Allie, joined our household. When I left the old homestead, and knew that my brother and sisters would soon have to go out in the cold world among strangers, I told them they should share my home with me whenever and just as long as they wished to. To accommodate my now increased household it became necessary to have more house-room. In August I erected an 18x41 two-story addition to my house, and finished the first floor finely for my store room. My business had increased to such an extent that I was now carrying a very large stock of musical goods. I remember of one week that my sales amounted to two thousand dollars. From a very small beginning, by hard work, perseverance and close attention to business, I had worked up a very large trade. I had a great deal of opposition to contend with, the worst of which was from unprincipled agents who were running over the country selling inferior instruments, not hesitating to use any means, however unfair or dishonest, to deceive the people and accomplish their object, even going so far as to try to malign and blacken the character of honorable local dealers. The following is an instance, of which I could give many. I had solicited an order for a Goodman cabinet pipe organ, from a gentleman near Prairie City. He desired me to get one built to order for him, which I agreed to do and deliver it in two months. Meantime one of those renegade agents, working for a firm then in Des Moines, hearing of this transaction, called on the gentleman two or three times and tried every means in his power to sell him one of his organs. He took one of the finest they had to his house and offered to give him fifty dollars to "go back on me" and purchase his. He said I could not and would not deliver the organ I had represented. When asked why, he said there was no such an organ company in existence; that the statements I made them were all false, for he *knew me*. The truth is, I had never spoken to this agent at all. When I delivered the organ, and while unpacking it, I heard such exclamations as: "Why, yes, there are the pipes;" "yes, and there is the glass panel, ma," etc. My curiosity being aroused I finally asked what they meant, when they explained the occurrence I have just related.

During leisure hours and odd moments I had been

working on an invention, upon which, in June, 1877, I received letters patent. Said invention is known as "Sallada's Combination Cupboard." It consists of two parts, and is detachable—each part complete in itself. The combination can be divided into five sections, and each section used independent of the other. All the drawers close air - tight, by means of rubber. The flour receptacles and victuals cupboard are provided with adjustable ventilators.

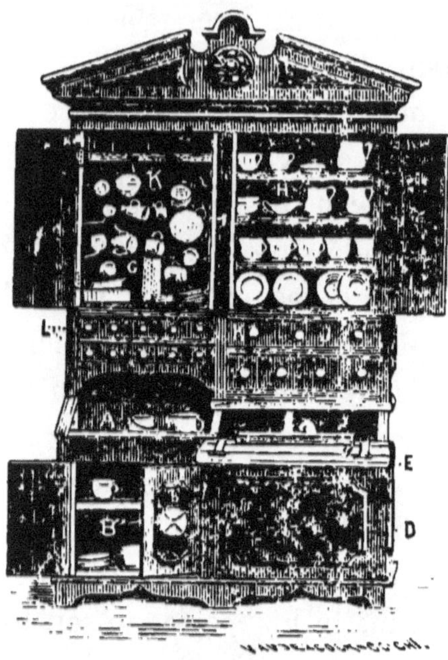

SALLADA'S COMBINATION CUPBOARD.

The whole combination contains thirty-six compartments, and only occupies 2x5 feet of space on the floor.

ODE TO SALLADA'S COMBINATION CUPBOARD.

BY REV. H. B. HARTZLER, CLEVELAND, O.

A song like this was never sung
By bird or beast or human tongue:
It fits the time, it suits the season,
Is full of sense and rhyme and reason,
　　And keeps in tune,
　　From March to June,
Through winter snow and harvest moon.

Here is a lasting household joy,   .
For daily service and employ;
A handy, pretty, useful thing,
Fit for the kitchen of a king:
A Combination Cupboard, madam,
Kept secret since the days of Adam.

Here is room for fruits, and bread and pies,
Secure against intrusive flies;
A place for butter, milk and flour—
For hot or cold, for sweet or sour:
A shelf for crystal, glass, or china,
In easy reach of Dan or Dinah;
      And all as clean,
      And neat, I ween,
As any wife has ever seen.

No less than sixteen drawers I see,
For sugar, coffee, spices, and tea;
For knives and spoons and table covers,
And dainty things for hungry lovers.
For pills and powders there's a nook,
For handled ware a handy hook;
For dishes, pots and pans a place,
With doors to close the ample space.
And if the busy housewife wishes
To bake her bread, or wash her dishes,
She'll find a board and sink and tray,
To keep her at it all the day.

Then sing this song with hearty cheer:
Proclaim the tidings far and near,
      In deed and word,
      With one accord,
All hail this Combination Cupboard.

In August, my youngest sister, Allie, was married to Mr. Howard, a worthy young man and enterprising furniture dealer of Monroe, where they went to housekeeping in a pleasant little home of their own. In September, my wife's mother, Mrs. Mary McGinnis, of Pennsylvania, who had been spending the summer with us, returned to her home. In October, my wife's health failed, and for more than a year she was in very poor health, which was a great calamity to me. In November, sister Lizzie was married. The departure of so many friends in so short a time, and my wife lying ill, I was for a time o'ershadowed with " clouds," but waited and hoped for the " sunshine " to come again. I was deprived of one great source of profit and pleasure—I refer to that of reading. We never let much time go by unimproved; for, when not otherwise employed, my wife would spend the time in the perusal of books, papers, etc. She is an elegant reader, and delights in reading as much as I do in hearing her read.

In January, 1879, Mr. H. Monroe and Judge Maxwell, temperance workers of Des Moines, came to Monroe, and began a series of meetings, which were continued for some time by J. Hardin, an eccentric, earnest worker, the pastors, and other workers of our city. We succeeded in procuring over 1,000 signatures to the pledge. I have in my mind now young men that were saved and reformed during that meeting who have since arisen to lucrative and honorable positions in the city. During my military career, and after I returned from the army, I had been addicted to tippling, or so-called moderate drinking, until about nine years ago I became awakened to the fact that it was an evil of no small magnitude; I finally resolved to abstain from all intoxicating drinks forever, and hope I shall yet see the day when this gigantic evil shall be eradicated from our land.

In February, Rev. J. W. Todd, and Mell and F. C. Brown started an eight-page weekly newspaper, called "The Reform," devoted to temperance reform, public morals and local news. Mr. Todd was very desirous that I should take charge of and edit the paper; and after repeated solicitations I consented to do so. I was to receive one-fourth the receipts of the office as my compensation for managing and editing the paper. Everything went along pleasantly and smoothly in this, to me, new departure, until after a few months my wife took sick again, and, as she was my amanuensis and proof-reader, I was compelled to resign my position. Thus ended my experience in the newspaper field.

On the 25th of June, I received letters patent on the Sallada carpet fastener and stair rods, a novel device for stretching and fastening down carpet without tacks. With this device carpet can be put down in one-tenth the time required by the old method; it obviates the injury carpet and floor sustain by the use of tacks; it entirely conceals the edge of carpet and gives a most elegant finish to the apartment; is easily adjusted to any sized room, and can be loosened in two or three minutes for speedy removal, as in case of fire.

The fastener possesses many novel features, which combined develop the true scientific principle of fastening down carpet.

Our stair rod, is in principle of construction and peculiar adaptability to the purpose desired, the most convenient, durable and handsome rod ever placed on the market.

Intending to go into the manufacture of these goods, I sold out my property and store to Messrs. Craft & Brown.

August 31, 1878, another sweet little cherub of a boy was added to our family.

My brother-in-law, Mr. Charley McGinnis, came from the East, and was so well pleased with the country and the business I was embarking in, that he concluded to remain, and entered into partnership with me in the manufacture of carpet fasteners and stair rods.

Craft & Brown being unable to meet their obligations, the property now came back to me. The few remaining musical goods I sold to a firm in Grinnell, at a tremendous sacrifice, and in September, I traded my property to Mr. J. J. Towne, of the Valley Bank, Des Moines, for property there, in order to have better manufacturing facilities and location; and, in November, bid adieu to Monroe and the many good, kind friends I had made during my eight years residence there, and took up my abode in the enterprising, flourishing city of Des Moines.

During the time I was engaged in the mercantile, book and music business, I had very good success. I have sustained the loss of over two thousand dollars in the past few months, which was in notes well secured and seemed perfectly good, but when the securities found that the principals would fail to meet their payments they then mortgaged their property to friends before the notes became due, thus leaving me without any recourse. My experience is, that while sympathy has been freely extended, I have found in every community and society those who seize every opportunity to take advantages that will result in their personal gain, no matter who suffers by it. I have learned that in order to keep pace with the spirit of the times, in this fast age, we have each got to paddle our own canoe.

Hoping that I may have said something in the preceding pages to inspire you, my reader, with new hope and greater zeal and perseverance amid the trials and afflictions of life, and that after this life is over, we may meet where the "sunshine is never marred by clouds," we will bid adieu to the stern realities of life, and wander for awhile through the poetical field of "Silver Sheaves."

PART SECOND.

MISCELLANEOUS COLLECTION.

MISCELLANEOUS COLLECTION

OF

PROSE AND POETRY.

SOLILOQUY OF THE AUTHOR OF SILVER SHEAVES.

BY W. W. FINK.

WHAT then is blindness? This and nothing more:
The window blinds are closed, the outer door
Close shut and bolted and the curtains drawn:
No more comes light of stars nor morning's dawn,
Nor one lone ray from day's meridian light,
And men pass by and say, "Within is night."
Not so; for memory's lamp, with steady blaze,
Shines on the hallowed scenes of other days,
While fancy's torch, prophetic, flashing through
The vistas of the future. brings to view
Scenes passing strange, but scenes that yet shall be,
Which I can see, and which *he* cannot see
Whose dazzled orbs find nothing hid away
Beyond the brilliant margin of to-day.

To me the radiant world forever gleams
With the rich halo of my boyish dreams;
The faces I have loved no wrinkles know;
My dear one's eyes ne'er lose their cherished glow;
The hair of gold ne'er turns to silver hair;
The young are young, the fair are always fair.

With reason strengthened, feelings more intense,
The senses, multiples of former sense,
Vicarious servants for dead sight become.
I *see* the city in the city's hum;
I catch its subtle undertone of trade;
I hear of fortunes lost and fortunes made,
In sounds to him a mystery profound,
Who, seeing, knows not vision muffles sound.

Go to the forest on a summer's day,
To some lone quiet nook where mossy pillows
Invite to dreamy wakefulness; now lay
Thyself beneath this canopy of willows,
And, gazing lazily among the trees
Whose leaves no quiver show of passing breeze,
Take note how silence reigns.   The drowsy world
Seems wrapped in slumber; e'en the brook lies curled
And sleeping among shadows cool and deep.
Now close thine eyes and listen; closely keep
Thy soul responsive to thy listening ear.
Hark to the sounds!   Soft, musical and clear,
Some insect beauty rings her silver bell
Within her grotto of an acorn shell,

While e'en the brook, deep sleeping at thy feet,
Moans in its slumbers mournfully and sweet;
And, as the sense intenser grows, there comes
The sound of bees through linden blossoms humming,
Upon his bark-guitar the woodcock strums
Responsive to the pheasant's distant drumming.

If, then, this act of self-dismissing sight,
With lids which only half obscure the light,
Brings sounds to thee thou couldst not hear before
When vision guided thought. then how much more
Distinct to him must sound become to whom
Life walks in darkness—call it not in gloom.
'Tis only an exchange of good for good,
A new plant growing where the old one stood,
Old blesssings taken and new blessings given;
Sweet compensation, thou wert born in heaven!

There is no silence unto him whose soul
In darkness sits and listens.   Like a scroll
On which the secrets of the world are traced,
Blindness is but a sea-shell kindly placed
Beside the ear, and from its varying tone,
Who will may make life's secrets all his own.

And thus misfortunes bless, for blindness brings
The power to pierce the depths of hidden things,
To walk where reason and fair fancy lead,
To read the riddle of men's thoughts, to read
The soul's arcana in each subtl'r tone,
And make man's joys and sorrows all my own.

Nor can I sit repining at my lot
As bitter and unjust, nor curse the shot
Which tore away my sight.   The world is kind
And gentle to her sons.   Though I am blind,
Smooth paths of enterprise have always stood
Open for me, and, doing what I could
With hand or brain, with simple earnestness,
Have gathered what was due me of success.

Oh, ye who sit in darkness, moaning o'er
Thy dead and vanished vision, mourn no more!
Keep in the current.   Be thou brave and strong.
The busy world is singing.   Join the song;
And thou shalt find, if thou no duty shirk,
Who *will* may prosper if he do but work.

NATIVITY.

No war or battle sound,
Was heard the world around;
   The idle spear and shield were high up hung,
The hooked chariot stood
Unstained with hostile blood;
   The trumpet spake not to the armed throng,
And kings sat still, with awful eye,
As if they surely knew their Sovereign Lord was by.

But peaceful was the night
Wherein the prince of light
    His reign of peace upon the earth began;
The winds, with wonder whist,
Smoothly the waters kist,
    Whispering new joys to the mild ocean,
Who hath now quite forgot,
While birds of calm sit brooding on the charm'd wave.

The stars, with deep amaze,
Stand fixed in steadfast gaze,
    Bending one way their precious influence;
And will not take their flight
For all their morning light,
    Or Lucifer, that often warned them thence;
But in their glimmering orbs did glow
Until their Lord Himself bespake and bid them go.

And though the shady gloom
Had given day her room,
    The sun himself withheld his wonted speed,
And hid his head for shame
As his inferior flame
    The new enlightened world no more should need:
He saw a greater Sun appear
Than his bright throne or axel-tree could bear.

The shepherds on the lawn,
Or e'er the point of dawn,
    Sat simply clothed in a rustic row;
Full little thought they then

14

That the mighty Dan
  Was kindly come to live with them below;
Perhaps their love, or else their sheep,
Was all that did their silly thoughts too busy keep.

When such music sweet
Their hearts and ears did greet,
  As never was by mortal finger struck;
Divinely warbled voice
Answering the stringed noise,
  As all their souls in blissful rapture took;
The air such pleasure loth to lose,
With thousand echoes still prolongs each heavenly
    close.

At last surrounds their sight,
A globe of circular light,
  That with long beams the shame-faced night arrayed;
The helmed cherubim
And sworded seraphim,
  Are seen in glittering ranks with wings displayed;
Harping in loud and solemn choir,
With unexpressive notes to heaven's new-born heir.

Such music as 'tis said
Before was never made,
  But when of old the sons of morning sung;
While the Creator great
His constellations set,
  And the well-balanced world on hinges hung;
And cast the dark foundation deep,
And bid the weltering waves their oozy channel keep.

Ring out, ye crystal spheres;
Once bless our human ears,
  If ye have power to touch our senses so;
And let your silver chime
Move in melodious time,
  And let the bass of heaven's deep organ blow;
And with your nine-fold harmony
Make up full concert to the angelic symphony.

For if such holy song
Enwrap our fancy long,
  Time will run back and fetch the age of gold;
And speckled vanity
Will sicken soon and die,
  And leprous sin will melt from earthly mould;
And hell itself will pass away
And leave her dolorous mansions to the peering day.

Yea, Truth and Justice then
Will down return to men,
  Orbed in a rain-bow; and like glories wearing,
Mercy will sit between,
Throned in celestial sheen;
  With radiant feet the tissued cloud down steering
And heaven, as at some festival,
Will open wide the gates of her high palace hall.

STANZAS ON MEMORY.

Oh 'tis a calm, a glorious night,
  A night that seemeth given
To call my thoughts from earth away,
  And woo me unto heaven.
From yon deep azure vault the snow
  In silence rolleth on;
I bow my head, and dreamily
  I muse on years agone.

Oh memory! majestic power!
  A monarch grand thou art;
Thou hast a throne of giant size
  Within the human heart.
There's not a soul that breathes but owns
  Thy firm unwavering sway;
Thou bringest tears to the broken heart,
  Smiles to the glad and gay.

To-night thou'st led me back again
  To childhood's sunny hours,
That golden age when life seemed but
  A pathway bright with flowers.
But sorrow's cloud stole o'er the sky
  That had been ever bright;
Alone—in anguish then I met
  Despair's dark moonless night.

Oh none were near to whisper words
  Of comfort or of love;
My grief was only known to one,
  The God in heaven above.

ONE BY ONE.

One by one the years are gliding
    Down the distant slope of time,
Leaving traces of their footprints
    In every land and clime;
Traces that we'll ere remember
    In our weary journey on
Life's pilgrimage of hopes and fears,
    That arise and fall anon,

One by one life's dearest treasures
    That enrapt our soul with joy,
And afford ecstatic pleasures
    Sink into its base alloy.
Perish like the golden beauties
    Of the silent hour of even'
Fade amid the coming twilight
    In the starry dome of heaven.

One by one the friends we cherish,
    Youthful hearts with us allied,
Like the transient flowers wither,
    And we miss them from our side.
Miss them in the joyous laughter,
    And the sunlight of their face;
The music of those happy voices
    Lingers not one single trace.

One by one the links are severed
    That enchain us to the past;

And more potent the enchantment
  Which memories o'er us cast;
Memories on whose golden pinions
  Fly we back in joy and pain
To those scenes of saddened pleasure,
  And we live them o'er again.

THOU ART GOD ALONE.

While standing on the ocean's shore
  And gazing o'er the deep,
Watching the billows' seething foam,
  While storms their revel keep,
My soul is filled with solemn awe
  While listning to their tone,
And David's words come o'er my mind,
  "Lord, Thou art God alone."
In all of nature's mighty works,
  The forest's gloomy shade,
The giant mountains' granite sides,
  All nature's vast arcade—
Thy praise in many a varied way
  To speak, are ever prone,
We listning hear it all around,
  Yes, "Thou art God alone."
Thou 'gravest it in living words
  Upon our inmost soul,

While dire misfortune's blast is heard,
  And clouds of anguish,
From out the thick and murky clouds,
  We hear Thy gentle tone,
"Fear not I'm with thee to the end,
  For I am God alone."
Take courage trembling, fearful saint,
  Though hosts of hell combine,
The Lord of Heaven is God alone,
  That God is ever thine.
He'll shield and guide thee, by and by
  Will claim thee as his own;
When nature sinks He'll raise thee up,
  For He is God alone.

THE BLACKSMITH'S STORY.

Well, no! My wife aint dead, sir, but I've lost her all
  the same;
She left me voluntarily, and neither was to blame.
It's rather a queer story, and I think you will agree—
When you hear the circumstances—'twas rather rough
  on me.
She was a soldier's widow, he was killed at Malvern
  Hill;
And when I married her, she seemed to sorrow for
  him still,

But I brought her here to Kansas. I never want to see
A better wife than Mary was, for five bright years to me.
The change of scene brought cheerfulness, and soon a
    rosy glow
Of happiness warmed Mary's cheeks and melted all
    their snow.
I think she loved me some, I'm bound to think that
    of her, sir,
And as for me, I can't begin to tell how I loved her.
Three years ago the baby came our humble home to
    bless.
And then I reckon I was nigh to perfect happiness.
'Twas her's, 'twas mine, but I've no language to ex-
    plain to you
How that litttle girl's weak fingers our hearts together
    drew.
Once we watched it through a fever; and with each
    gasping breath,
Dumb with an awful worldless woe, we waited for its
    death.
And though I am not a pious man, our souls to-
    gether there,
For Heaven to spare our darling, went up in voiceless
    prayer.
And when the doctor said 'twould live, our joy what
    words could tell;
Clasped in each other's arms, our grateful tears to-
    gether fell.
Sometimes, you see, the shadow fell across our little
    nest,

But it only made the sunshine seem a doubly welcome
    guest.
Work came to me plenty, and I kept the anvil ringing;
Early and late you'd see me there a hammering and
    singing.
Love nerved my arm to labor, and turned my tongue
    to song,
And though my singing wasn't sweet, it was almighty
    strong.
One day a one-armed stranger stopped to have me nail
    a shoe,
And while I was at work we passed a compliment or two.
I asked him how he lost his arm, he said 'twas shot
    away
At Malvern Hill. "At Malvern Hill! Did you know
    Robert May?"
"That's me!" said he. "You! You!" I gasped, chok-
    ing with horrid doubt,
"If you're a man, just follow me; we'll try this mys-
    tery out."
With dizzy steps I led him to Mary. God! 'Twas true!
Then the bitterest pangs of misery unspeakable I knew.
Frozen with deadly horror, she stared with eye of stone,
And from her quivering lips there broke one wild,
    despairing moan.
"'Twas he! the husband of her youth, now risen from
    the dead,
But all too late!" and with that bitter cry her senses
    fled.

What could be done; he was reported dead. On his
      return
He strove in vain some tidings of his absent wife to learn.
'Twas well that he was innocent, else *I'd* have killed
      him too,
So dead he never would have riz till Gabriel's trumpet
      blew.
It was agreed that Mary then between us should decide,
And each by her decision would sacredly abide.
No sinners at the judgment seat waiting eternal doom
Could suffer what I did while waiting sentence in that
      room.
Rigid and breathless there we stood, with nerves as
      tense as steel,
While Mary's eyes sought each white face in piteous
      appeal.
God! Could not woman's duty be less hardly reconciled
Between her lawful husband and the father of her child?
Ah, how my heart was chilled to ice when she knelt
      down and said,
"Forgive me, John! He is my husband! Here, alive
      not dead."
I raised her tenderly and tried to tell her she was right,
But somehow in my aching breast the prisoned words
      stuck tight.
"But, John, I can't leave baby." "What! wife and
      child," cried I
"Must I yield all? Ah, cruel! Better that I should die.
Think of the long, sad lonely hours waiting in gloom
      for me;

No wife to cheer me with her love, no babe to climb
  my knee.
And yet you are her mother, and the sacred mother love
Is still the purest, tenderest tie that Heaven ever wove.
Take her, but promise, Mary, for that will bring no
  shame,
My little girl shall bear, and learn to lisp her father's
  name."
It may be, in the life to come I'll meet my child and
  wife,
But yonder by the cottage gate we parted for this life.
One long hand clasp from Mary, and my dream of
  love was done;
One long embrace from baby, and my happiness was
  gone.

I'LL KNOW THEE THERE.

Pale star, that with thy soft, sad light,
  Came out upon my bridal eve,
I have a song to sing to-night,
  Before thou takest thy mournful leave;
Since then so softly time has stirred,
  That months have almost seemed like hours;
And I am like a little bird,
  That slept too long among the flowers;
And waking, sits with waveless wing,
  Soft singing 'mid the shades of even';

But, oh! with sadder heart I sing—
   I sing of one who dwells in heaven.

The winds are soft, the clouds are few,
   And tenderest thought my heart beguiles;
As floating up through mist and dew,
   The pale young moon comes out in smiles;
And to the green resounding shore,
   In silvery troops the riplets crowd;
Till all the ocean dimpled o'er,
   Lifts up its voice and laughs aloud;
And star on star, all lost and calm,
   Floats up yon arch serenely blue,
And lost to earth and steeped in balm,
   My spirits float in ether, too.

Loved one! though lost to human sight,
   I feel thy spirit lingering near;
And, softly—as I feel the light
   That trembles through the atmosphere,
As in some temple's holy shades,
   Though mute the hymn and hushed the prayer,
A solemn awe the soul pervades,
   Which tells that worship has been there;
A breath of incense, left alone,
   Where many a censer swung around;
Which thrills the wanderer, like to one
   Who treads on consecrated ground.

I know thy soul from worlds of bliss,
   Yet stoops awhile to dwell with me;

Hath caught the prayer I have breathed in this;
    That I at least might dwell with thee;
I hear a murmur from the seas,
    That thrills me like the spirit's sighs;
I hear a voice on every breeze,
    That makes to mine its low replies—
A voice all low and sweet like thine!
    It gives an answer to my prayer,
And brings my soul from heaven a sign
    That I will know and meet thee there.

I'll know thee there by that sweet face,
    'Round which a tender halo plays,
Still touched with that expressive grace
    That made thee lovely all thy days;
By that sweet smile that o'er it shed
    A beauty like the light of even',
Whose soft expression never fled,
    Even when its soul had fled to heaven.
I'll know thee by thy starry crown,
    That glitters in thy raven hair;
Oh, by these blessed signs alone
    I'll know thee there!—I'll know thee there.

For, ah! thine eye, within whose sphere
    The greatest youth and beauty met,
That swam in love and softness here,
    Must swim in love and softness yet;
For, Oh! it's dark and liquid beams,
    Though gladdened by a thousand sighs,

Never holier than the light that streams
    Down from the gate of Paradise—
Were bright and radiant like the moon,
    Yet soft and dewy as the eve;
Too sad for eyes where smiles are born,
    Too young for eyes to learn to grieve.

I wonder if this cold, sweet breeze
    Hath touched thy lips and fanned thy brow;
For all my spirit hears or sees,
    Recalls thee to my memory now;
For every hour we breathe apart
    Will but increase.   If that be
The love that fills this lonely heart,
    Already filled so full of thee;
Yet many a tear these eyes must weep,
    And many a sin must be forgiven,
Ere these pale lids shall sink to sleep,
    And you and I shall meet in Heaven.

ALICE CARY'S SWEETEST POEM.

Of all the beautiful pictures
    That hang on memory's wall,
Is one of a dim old forest,
    That seemeth best of all.
Not for its gnarled oaks olden,
    Dark with the mistletoe;

Not for the violets golden,
　That sprinkle the vale below;
Not for the milk-white lillies,
　That lean from the fragrant hedge,
Coquetting all day with the sunbeams,
　And stealing their golden edge;
Not for the vines on the uplands,
　Where the bright red berries rest;
Not for the pinks, nor the pale, sweet cowslips,
　It seems to me the best.

I once had a little brother,
　With eyes that were dark and deep—
In the lap of that olden forest
　He lieth in peace asleep.
Light as the down on the thistle,
　Free as the winds that blow,
We roved there the beautiful summers,
　The summers of long ago;
But his feet on the hills grew weary,
　And one of the autumn eves,
I made for my little brother
　A bed of yellow leaves.

Sweetly his pale arms folded
　My neck in a meek embrace,
As the light of immortal beauty
　Silently covered his face;
And when the arrows of sunset
　Lodged in the tree-tops bright,

He fell, in his saint-like beauty,
　Asleep by the gates of Light.
Therefore, of all the pictures
　That hang on memory's wall,
The one of the dim old forest
　Seemeth best of all.

THE FUTURE OF AMERICA.

BY A. P. DUTCHER, M. D.

This is a grand problem! If we could unseal the book of God's decree its solution would be easy.

Although we cannot read the folded leaves of this book, yet we may gather much from the history of the past and the character of our people, that will aid us greatly in our work. From a careful study of our history, we cannot repress the conviction that our land is destined to be the light of the world; and her people, if true to themselves, a blessing to mankind. Her beginning, her advancement, and her institutions, are so many tokens that the time-worn things of caste will vanish from her presence, and political and religious freedom reign supremely in their stead.

What a glorious future awaits this favored land. Some one has said that "war is an antiquated pageant." Man may never surpass the Macedonian, the Roman, or the Corsican, in feats of valor; but here is a field almost without competitors, of love and mercy. Its trophies are not banners wrested from a bleeding foe, nor territory grasped by conquering hands, but the blessings of the nations. Wherever the Star-spangled Banner floats on the breeze the poor shall hail it as the flag of freedom, and all the oppressed bless it as the symbol of deliverance. America shall be earth's asylum. If famine or pestilence waste distant isles or remote climes, the stricken shall turn to her, and never in vain. Light shall go forth from her to the benighted, bread to the hungry, succor to the distressed, help to all mankind. What a noble destiny! And we, of all nations, are in the best condition for reaching it. Would that the national heart and conscience were thoroughly prepared for it! Would that this may become the end and aid of the administration of our national affairs, and the united endeavors of the whole people of the land. Then might we hope for permanent greatness, for nothing so binds a people together as morality and religion. The history of the past furnishes ample testimony on this point. Thus the Roman Empire was the product of the religious sentiment of the people, and it was the most abiding. It endured for centuries, while the Macedonian, framed only by war, perished at the death of its founder.

In modern times, Sweden never assumed so high a rank as when under the lion-hearted Adolphus, she stood the bulwark of the Protestant faith. Spain attained her highest glory when arrayed against the Moors. England may date her advancement from

15

Cromwell, who placed her in the front rank of Protestantism. In these cases error and truth were mingled, and could not therefore form a perfect union. There was a fatal element which hastened their decay. That element was war, and it sapped the life. England alone yet lives, and she is crippled and exhausted by the disease engendered by war, so that the prodigious energy of the vital principal in her alone saves her from dissolution.

But the most remarkable of the power of religious bonds is seen in the case of the Jews. Exiles without home or country, they are still one people, because of one faith. They are, and always have been, a people of destiny. And what a profound impression they have made upon the world! Conquered and despised, they have yet given their sacred books to their conquerors. Moses and the Prophets are read in costly cathedrals and churches, across whose threshhold the Jew may not pass; and the nation lives in faith, strong in destiny, while other kingdoms pass off into oblivion.

Give, then, this idea to our land and it will live, and the next Centennial will be more glorious than this. It is true we are many tribes, divided in many States, and can continue one only as we are one in purpose and destiny. Let this destiny be worthy of us and we can never be destroyed. Let it be an holy end which will elevate every man, and purify each heart and conscience. Then it will be an unbroken band of union, and each citizen will feel himself clothed with high responsibility, as a member of a state whose divine distinction is one of loving kindness and mercy to mankind. The Bible, like the ark and tabernacle in the wilderness, will be the grand central point of attraction, and all the tribes marshalled around it will move by its summons, and cleave together because one power controls them. This is a destiny peculiarly fitted to the character of our institutions. The despot dare not attempt to accomplish it. It would tear up the foundations of his throne, it must be done by a people among whom all are free to think and act, and where all may labor for its accomplishment. Let it fill the mind and heart of the nation and each individual may do his part. No one so poor and humble as not to be able to effect something toward this noble end. The statesman in the hall of legislation, with eloquent lips and discerning wisdom, may build up a new frame of policy, bounded upon principles of justice and piety, and affording a sure refuge to earth's long oppressed and degraded nations. The guardians of the press, that mighty engine of good or evil, shaking off political bigotry and partisan proscription may make it the organ of truth, the servant of mankind and not the slave of faction. The minister of God may from every altar publish peace and salvation. The teacher of youth may train children for useful action and benevolent enterprise. The man of business may devote himself to commerce or manufactures, not to hoard or to squander his gains, but to consecrate them to God, his country and the world. The mother in her retirement as she bends over her babe and teaches his infant lips to pray, may aid in rearing a people worthy of our destiny. The reaper on the wide prairie of the West, while he binds his golden sheaves, the distant emigrant by the Rocky Mountains or the Pacific slopes, the sailor as he launches on the Atlantic or Pacific wave, one and all, the people, the whole people, may thus move on by one impulse and labor by one destiny, and make our land the light of nations diffusing over the earth the mingled radiance of peace, liberty and religion.

GOD.

O thou Eternal One! whose presence bright
   All space do occupy, all nations guide;
Unchanged through time's all devastating flight;
   Thou only God! there is no God beside.
Being above all beings! Mighty One!
   Whom none can comprehend and none explore.
Who fillest existence with thyself alone,
   Embracing all, supporting, ruling o'er,
   Being whom we call God and know no more,

In its sublime research, philosophy
   May measure out the ocean deep; may count
The sands, or the sun rays, but God, for Thee
   There is no weight nor measure. None can mount
Up thy mysteries. Reason's brightest spark
   Though kindled by the lights, in vain would try

To trace thy counsels infinite and dark;
  And thought is lost ere thought can soar so high,
Even like past moments in eternity.

Thou from primeval nothingness didst call,
  First chaos, then existence.   Lord on Thee
Eternity has its foundation; all
  Spring forth from Thee; of joy, light, harmony,
Sole origin—all life, all beauty thine,
  Thy word created all space with rays divine;
Thou art and wert and shall be glorious, great,
Life giving, life sustaining potentate.

Thy chains the unmeasured universe surround,
  Upheld by Thee, by Thee inspired by breath.
Thou the beginning with the end hast bound
  And beautifully mingled life and death.
As sparks mount upward from the fiery blaze,
  So suns are born, so worlds spring forth from Thee,
And as the spangles in the sunny rays
  Shine round the silver snow, the pageantry
Of heaven's bright array glitters to thy praise.

A million torches lighted by thy hand
  Wander unwearied through the blue abyss,
They own thy power, accomplish thy command;
  All gay with life, all eloquent with bliss,
What shall we call them, piles of crystal light,
  A glorious canopy of golden streams,
Lamps of celestial ether, burning bright
  Suns lighting systems with their joyous beams?
But thou to these art as the moon to night.

Yes! as a drop of water on the sea,
   All this magnificience in Thee is lost!
What are a million worlds compared with Thee,
   And what am I then?   Heaven's unnumbered host,
Though multiplied by myriads and arrayed
   In all the glory of sublimest thought,
Is but an atom in the balance weighed
   Against thy greatness, is a cipher brought
   Against infinity!   What am I, then?   Naught.

Naught, but the effulgence of thy light divine,
   Pervading worlds hath reached my bosom too:
Yes! in my spirit doth thy spirit shine,
   As shines the sunbeam in a drop of dew.
Naught but I live, and on hope's pinions fly
   Eager toward thy presence, for in Thee
I live and breathe and dwell; spring high,
   Even to the throne of thy divinity
   I AM, O God! and even thou MUST BE.

Thou art directing, guiding all, thou art.
   Direct my understanding then to Thee;
Control my spirit, guide my wandering heart;
   Though but an atom 'midst immensity,
Still I am something fashioned by thy hand;
   I hold a middle rank 'twixt heaven and earth;
On the last verge of mortal being stand,
   Close to the realms where angels have their birth,
Just on the boundaries of the spirit land.

The chain of being is complete in me;
　　In me is matter's last gradation lost,
And the next step is spirit, Deity.
　　I can command the lightning, and am dust,
A monarch and a slave, a man, a God!
　　Whence came I here and how so marvelously
Constructed, and conceived? This clod
　　Lives through some higher energy,
　　For from itself it could not be.

Creator? Yes! thy wisdom and thy word
　　Created me, thou source of life and good!
Thou spirit of my spirit and my Lord
　　Thy light, thy love, in all their brightest plentitude.

THERE REMAINETH THEREFORE REST.

　　Watchman, are you growing weary,
　　　　Watching night and watching day?
　　Do the hours seem long and dreary
　　　　Till the shadows clear away?
　　Grasp the standard, hold it tighter,
　　　　Meet the foe 'midst shot and shell;
　　Heavenly rest will be the lighter
　　　　If you do your duty well.

　　Burdened heart, by sorrow shaken,
　　　　Left alone in tears to grieve,
　　By the friends of youth forsaken
　　　　Whom you dreamed would never leave,

Let your hopes be centered only
 On the Saviour's changeless love!
There's a rest for all the lonely
 In the heavenly home above.

Christian, are thy crosses growing
 Heavier, and the journey long?
Art thou saddened with the knowing
 Right is conquered by the wrong?
Strive a little longer, bearing
 All, though drooping spirits mourn;
Crowns will be more worth the wearing
 If the cross is only borne.

Brothers, sisters, toiling, praying,
 Seeking for the higher rest!
Oh, the joy of weary laying
 Ever on the Saviour's breast,
Where the severed friends are meeting,
 Never more to parted be,
Where the angels shout their greeting
 All across the deeper sea.

Here is but the time of testing,
 Time of battle, tears and pain;
There the joy of sweetly resting,
 Never more to toil again.
Let us then bear all the sorrow
 God shall deem it wise and best;
Soon will dawn the glorious morrow
 With the sweet eternal rest.

PAUL REVERE'S RIDE.

BY H. W. LONGFELLOW.

The Battle of Lexington, April 19, 1775.

Listen, my children, and you shall hear
Of the midnight ride of Paul Revere,
On the eighteenth of April seventy-five.
Hardly a man is now alive
Who remembers that famous day and year.

He said to his friend: " If the British march
By land or sea from the town to-night,
Hang a lantern aloft in the belfry arch
Of the north church-tower, as a signal light—
One if by land, and two by sea—
And I on the opposite shore will be
Ready to ride and spread the alarm
Through every Middesex village and farm,
For the country folk to be up and arm."
Then he said "good night," and with muffled oar
Silently rowed to the Charlestown shore.
Just as the moon rose over the bay
Where swinging wide at her moorings lay
The Somerset British man of war;
A phantom ship, with each mast and spar
Across the moon like a prison-bar,
And a huge black hulk, that was magnified
By its own reflection in the tide.

Meanwhile, his friend through alley and street
Wanders and watches with eager ears

Till in the silence around he hears
The muster of men at the barrack door,
The sound of arms and the tramp of feet,
And the measured tread of the grenadiers
Marching down to their boat on the shore.

Then he climbed the tower of the Old North Church
By the wooden stairs, with stealthy tread,
To the belfry chamber overhead,
And startled the pigeons from their perch
On the sombre rafters, that round him make
Masses of moving shapes of shade—
By the trembling ladder steep and tall,
To the highest window in the wall,
Where he paused to listen and look down
A moment on the roofs of the town;
And the moonlight flowing over all.
Beneath, in the churchyard, lay the dead,
In their night encampment on the hill,
Wrapped in silence so deep and still,
That he could hear, like the sentinel's tread,
The watchful night wind, as it went
Creeping along from tent to tent,
And seeming to whisper, "All is well!"
A moment later he feels the spell
Of the place and the hour and the secret dread
Of the lonely belfry and the dead;
For, suddenly all his thoughts are bent
On a shadowy something far away,
Where the river widens to meet the bay—

A line of black that bends and floats
On the rising tide like a bridge of boats.
Meanwhile, impatient to mount and ride,
Booted and spurred, with a heavy stride,
On the opposite shore walked Paul Revere.
Now he patted his horse's side,
Now he gazed at the landscape far and near;
Then, impetuous stamped the earth,
And turned and tightened his horse's girth;
But mostly he watched with eager search
The belfry tower of the Old North Church,
As it rose above the graves on the hill,
Lonely and spectral, and sombre and still;
And, lo! as he looks at the belfry's height,
A glimmer and then a gleam of light!
He springs to the saddle, the bridle he turns;
But lingers and gazes, till full on his sight
A second lamp in the belfry burns.

A hurry of hoofs in a village street;
A shape in the moonlight, a bulk in the dark,
And beneath from the pebbles in passing,
Struck out by a steed flying fearless and fleet.
That was all! And yet through the gloom and the
    light,
The fate of a nation was riding that night;
And the spark struck out by that steed in his flight,
Kindled the land into flame with its heat.

He has left the village and mounted the steep,
And beneath him tranquil and broad and deep,

Is the mystic meeting of the ocean-lids;
And under the alders that skirt its edge,
Now soft on the sand, now loud on the ledge,
Is heard the tramp of his steed as he rides.
It was twelve by the village clock,
When he crossed the bridge into Medford town;
He heard the crowing of the cock,
And the barking of the farmer's dog,
And felt the damp of the river fog
That rises after the sun goes down.

It was one by the village clock,
When he galloped into Lexington;
He saw the gilded weather-cock
Swim in the moon-light as he passed,
And the meeting-house window, blank and bare,
Glance at him with spectral glare,
As if they already stood aghast
At the bloody work they would look upon.
It was two by the village clock,
When he came to the bridge in Concord town;
He heard the bleating of the flock,
And the twitter of birds among the trees,
And felt the breath of the morning breeze
Blowing o'er the meadows brown.
And one was safe and asleep in his bed
Who at the bridge would be first to fall,—
Who that day would be lying dead,
Pierced by a British musket-ball.

You know the rest.   In the books you have read
How the British regulars fired and fled;
How the farmer gave him ball for ball
From behind each fence and farm-yard wall,
Chasing the red coats down the lane,
Then crossing the fields to emerge again,
Under the trees at the turn of the road,
And only pausing to fire and load.
So, through the night rode Paul Revere;
And so through the night went his cry of alarm
To every Middlesex village and farm;
A cry of defiance, and not of fear,
A voice in the darkness, a knock at the door,
And a word that shall echo for evermore.
For, borne on the night-wind of the past,
Through all our history to the last,
In the hour of darkness, and peril and need,
The people will waken and listen to hear
The hurrying hoof-beats of that steed,
And the midnight message of Paul Revere.

WHAT IS TROUBLE?

A company of Southern ladies were one day assem-
bled in a lady's parlor when the conversation chanced
to turn on the subject of earthly affliction.   Each had
her story of peculiar trial and bereavement to relate,
except one pale, sad looking woman whose lustreless

eye and dejected air showed that she was a prey to the deepest melancholy. Suddenly arousing herself, she said in a hollow voice "not one of you know what trouble is." "Will you please, Mrs. Gray," said the kind voice of a lady who well knew her story, "tell the ladies what you call trouble?" "I will if you desire it," she replied, "for I have seen it. My parents possessed a competence, and my girlhood was surrounded by all the comforts of life. I seldom knew an ungratified wish, and was always gay and light hearted. I married at nineteen one I loved more than all besides. Our home was retired, but the sunlight never fell on a lovelier one or a happier household. Years rolled on peacefully; five children sat around our table and a little curly head still nestled in my bosom. One night about sundown one of those black storms came on which are so common to our southern clime. For many hours the rain poured down incessantly. Morning dawned, but still the elements raged. The whole Savanah seemed afloat. The little stream near our dwelling became a raging torrent. Before we were aware of it our house was surrounded by water. I managed with my babe to reach a little elevated spot on which a few wide spreading trees were standing, whose dense foliage afforded some protection, while my husband and sons strove to save what they could of our property. At last a fearful surge swept away my husband, and he never arose again. Ladies, no one ever loved a husband more, but that was not trouble. Presently my sons saw their danger, and the struggle for life became the only consideration. They were as brave, loving boys as ever blessed a mother's heart, and I watched their efforts to escape with such agony as only mothers can feel. They were so far off I could not speak to them, but I could see them closing nearer and nearer each other as the little island grew smaller and smaller. The sullen river raged around the huge tree, dead branches, upturned trunks, wrecks of houses, drowning cattle, masses of rubbish, all went floating past us. My boys waved their hands to me, then pointed upward; I knew it was a farewell signal, and you mothers can imagine my anguish. I saw them all perish, and yet that was not trouble.

I hugged my babe close to my heart, and when the water arose to my feet I climbed into the low branches of the tree, and so kept retiring before it till an All-Powerful Hand staid the waves that they should come no further. I was saved; all my worldly possessions swept away; all my earthly hopes blighted, yet that was not trouble. My babe was all I had left on earth. I labored night and day to support him and myself, and sought to train him in the right way, but as he grew older evil companions won him away from home. He ceased to care for his mother's counsel; he would sneer at her entreaties and agonizing prayers. He left my humble roof that he might be unrestrained in the pursuit of evil, and at last when heated by wine one night he took the life of a fellow being, and ended his own upon the scaffold. My Heavenly Father had filled my cup before, now it ran over. This was trouble, ladies, such as I hope His mercy will save you from ever experiencing." There was not a dry eye among her listeners, and the warmest sympathy was expressed for the bereaved mother, whose sad history had taught them a useful lesson.

TYPHLOTES.

I hear thee speak of beauty's countless forms
    And color's prismal tints in earth and sky,
The works of God and works of man, whose charms
    Forever fill and please the seeing eye.
The mighty sun that gleams in morning gray
.   And ev'ng gold, and glares in midday height;
The twinkling stars and moon, with pensive ray
    That bless the near and distant worlds with light;
    But oh, for me all is rayless night!

I hear thee speak of cloud with tempest black,
    And lightnings fiery in instant blaze,
Leading the thunder in its deadly track,
    And rain shrouding the earth in watery haze;
The snow in feathery flake or spotless fleece,
    And sky so clear and blue to heaven's height,
    But these for me are all engulfed in night.

I hear thee speak of mountain's snowy crest,
    And rivers decked with foam and sparkling wave,

Of isle-gemmed seas sublime in rage or rest,
   Of silvery lake and torrents' misty lave,
And spheric mound and grassy width of plain,
   And myriad flowers that bloom in dewy sheen,
The fields with verdant blade and yellow grain,
   And forest pillars crowned with leafy green:
   Yet oh, for me 'tis told, but all unseen!

I hear thee speak of cities great and proud,
   Vast heaps of art and homes of toiling hearts,
And spacious streets where beats the medly crowd;
   Of restful parks and grimy mammon's marts,
And marble snowy walls seen frowning high,
   With cornice shade and window's glint of light,
Within the spacious hall from far and nigh;
   The fruits of genius' toil in pictures bright;
   I hear the winsome song, but all is night.

I hear thee speak of mother's thoughtful face,
   And father's stooping form and silvery hair,
And sister's eyes all filled with tearful grace,
   And in my brother's look a brother's care.
I hear thy voice, O friend! thy every tone,
   And on thy kindly words I helpless lean.
For all to me is gloom—a dark unknown;
   I grope in night—no ray can pierce the screen—
   For me no star, no sun; all are unseen.

I tell to thee a story sad and brief
   On my young eyes entranced with the first light:
16

There fell a stroke of crushing pain and grief,
  Which once forever swept from me my sight,
And now for years and years all dark has been
  This world to me; for me no vision blest.
And thus until I pass that shore unseen
  And Christ robes me in my immortal dress—
  Then changeless beauty, light, sight, and rest!

MY INDIAN LOVE.

BY JOAQUIN MILLER.

        I love
A forest maiden; she is mine;
And on sierra's slopes of pine
The vines below, the snow above,
A solitary lodge set
Within a fringe of watered firs—
And there my wigwam fires burned,
Fed by a round brown patient hand.
That small brown faithful hand of hers,
That never rests till my return;
The yellow smoke is rising yet;
Tip-toe and see it where you stand,
Lift like a column from the land.

There are no sea-gems in her hair,
No jewels fret her dimpled hands,
And half her bronzed limbs are bare,
But round brown arms have golden bands,

Broad, rich, and by her cunning hands
Cut from the yellow virgin ore,
And she does not desire more.
I wear the beaded wampum belt
That she has wove—the sable pelt
That she has fringed red threads around:
And in the room, where men are not,
I wake the valley with the shot
That brings the brown deer to the ground;
And she beside the lodge at noon
Sings with the wind, while baby swings
In sea-shell cradle by the bough—
Sings low, so like the clover sings
With swarm of bees.   I hear her now;
I see her sad face through the moon;
Such songs!   Would earth had more of such.
She has not much to say, and she
Lifts never voice to question me
In aught I do—and that is much.
I love her for her patient trust,
And my love's forty-fold return—
A value I have not to learn
As you—at least as many must.
She is not o'er tall or fair;
Her breasts are curtained in her hair,
And sometimes through the silken fringe
I see bosom's wealth, like wine,
Burst through, in luscious rudy tinge—
And all its wealth and worth are mine.
I know not that one drop of blood

Of prince or chief is in her veins;
I simply say that she is good
And loves me with pure womanhood.
When that is said, why, what remains?

CENTENNIAL HYMN.

BY JOHN G. WHITTIER.

[Sung at the Opening of the Centennial Exhibition, May 10, 1876.]

Our Fathers' God, from out whose hand
The centuries fall like grains of sand,
We meet to-day, united, free,
And loyal to our land and Thee,
To thank Thee for the era done,
And trust Thee for the opening one.

Here, where of old, by Thy design
The fathers spake that word of Thine,
Whose echo is the glad refrain
Of rended bolt and falling chain,
To grace our festal time, from all
The zones of earth our guests we call.

Be with us while the New World greets
The Old World thronging all its streets,
Unvailing all the triumphs won
By art or toil beneath the sun;
And unto common good ordain
This rivalship of hand and brain.

Thou who hast here in concord furled
The war-flags of a gathered world
Beneath our western skies, fulfill
The Oriental's mission of good will,
And, freighted with love's Golden Fleece,
Send back the Argonauts of peace.

For art and labor met in truce,
For beauty made the bride of use,
We thank Thee; while withal, we crave
The austere virtues strong to save
The honor proof to place or gold,
The manhood never bought nor sold!

O! make thou us, through centuries long,
In peace secure, in justice strong:
Around our gift of Freedom draw
The pageants of Thy righteous law;
And, cast in some diviner mould,
Let the new cycle shame the old!

ON THE DEATH OF NETTIE.

(SISTER OF THE AUTHOR.)

Carefully, carefully close her blue eyes,
  Speed not the words of your sorrow;
Silently, gladly her spirit shall rise.

Tearfully, sadly we watched through the hours,
　Watched for the angel's pinions,
That like the breeze from a garden of flowers,
　Came bearing her to its dominions.

Beautiful, beautiful, even in death,
　Calm as the blue sky at even';
For, with the last faint expiring breath,
　Came the glad, bright smile of heaven.

Quietly, quietly brush them away,
　Ringlets of golden lustre;
O'er her forehead they fain would play,
　In a soft shining cluster.

Here is her path by the mountain brook,
　Here had she gathered wild flowers,
Here in the cool and shady nook,
　Played through the rosy hours.

Here are her play-things, all scattered around,
　Here are her flowers all dying;
There flows the brook with its sad moaning sound,
　And the low night breeze is sighing.

Sighing for her who shall wander no more,
　Down where it kisses the water;
Courting the ripples that dance to the shore,
　Nature's own beautiful daughter.

Nettie, sister Nettie! can it be,
　Thou shalt return again never;

Say not the cold grave has swallowed thee,
   Thou art an angel ever.

Silently, silently close her blue eyes,
   Brush back her ringlets so golden;
Over her pure snowy features there lies,
   A smile, oh! so calm, like the olden.

LIGHT FOR ONE STEP MORE.

What, though before me it is dark—
   Too dark for me to see;
I ask but light for one step more,
   'Tis quite enough for me.

Each little humble step I take,
   The gloom clears from the next;
So, though 'tis very dark beyond,
   I never am perplexed.

And, if sometimes the mist hangs close,
   So close I fear to stray,
Patient I wait a little while,
   And soon it clears away.

I would not see my future path,
   For mercy veils it so;
My present steps might harder be,
   Did I the future know.

It may be that my path is rough,
    Thorny and hard and steep;
And, knowing this, my strength might fail,
    Through fear and terrors deep.

It may be that it winds along
    A smooth and flowery way,
But, seeing this, I might despise
    The journey of to-day.

Perhaps my faith is very short,
    My journey nearly done;
And I might tremble at the thought,
    Of ending it so soon.

Or if I saw a weary length
    Of road that I must wend,
Fainting, I'd think my feeble powers
    Would fail me ere the end.

And so I do not wish to see,
    My journey or its length;
Assured that through my Father's love,
    Each step will bring it's strength.
Thus, step by step, I onward go,
    Trusting that I shall always have
Light for just one step more.

THE WORLD OF BLISS.

A COLLOQUY FOR FIVE YOUNG LADIES.

Is life a reality or a dream? The bright sun of morning wakes my senses and I see a moving mass; people going up and down, some doing this, others that; all is motion. Even the cattle "upon a thousand hills," every bird on the wing, the finny tribe that glide over the bosom of the clear waters, or dive beneath its turbid waves, the waving grain and foliage all add their voices in a testimony of a real existence.

I draw aside the curtain and examine more closely, and my eyes would fain turn aside from looking at the scene. Men and women taking by the hand innocent youth and guileless children and making for them and themselves a pathway where poverty, misery and guilt stalk about, and grim spectres and dispair sit brooding like a storm king. But methinks I have been told of other worlds far away; one of infinite beauty, whose inhabitants drink their fill of joys, and dwell in light far surpassing terrestrial lights. That darkness never obscures the vision of pearly gates and golden streets; that the King immortal sits there upon his throne, and all delight to honor him.

Tell me ye maidens who wear the emblem of purity, is there such a world of bliss?

FIRST VOICE.

There is a world above
Where sorrow is unknown;

A long eternity of love,
  Formed for the good alone;
And faith beholds the dying here,
Transplanted to that glorious sphere.

SECOND VOICE.

There no shadow shall bewilder,
  There life's vain parade is o'er,
There the sleep of sin is broken,
  And the dreamer dreams no more.
There the bond is never severed,
  Partings, claspings, sob and moan,
Midnight waking, twilight weeping,
  Heavy noontide, all are done.

THIRD VOICE.

There is a region lovlier far
  Than sages tell or poets sing,
Brighter than noonday glories are,
  And softer than the tints of spring.
It is all holy and serene,
  The land of glory and repose;
No cloud obscures the radiant scene,
  And not a tear of sorrow flows.

FOURTH VOICE.

A gentle air, so sweet, so calm,
  That sometimes from that viewless sphere
The mourner feels their breath of balm,
  And soothed sorrow dries the tear.

And sometimes ltstening ear may gain
　　Entrancing sound that hither floats,
The echo of a distant strain,
　　Of harps and voices, blended notes,
　　　　Beyond the river.

SOLILOQUIZER.

Tell me ye maidens fair, how I may gain that blest
abode?

FIRST VOICE.

Repent, return and live;
　　He who no penitent disdains,
New heavens, new earth can give.
　　Simple obedience shall restore
Green fields and sunny skies,
　　And harkening to His voice, brings more
Than Eden to your eyes.

SECOND VOICE.

Oh blest Repentance in thy weeping eye
Swim the pure beams of embryo ecstacy,
And faith and hope and joy and love prepare
To still thy heart and wipe thy bitter tears.
To thee alone the privilege is given,
By earthly woe to kindle joy in heaven.

THIRD VOICE.

To thy heart take faith,
Soft beacon light upon a stormy sea,

A mantle for the pure in heart to pass
Through a dim world untouched by living death;
  A cheerful watcher through the spirit's night,
Soothing the grief from which she may not flee;
  A herald of glad news, a seraph bright,
Pointing to sheltering heavens yet to be.

FOURTH VOICE.

"'Till death the weary spirit free,"
Thy God hath said "'tis good for thee
  To walk by faith and not by sight."
Take on trust a little while,
  Soon shall thou read the mystery right,
n the full sunshine of his smile.

SOLILOQUIZER.

With faith our guide,
  White robed and innocent to lead the way,
We will not fear to plunge in Jordan's tide,
  And find the heaven of eternal day.

A WESTERN SKETCH.

BY ESTHER DREISBACH CONDO.

The sun was low, the air was cold, the day was almost
    flown,
October's breath across the path a few red leaves had
    blown;

Where brown-faced, black-maned Dick, the parson's
    faithful horse,
Reflectively pursued his solemn, slow-paced course.

Whilst his master high did sit in most triumphant
    state,
In one-horse open chaise; the meanwhile through his
    pate
Busy thoughts went trooping through of the country
    then so new,
And the people dwelling there who claimed his kindly
    care.

The prairies stretching wide he saw on every side,
So, the vision seemed to be like the billows of the sea;
And, looking far ahead, over knolls and over the mead,
Behind the tall poplar tree, near the home of Farmer
    Lee.

When we at last did enter through rough gate into the
    yard,
With dogs and kittens swarming 'round his feet and
    body-guard;
We met a hearty welcome — a greeting warm and
    true,
As the farmer gave his brown hand, with, "Why,
    brother, how d' ye do?"

The house, although a log one, was cleanly, quiet and
    new;
Outside some shining milk-pans had been sunning
    pure and sweet;

Hard by stood rows of bee-hives, with the bees' low
    droning sound:
All hushed they were and quiet in the twilight closing
    'round.

Arching o'er the pathway, a grape-stalk hung with
    fruit;
Green hop-vines clambered o'er the dark old clap-
    board roof;
There were morning-glories, pinks and striped ribbon
    grass so long,
Their summer beauty faded, their bloom and freshness
    gone.

Let us turn our glance again to the circle now within,
As they gathered 'round the pastor and bid him wel-
    come in;
And while they are discussing health, farms, church
    and weather,
Can we not describe for you a western country supper?
Dame Lee is turning "flannel cakes" with shining
    copper ladle;
Yudie Jane, a little maid, spreads on scoured wooden
    table,
A snowy cloth, mug of cream, dark crullers piled so
    high,
Pink bowl of quince preserves, and rich brown pump-
    kin pie;
While blue-edged plates, cheese, pickles, a pat of but-
    ter yellow,

Fresh comb of dripping honey, canned peaches large
    and mellow;
Fresh golden sweet potatoes, and fresh fish are in the
    oven waiting,
Tea, and hungry-smelling coffee the olfactories are
    regaling.
The round-faced, black-eyed boys, all eager, listening
    stand,
And a chubby little girl, clutching mamma's dress in
    hand;
For the conversation flagged not — it ran most steadily
    on
About the "up North meetin's" in country and in
    town.

"Oh, yes; I'm glad you came," said honest Farmer
    Lee,
"We were getting quite discourged — no churches do
    we see;
We've no soulism, and isms I can't nor wouldn't join,
But I tell ye now 'tis hard work to live God's will
    alone.

"We will most surely all come next holy Sabbath day
Up to the new big school house — you passed it on
    your way;
And I will tell the neighbors and rouse the country
    'round,
To come and listen, while you preach a doctrine that
    is sound.

"We have much to wait and pray for, but I hope it
　　won't be long
Ere we will have a church-house for hallowed prayer
　　and song;
The country yet is new and rough, some of the people
　　very wild,
Though many good folks here I've met, real christians
　　true and mild."

The preacher, as he answered to the words of Farmer
　　Lee,
Said: "The Lord can save his children wherever they
　　may be;
It is not in the surroundings, so much as in the faith,
That draws our Savior to us and strengthens our be-
　　lief."

*　　*　　*　　*　　*　　*　　*　　*

On the morrow, then, they parted, when God's bless-
　　ing had been asked,
And the hearts of all were strengthened for their own
　　appointed tasks;
And where are found co-workers, as this man Farmer
　　Lee,
The weary, traveling preacher good results may surely
　　see.

THE MOTHER'S MOTTO—"TOUCH NOT TASTE NOT."

When this cruel war is over
  And our boys come home again,
Will they come—our James and Roger—
  Staunch and steadfast temp'rance men?
Will they bring the temp'rance banner
  Floating freely on the wind,
Or in vile and base dishonor
  Trailing in the dust behind?

Earnestly dear mother's praying,
  Praying for her sons to-night;
Are those sons to-night betraying
  Her fond teachings of the right?
Whatsoever 's the temptation,
  Touch not taste not is her word,
For it leads to condemnation
  And dishonor of the sword.

When the march is long and weary,
  Or the day is dull in camp,
When you pass the night so weary
  In the guardsman's lonely tramp,
When the grape and shell are flying
  Round you with their deadly aim,
And your comrades falling, dying,
  Breathe the fondest, dearest name,

You may hear the syren singing
   "Drink! 'twill nerve and cheer you up;"
Then hear mother's motto ringing
   "Touch not, taste not, dash the cup!"
There is safety in refraining,
   Bravely, soldierly to die?

But we hope ere long to greet you,
   Mother, maiden, wife and friend,
Praying that no evil meet you
   Till this cruel war shall end.
Maimed or scarred with fair escutcheon,
   Upright, temp'rate, brave and true,
Come to us who set our hearts on
   Victory, through such as you.

LINES.

*[Written on the cover of an old Bible, at the time when many
Banks stopped payment.]*

This is my never-failing bank,
   My more than golden store.
No earthly bank is half so rich,
   How can I then be poor?

'Tis when my stock is spent and gone
   And I without a groat,
I'm glad to hasten to my bank
   And beg a little note.

Sometimes my banker smiling, says,
  Why don't you oftener come?
And when you draw a little bill,
  Why not a larger sum?

Why live so niggardly and poor?
  The bank contains a plenty.
Why come and take a one pound note
  When you may take a twenty?

Nay, twenty thousand, ten times told,
  Is but a trifling sum
To what my bank contains for me,
  Secured in God the Son.

Since then my Banker is so rich,
  I have no need to borrow,
But live upon my notes to-day
  And draw again to-morrow.

I've been a thousand times before
  And never was rejected;
Those notes can never be refused,
  They are by grace accepted.

All forged notes will be refused,
  They're sure to be detected.
All those will deal in forged notes
  Who are not God's elected.

'Tis only those beloved of God,
  Redeemed by precious blood,

That ever have a note to bring—
  They are the gift of God.

There's thousand ransomed sinners fear
  They have no note at all
Because they feel the plunge of sin,
  So beggar'd by the fall.

Though thousand notes lie scattered round
  All signed, and sealed and free,
Yet many a doubting soul will say
  " Ah, they are not for me."

Base unbelief will lead the soul
  To say what is not true;
I tell the poor, emptied man
  Those notes belong to you.

Should all the banks in Britain break,
  The Bank of England smash,
Bring in your notes to Zion's Bank;
  You are sure to get the cash.

Nay, if you have but one small note
  Fear not to bring it in:
Come boldly to the Bank of Grace,
  The banker is within.

I'll go again; I need not fear
  My notes should be neglected:
Sometimes my banker gives me more
  Than asked for, or expected.

Sometimes I felt a little proud,
  I managed things so clever;
Perhaps before the day was gone
  I felt as poor as ever.

Sometimes, with blushes in my face,
  Just at the door I stand;
I know if Moses kept the bank
  I am sure I must be damn'd.

But ah! my bank can never break,
  My bank can never fall;
The firm—three persons in one God—
  Jehovah, Lord of All.

Should all the bankers close their doors,
  My bank stands open wide
To all the chosen of the Lord,
  For whom the Saviour died.

We read of one young man, indeed,
  Whose riches did abound,
But in the banker's Book of Life
  His name was never found.

The leper had a little note:
  "Lord, if thou wilt thou canst."
The banker paid this little note
  And healed the dying man.

Behold and see the dying thief,
  Hang by his Banker's side;

He cried, "Dear Lord, remember me":
  He got his cash and died.

His Blessed Banker took him home
  To everlasting glory,
And there to share his Banker's grace
  And tell his endless story,

With millions more—Jehovah's choice—
  Redeemed with precious blood;
With Peter, Paul, and Magdalene,
  And all the elect of God.

A PRAYER.

Jesus of Heaven, condescend
Thy grace and pity for to lend,
Awhile my aching heart to cheer,
With love that all mankind should fear.

My sins forgive, thy love bestow,
That I may happy live below,
Or, dying, soar to Thee above,
To dwell in endless peace and love.

VASTNESS AND GRANDEUR OF THE SOLAR SYSTEM.

PROF. GRANT, of Glasgow University, in a recent lecture on Stars. said that a railway train traveling night and day at the rate of fifty miles an hour, would reach the moon in six months, the sun in two hundred years, and the *Alpha Centauri* in forty-two millions of years. A ball from a gun, traveling at the rate of 900 miles an hour, would reach *Alpha Centauri* in 2,900,000 years; while light, traveling as it did at the rate of 185,000 miles a second, would not reach it in less than three years. Light from some of the telescope stars would take 5,760 years to reach the earth; and from some of these clusters the distance was so great that light would take half a million years to pass to the earth, so that we see objects not as they really are but as they were half a million years ago. These stars might have become extinct thousands of years ago, and yet their light might present itself to us.

As to the magnitude of the stars, he noticed that it was computed that *Alpya Lyra* was a hundred billions of miles distant from the earth, and its magnitude and splendor was as twenty to one when compared with our sun. Similar investigations brought out the fact that our sun was neither vastly greater nor vastly less than the great majority of our stars.

ANGELS MET HIM AT THE GATE.

[This elegant Song was written in tribute to the Memory of
P. P. Bliss, the Evangelist.]

Angels met him at the gate,
   Humble singer of earth's song,
Welcomed to their bright estate,
   By the fair immortal throng.
Sweetly singing, strains of mirth
   Ringing through high heaven's dome,
To the wayfarer from earth
   Who at last had wandered home.

CHORUS.

Angels bright and angels fair
   Gladly meet him at the gate,
Sweetly singing he shall wear
   Brightest crown of our estate.

Angels met him at the gate,
   Bearing robes of snowy white
For the wanderer long and late,
   Out of darkness into light;
Out of pain and into rest;
   Sweetest rest forever more,
'Mid the mansions of the blest
   Over on that sunny shore.

Angels met him at the gate,
   And his pilgrimage was done;
Ev'ry joy of heaven's estate
   By the christian soldier won.

After night the golden day;
  After seed-time harvest-home;
Pilgrim from life's thorny way,
  Never more thy feet shall roam.

CENTENNIAL ODE.

BY WILLIAM CULLEN BRYANT.

Through storm and calm the years have led
  Our nation on, from stage to stage,
A century's space, until we tread
  The threshold of another age.

We see there, o'er our pathway swept,
  A torrent stream of blood and fire,
And thank the Ruling Power who kept
  Our sacred league of States entire.

Oh, checkered train of years, farewell!
  With all thy strife and hopes and fears:
But with us let thy memories dwell,
  To warn and lead, the coming years.

And thou, the new-beginning Age,
  Warned by the past, and not in vain,
Write on a fairer, whiter page,
  The record of thy happier reign.

BEND BENEATH THE BLAST.

When sorrow's tempests round us roar,
   And overwhelm the soul,
O trust thou not in worldly pride,
   Or seek the tempest's bowl;
But with a firm and trusting heart
   Bend low beneath the blast,
And He above who chasteneth thee
   Will raise thee when 'tis past.

The lofty oak, the mountain pine,
   So stately in their pride,
Must bend or break before the storms
   That on the night winds ride;
While the meek willow lowly stoops
   Before the raging blast,
And lifts it's head in beauty decked,
   When storms and clouds are past.

So thou, O man, must lowly bend
   When sorrows round thee press;
They may be angels in disguise,
   To lead to happiness.
O trust to Him who rules above,
   And bend beneath the blast,
And He will raise thy drooping soul
   When storms of life are past.

A TOUCH OF NATURE.

MUSIC IN CAMP.

*[This beautiful poem was written during the war by John R.
Thompson, a Southern poet, who died on the first of May, 1862.]*

Two armies covered hill and plain
   Where Rappahannock's waters
Ran deeply crimsoned with the stain
   Of battle's recent slaughter.

The summer clouds lay pitched like tents
   In meads of heavenly azure,
And each dread gun of elements
   Slept in his hid embrasure.

The breeze so softly blew, it made
   No forest leaf to quiver,
And the smoke of the random cannonade
   Rolled slowly from the river.

And now where circling hills looked down
   With cannon grimly planted,
O'er listless camp and silent town
   The golden sunset slanted—

When on the fervent air there came
   A strain, now rich, now tender—
The music seemed itself aflame
   With day's departing splendor.

A Federal band, which eve and morn
   Played measures brave and nimble,

Had just struck up with flute and horn
    And lively clash of cymbal.

Down flocked the soldiers to the bank
    Till margined by its pebbles,
One wooded shore was blue with 'Yanks;'
    And one was gray with 'Rebels.'

Then all was still; and then the band,
    With movement light and frisky,   ·
Made stream and forest, hill and strand
    Reverberate with 'Dixie.'

The conscious stream, with burnished glow,
    Went proudly o'er the pebbles,
But thrilled throughout its deepest flow
    With yelling of the Rebels.

Again a pause, and then again
    The trumpet pealed sonorous,
And "Yankee Doodle" was the strain
    To which the shore gave chorus.

The laughing ripple shoreward flew
    To kiss the shining pebbles—
Loud shrieked swarming boys in blue
    Defiance to the Rebels.

And yet once more the bugle sang
    Among the stormy riot;
No shout upon the evening rang—
    There reigned a holy quiet.

The sad, slow stream its noiseless flood
   Pouring o'er the glistening pebbles;
And silent now the Yankees stood—
   And silent stood the Rebels.

No unresponsive soul had heard
   That plaintive note's appealing,
So deeply "Home, Sweet Home," had stirred
   The hidden founts of feeling.

Of blue or gray, he sees,
   As by the wand of fairy,
The cottage 'neath the live oak trees,
   The cabin by the prairie;

Or cold or warm his native skies
   Bend in their beauty o'er him;
Seen through the tear-mist in his eyes
   His loved ones stand before him.

As fades the iris after rain
   In April's tearful weather,
The vision vanished as the strain
   And daylight died together.

But memory waked by music's art,
   Expressed by simplest numbers,
Subdued the sternest Yankee's heart,
   Made light the Rebel's slumbers.

And fair the form of Music shrines—
   That bright, celestial creature—
Who still 'mid war's embattled lines,
   Gave this one touch of nature.

GOD BLESS THE UNION SOLDIER.

BY ROBERT G. INGERSOLL.

The past rises before me like a dream. Again we are in the great struggle for national life. We hear the sounds of preparation, the music of the boisterous drums, the silver voices of heroic bugles. We see thousands of assemblages, and hear the appeals of orators; we see the pale cheeks of women and the flushed faces of men; and in those assemblages we see all the dead whose dust we have covered with flowers. We lose sight of them no more. We are with them when they enlist in the great army of freedom. We see them part with those they love. Some are walking for the last time in quiet, woody places with the maidens they adore. We hear the whisperings and the sweet vows of eternal love as they lingeringly part forever. Others are bending over cradles, kissing babies that are asleep; some are receiving the blessings of old men; some are parting with mothers who hold them and press them to their hearts again and again, and say nothing, and some are talking with wives, and endeavoring with brave words spoken in the old tones to drive from their hearts the awful fear. We see them part. We see the wife standing in the door, with the babe in her arms—standing in the sunlight sobbing—at the turn of the road a hand waves— she answers by holding high in her loving hands the child. He is gone, and forever. We see them all as they march proudly away under the flaunting flags, keeping time to the wild, grand music of war, marching down the streets of the great cities, through the towns and across the prairies, down to the fields of glory, to do and to die for the eternal right. We go with them, one and all. We are by their side on all the gory fields, in the hospitals, on all the weary marches. We stand guard with them in the wild storm, and under the quiet stars. We are with them in ravines running with blood, in the furrows of old fields; we are with them between contesting hosts unable to move, wild with thirst, the life ebbing slowly away among the withered leaves. We see them pierced by balls and torn with shells in the trenches by forts, and in the whirlwind of the charge, where men become iron with nerves of steel.

We are with them in the prisons of hatred and famine; but human speech can never tell what they endured. We are at home when the news comes that they are dead. We see the maiden in the shadow of her first sorrow. We see the silvered head of the old man bowed with the first grief.

The past rises before us, and we see four millions of human beings governed by the lash; we see them bound hand and foot; we hear the strokes of cruel whips; we see the hounds tracking women through the tangled swamps; we see babes sold from the breasts of mothers. Cruelty unspeakable! Outrage infinite! Four million bodies in chains—four million souls in fetters. All the sacred relations of wife, mother, father and child trampled beneath the brutal feet of might. All this was done under our own beautiful banner of the free. The past rises before us; we hear the roar and shriek of the bursting shell; the broken fetters fall; these heroes died. We look, instead of slaves we see men, women and children. The wand of progress touches the auction block, the slave pen, the whipping post, and we see homes and firesides, and school-houses and books, and where all was want and crime and cruelty and fetters, we see the faces of the free. These heroes are dead; they died for liberty; they died for us; they are at rest; they sleep in the land they made free under the flag they rendered stainless, under the solemn pines, the sad hemlocks, the tearful willows and the embracing vines; they sleep beneath the shadows of the clouds, careless alike of sunshine or storm, each in the windowless palace of rest. Earth may run red with other wars, they are at peace. In the midst of battle, in the roar of conflict, they found the severity of death. I have one sentiment for the soldiers, living and dead—cheers for the living and tears for the dead.

THE BIVOUAC OF THE DEAD.

BY COL. THEODORE O'HARA.

I.

The muffled drum's sad roll has beat
    The soldier's last tattoo;
No more on life's parade shall meet
    The brave and fallen few.
On Fame's eternal camping ground
    Their silent tents are spread,
And Glory guards, with solemn round,
    The bivouac of the dead.

II.

No rumor of the foe's advance
    Now swells upon the wind,
Nor troubled thought at midnight haunts
    Of loved ones left behind.
No vision of the morrow's strife
    The warrior's dream alarms;
No braying horn, no screaming fife,
    At dawn shall call to arms.

III.

Their shivered swords are red with rust,
    Their plumed heads are bowed,
Their haughty banner, trailed in dust,
    Is now their martial shroud—
And plenteous funeral tears have washed
    The red stains from each brow,

18

And the proud forms by battle gashed
    Are free from anguish now.

IV.

The neighing troop, the flashing blades,
    The bugle's stirring blast,
The charge, the dreadful cannonade,
    The din and shout are passed;
Nor War's wild notes, nor Glory's peal,
    Shall thrill with fierce delight
Those breasts that never more may feel
    The rapture of the light.

V.

Like the fierce Northern hurricane
    That sweeps his great plateau,
Flushed with the triumph yet to gain,
    Come down the serried foe.
Who heard the thunder of the fray
    Break o'er the field beneath,
Knew well the watchword of that day
    Was "Victory or death!"

*   *   *   *   *   *   *

VI.

Thus 'neath their parent turf they rest,
    Far from the gory field,
Borne to a Spartan mother's breast
    On many a bloody shield.

The sunshine of their native sky
  Smiles sadly on them here,
And kindred eyes and hearts watch by
  The hero's sepulchre.

VII.

Rest on, embalmed and sainted dead!
  Dear is the blood you gave—
No impious footsteps here shall tread
  The herbage of your grave.
Nor shall your glory be forgot
  While fame her record keeps,
Or Honor points the hallowed spot
  Where Valor proudly sleeps.

VIII.

Yon marble minstrel's voiceful stone,
  In deathless song shall tell,
When many a vanished year hath flown,
  The story how you fell;
Nor wreck, nor change, nor winter's blight,
  Nor Time's remorseless doom,
Can dim one ray of holy light,
  That gilds your glorious tomb.

EPISODE.

'Twas on a stormy winter's day,
Upon the ground snow thickly lay;
December winds were whistling by,
Dark clouds were flitting o'er the sky,
And nature put forth every token,
As plainly as if words were spoken:
The blast is near—hie to your cot;
Nor venture from that hallowed spot.
One weary traveler on the road
Employs in vain both whip and goad,
To force his jaded, way-worn beast
Into a faster walk, at least;
But, notwithstanding whip and spur,
From off a walk he would not stir.
The blast sweeps on with all its force,
Snow-laden Boreas hides his course;
The night now taking place of day,
In vain he tries to find the way.
Long hours he wanders through the gloom,
Fearing each hour may fix his doom,
Until hope dies within his heart;
" Must I," he cries, " with earth thus part?
My God! is this Thy stern decree—
My kindred never more to see?
Why hast Thou kept me thus alive,
So near my father to arrive,
And brought me here to be ov'rthrown,
While friends are near to die alone?"

And bewildered with the blast,
One hopeful look toward heaven he casts;
Then yielding up his frozen breath,
Sinks from his horse all cold in death.
Relieved at once of all its load,
Again the horse soon finds his way—
Brute instinct now assuming sway,
The beast again plods on his way;
And ere another hour goes by,
To the old homestead he draws nigh.
Stopping at the barn-yard gate,
Long time with patience does he wait,
Until the new returning light
Dispels the gloomy shades of night.

'Tis morn: The cock with trumpet shrill,
Makes music o'er each vale and hill,
And brings each sturdy yeoman forth
To tend his herd; while from the North
Old Boreas comes with furious tread,
That drives each beast to stall and shed.
And now, unconscious of his loss,
The sire goes forth through snow and frost,
To milk the kine and feed the stock,
And mind the welfare of his flock.
He stands aghast in mute surprise,
When he the faithful beast espies,
Who, neighing, runs to where he stands,
And smells his kind old master's hands;

The father speeds from cot to cot,
His story tells and tarries not,
Till twenty sturdy yeomen meet
To scour the ground with nimble feet.

An hour goes by, and in their search
They wander past the ruined church,
Into a wild, untraveled way,
Where the light snow in mountains lay;
When with a mournful howl that sounds
O'er hill and mountain crag around,
The faithful watchdog snuffs the breeze,
Then darts away among the trees.
Sinking each moment to the waist,
They follow on with breathless haste;
Till 'neath an old and spreading pine,
He paws the snow with piteous whine.
The mantling snow is torn away,
And there in icy windings lays,
That weary traveler's form,
Who perished in the midnight storm.
"O God!" the aged sire exclaims;
It is my son — my noble James!"
Then low, upon the frozen ground,
Beside the corpse he sat him down.
" Alas, my boy! that I should find
Thee here in death's embrace entwined;
My son, my son, my only born!
Why didst thou leave me here forlorn?

I loved thee tenderly, my son;
But now, alas, thy race is run!
And I am left an aged man,
Amid the wrecks of life to stand
Alone.   The partner of my joy
Expired in bearing thee my boy;
And now thou 'rt gone, upon whose breast
I thought my dying head to rest,
And I am left all alone to bear
This weary burden of despair.

Come, welcome death, O, give relief!
And in oblivion end my grief."
He ceased, and low upon his breast
His head sank down, as if in rest.
They lifted softly his drooping head,
'Twas vain — the stricken sire was dead.

LINES ON THE MYSTIC TIE.

BY CAPT. S. WHITING.

When far in distant lands we roam,
    And no loved faces we descry;
This bond makes every place a home—
    The " mystic tie "—the " mystic tie."
When tossed upon the stormy sea,
    Or sick in distant lands we lie;
A thought consoling, 'tis that we
    Are brethren of the " mystic tie."

It brings kind friends around our bed—
　　It bids us look to God on high;
By it our thoughts to heaven are led,
　　Dear "mystic tie"—sweet "mystic tie."
When turning homeward o'er the main,
　　We watch our bark with gladness fly;
To bear us to our friends again—
　　Our brethren of the "mystic tie."

O! may this bright, fraternal chain,
　　That binds us heart to heart below,
Unweakened and undimmed remain,
　　When to the heavenly lodge we go;
There by this bond, that e'er shall last,
　　Eternal as the starry sky,
May be linked when life is past,
　　Sweet "mystic tie"—sweet "mystic tie."

To L. M. W.

The mind still retains
　　After years have departed,
Some precious remains
　　Of the generous hearted;
And brings back to view,
　　From the shore of time's ocean,
The good and the true,
　　We have crowned with devotion.

The flash of a smile,
  Or the ripple of laughter,
That rang for awhile,
  Will revive in years after;
Though the voice may be hushed,
  And the smile may be faded,
And flowers may be crushed,
  O'er the forms they have shaded.

So this faithful heart
  Will forget thee, no never!
Till life's scenes depart
  And existence shall sever;
Then, constancy's gem,
  You must give while I ask it,
And grant me the same
  From thy memory's casket.

ODE ON THE SEA OF GALILEE.

BY N. P. WILLIS.

As o'er thy past my fancy strays,
  Blue sea amidst the lonely hills!
Sweet thoughts of other, brighter days
  With holy calm my spirit fills.

'Twas on the hills that round thee swell,
  And on thy narrow, verdant shore

The Saviour whom I love so well
    Oft journeyed in the days of yore.

And there He brake the living bread,
    And bade the streams of mercy flow;
To heaven true life waked up the dead,
    And turned to joy the mourner's woe.

Oh, would that I were with them amid their shining
    throng,
Mingling in their worship, joining in their song.
The friends that started with me have entered long
    ago;
One by one they left me struggling with the foe;
Their pilgrimage was shorter, their triumph sooner
    won;
How lovingly they'll hail me when my toil is done!

With them the blessed angels that know no grief nor
    sin,
I see them by the portal, prepared to let me in.
Oh, Lord! I wait thy pleasure; thy time and way are
    best;
But I am wasted, worn and weary, Oh Father bid me
    rest.

THERE'S REST BY AND BY.

When faint and weary toiling,
  The sweat drops on my brow
I long to cease from labor
  And drop the burden now.
There comes a gentle chiding
  To quell each murmuring sigh:
Work while the day is shining
  "There's resting by and by."

'Tis not to hear thy groaning
  Thy task is heavy made,
Nor adding to thy sorrow
  That succor is delayed.
When bending neath the burden
  You toil, and sweat, and cry,
"Be patient" is the answer,
  "There's resting by and by."

The way is rough and thorny,
  The day is dark and drear,
My step is growing weary,
  The night is drawing near;
Behold this verdant wayside,
  How cool the shadows lie!
"Nay, pause not in thy journey,
  There's resting by and by."

Ah! when the crown is waiting,
  And room enough in heaven,

Why wage a further warfare
  Where dreadful wounds are given?
O give me now the trophy!
  Why not my Saviour, why?
" Still bear the cross a season,
  There's resting by and by."

This life to toil is given,
  And he improves it best
Who seeks by cheerful labor
  To enter into rest.
Then pilgrim worn and weary
  Press on! the goal is nigh!
" The prize is straight before thee;
  There's resting by and by."

ON THE DEATH OF MY BUNK-MATE, G. A. BLANK,

Whose heart was hushed in the Battle of the Wilderness, May 5, 1864.

In the battle cloud's eclipse,
  'Mid a shower of shot and shell,
With his soul upon his lips,
    George fell;
And we laid him, stiff and cold,
  'Neath the sod; yet, why repine?
When he reached the Gates of Gold,
  If he had the countersign,
    All is well!

Hallowed is the path he trod,
  And the little nameless knoll;
Earth has claimed his form, but God
      Claimed his soul!
And, like Samuel of old,
  When he called him, wounded, grieved,
Quick he answered: " Lord, behold,
  Here am I!" and God received
      George's soul.

Pilgrim clouds in mourning deep,
  As they journey through the skies,
Pause upon their way to weep
      Where he lies;
And, salutes of thunder roll
  O'er the hero's burial sod,
But his young unimprisoned soul
  Has joined the hosts of God,
      In the skies.

MORNING SUPPLICATION.

Thou who watchest in the darkness,
  Who dost give the morning light;
During sleep's defenseless hours,
  Who hast kept me through the day.

Wilt thou suffer me to praise Thee?
  Wilt thou hear my morning song?

I who have so often wandered
From the right and chose the wrong.

Father wilt thou let me thank Thee,
Bowing at thy mercy seat,
For thy mercies and thy patience,
Prostrate here before thy feet?

Shall I go *alone* to struggle
In the conflicts of this day?
Grant thy all sufficient favor—
Father aid me lest I stray.

May my praises be accepted,
And my thanks be all sincere,
Though as poor and undeserving—
Gracious Being! wilt Thou hear.

·LINES ON THE OLD SHOOL-HOUSE.

Whatever else to the night has gone—
The night that never shall know a dawn—
It stands undimmed in my memory still,
The old brown school-house on the hill.

I see the briers beside the door;
The rocks where we played in keeping store;
The steps we dug in the bank below,
And the "bear track trod in the winter's snow.

The corner brick on the chimney lies
Just as it did to my boyish eyes,
And in dreams I throw the stones again
I threw at the toppling brick in vain.

The names on the weatherboards are part
Of the sacred treasures of my heart;
Some yet a place with the earth-sounds keep,
And some in the holds of silence sleep.

I hear the growl from his central lair
Of the swiftest boy who stood for "bear,"
And the sound brings back the joy and glow
Of the chase around the ring of snow.

Often again in thought I slide
On the stone-boat down the long hill side;
The breathless speed and the dizzy reel,
And the wind in my lifted hair I feel.

Ah me! there are spots that hold my dead
In a sleep unstirred by memory's tread;
And many a scene of life's triumph lies
Deep in the mists that never rise.

And things of rapture and things of tears,
Are hidden within the veil of years;
But the old brown school-house on the hill—
It stands undimmed in my memory still.

LINES ON THE DEPARTING YEAR.

A sad farewell to thee, Old Year!
  Thoul't soon be numbered with the past,
And from thy grasp so white and drear
  Thy few short hours are slipping fast.
Thou'rt leaving still a careless world,
  That does not mark thy rapid flight;
Heedless they live till they are hurled
  Into the grave and out of sight.

Old Year, I will not thee forget,
  For thou hast been a friend to me;
Only it makes this heart regret
  How sadly I have misused thee.
You brought me stores of joy and pain,
  And taught me many lessons, too,
How deeper pleasures to attain,
  And gave me friendship lasting, true.

The clock strikes twelve and now thour't gone;
  Another quickly takes thy place,
Until like thee, as old and wan,
  He hurries from this world of space.
The earth pursues its onward track—
  The sun still rises just to set;
Oh! if I could I'd call thee back,
  But thou art now beyond regret.

Thy life was shorter yet than mine
  I have lived recklessly with thee;

But this much I have learned of thine:
  Time may not linger long for me.
Many have died and many born,
  Though some of these that passed away
Were not the old and weary-worn,
  Nor ready for the last great day.

Nations have shook and nations fell
  Since thou wast ushered into life,
But now a calm pervades— 'tis well,
  For all seemed weary—tired of strife.
I mourn that thou hast left our sight:
  Let others sound thy loud death knell;
Oh! these may seem our parting bright;
  Departing year! a long farewell!

BREEZES OF THE SUMMER EVE.

Breeze of the summer eve, from whence is thy flight?
And whither art straying so gently to-night?
Oh, soft are thy whispers and balmy thy breath,
And peaceful, O peaceful, thy song on the heath.

Say, where hast thou been in thy journey to-day?
Say, what hast thou seen on thy sun-lighted way?
What happiness prompts thee, sweet zephyr, to pour
Forth thy burden of gladness and hope at my door?

19

"I have come from the clime where the incense of
    flowers
Is kissing to heaven, through all the bright hours;
Where the vine spreads its leaves in the midsummer's
    ray;
Where the orange groves bloom and the cool foun-
    tains play;

" Where a bright river winds by an ever green shore,
And the song of the bulbul is heard evermore;
And for many a blessed and beautiful day,
No storm-cloud nor shadow has darkened my way.

"And I saw on the deep, as I journeyed to-day,
A vessel becalmed on her watery way;
I filled her white sails and she sped on her flight,
And she rides at her anchor in safety to-night.

"And again, as I wandered through forest and glade,
I came by the bower of a beautiful maid;
A sunbeam was tinging her cheek with its glow,
And I kissed her ripe lips and caressed her fair brow.

"And then through a lattice I noiselessly crept,
And passed by a couch where an invalid slept;
I fanned his hot cheek with the breath of a rose, .
And a bright dream of pleasure passed o'er his repose.

"And I saw a young bride, whose bloom would outvie
The blush of the rose in its ruddiest dye,
And she heard with delight my low sigh in the grove
As I blended my song with her day-dream of love.

"And I came where an innocent babe, on the breast
Of a happy young mother, was taking a rest,
And I tossed its bright ringlets of gold as I passed,
And o'er its calm sleep sweet visions I cast.

"And a toiler had paused by the side of a rill
To allay his fierce thirst, as I swept o'er the hill;
A silvered-haired man, with a sorrowful air,
All encumbered with years and encompassed with
    care—

"And then, as he eagerly bowed down his head
To quaff from the stream, in its pebbly bed,
I cooled the bright drops as they playfully ran
To meet the parched lips of the weary old man.

"And thus as I wander by cottage and grove,
I bear on my wings a blest mission of love;
And the children of men in their joy shall reply,
As I turn my glad song through the midsummer sky."

"OUR HEROIC THEMES."

*[This poem was read at the Annual Reunion of the Society of the
Army of the Potomac, by Geo. H. Boker.]*

Turn as I may in search of worldly themes
To fill with life the poet's solemn dreams,
Some hint from Rome, some retrospect of Greece
Red with their war, or golden with their peace;

Some thought of Lancelot and Guinevere,
The "Arm in samite" and the "mystic mere,"
Or those grand echoes that forever flow
From Roland's horn through narrow Roncesvaux.
Some spark yet living of the strange romance
Whose flame illumed the Crusader's lance;
Or that strong purpose which inclosed the seas
Before the vision of the Genoese;
Or when the love lock and the close cropped crown
Died with a laugh, or triumphed with a frown;
Or the frail mayflower poured her prayerful flock, ·
Upon the breast of Plymouth's wintry rock;
Or, when the children of those hardy men
Bearded the throne they never loved again.
Those splendid themes, so sacred to my youth,
Those dreams of fancy with their heart of truth,
Paled, as I viewed them in the fresher rays
That light the scenes of these heroic days;
Shrank, as the young Colossus of our age
With scornful finger turned the historic page, ·
And sought through pigmy chiefs and pigmy wars
To peer his stature and his studious frown;
Then razed the records as he wrote his own,
Matchless in grandeur—product of a cause
As deep and changeless as those moral laws
That base themselves upon the throne of God,
Fair with his blessings, awful with his rod.

But why explore the sources of the flood,
Whence all the land ran steel and fire and blood.

My heart is fretting like a tethered steed's,
To join the heroes in their noble deeds.
A noise of armies gathers in my ears,
The Southern yells! the Northern battle cheers;
The endless volleys, ceaseless as the roar
Of the vexed Ocean brawling with its shore;
The groaning cannon, puffing at a breath
Man's shreds and fragments through the jaws of death;
The rush of horses and the wherring sway
Of the keen sabre cleaving soul from clay;
And over all intelligible and clear
As spoken language to a listning ear,
The bugle orders the tumultuous herds,
And leads the flocks of battles with its words.

'Twas mine to witness and to feel the shame
Manassas cast upon our early fame,
When the raw greenness of our boastful bands
Yielded a victory almost in their hands;
Fled from the field before a vanished foe,
And lied about it, to complete the woe.
Since then, through all the changes of the war,
My eyes have followed our ascending star.
Ascending ever, though at times the cloud
Of dark disaster cast its murky shroud
About our guide, oppressing men with fear
Lest the last day of liberty draw near.
Through all I knew, and with my faith upborne,
Turned on the weak a smile of pitying scorn,

That our calm star still filled its destined place,
Lost to our sight, but shining in God's face.
With growing courage day by day I hung
Above the soldier with the quiet tongue.
Sneers hissed about him, penmen fought his war,
Here he was lacking, there he went too far,
Alas! how bloody, but alack how tame;
O for Lee's talent! O ye fools for shame!
From the first move this foe defensive stood,
And was that nothing? It was worth the blood,
O chief supreme, the head of glory's roll,
O will of steel, O lofty, generous soul,
Sharing thy laurels lest a comrade want,
Why should I name thee? Every mouth cries Grant!

Time was my faith in him whose sturdy skill
Three dreadful days had held the quaking hill,
Stood like a rock on which the fiery spray
Beat out its life, then slowly ebbed away;
Saved our domain from rapine, waste and wrath,
And taught the foe an unreturning path—
Light of our darkness, succor our need;
God of our country, bless the name of Mead!

I saw with wonder Sherman's Titan line
Pour from the mountains to the distant brine,
Sweep treason's cradle bare of all its brood,
And turn its garden to a solitude;
Fear ran before him, Famine groaned behind,
And following Famine came the humble mind.

Who felt a care within his bosom grow
Of more than pity for the hapless foe,
Or spent a fear on that which Fate's decrees
Already wrote among her victories.
When in the tumult of the battle van
Shone fortune's darling, mounted SHERIDAN,
Rapid to plan, and peerless in the fight,
He plucked Fame's chaplets as by sovereign right;
Emerged triumphant from a wild retreat,
And blazoned victory's colors on defeat.

I watched with THOMAS while his wary glance
Marked the rash foes their heedless lines advance;
Step after step he lured their willing feet
Into the toils from which was no retreat;
Then with a swoop, as when the eagle swings
Out of his eyrie with the roar of wings,
The veteran fell upon his venturous prey,
And rolled his lines to mobs in wild dismay.
But hark! what tidings from the west advance
To choke Fame's voice and dim her shining glance?
Still are the lips that gave the wise command,
Dark the controlling eye and cold the hand,
That as the needle toward the northern sky,
Pointed one way — the way to victory.
Our annals hold secure the soldier's fame,
A nation's glories cluster 'round his name;
No deeds of his require the grace of song —
Mere praise would do their simple grandeur wrong;

Turn from his honors, which he left to earth,
And ponder what he bore to heaven: His worth?
A simple nature in antique mould,
Gentle, serene, child-tender, lion-bold;
A heart with sympathies so broad and true
That trust and love grew 'round him ere they knew;
Open, sincere, uncovetous and pure,
Strong to achieve and patient to endure;
Heedless of Fame he looked within himself,
For that reward that neither prise nor pelf
Can give the soul, whose naked virtues stand
Before God's eye, beneath God's lifted hand.
In the long future of this mortal hive,
Who may predict what records will survive?
A little shudder of earth's brittle crust,
And man and man's renown were scattered dust.
But in his day to THOMAS it was given
To sow his fields and gather fruits for heaven,
Which neither worm can gnaw nor care make dim,
And these are deathless: these he took with him.

Through anxious years I saw the martial flood
Surge back and forth in waves of fire and blood;
Sometimes it paused, and sometimes seemed to reel,
Spent and exhausted from the rebels' steel;
But every shock was sapping, blow by blow,
The bars that backward held the overflow,
Till suddenly the vein cracked and roared,
And over all the human torrent poured;

Then bloomed the harvest of our patient aims,
Then bowed the world before our deeds and names,
Then on the proudest of Fame's temple gates
Shone novel records and thick crowded gates;
New wreaths were hung upon her horned shrines,
New clarions blow before her martial lines;
Fresh incense smoked, and fresh libations dripped;
The vernal laurels from the hills were stripped,
And woven in chaplets.   Far and near the hum
Of gladness ushered the returning drum —
Welcome stood beckoning, looking toward the South,
With cheers of welcome brimming in the mouth;
Till came the rapture of that crowning hour,
When the vast armies proved their awful power.
In dense procession through the marble banks,
That rang and quivered with a nation's thanks;
While, like a temple of the morning sky,
August, sublime, refulgent, calm and high,
Towered in its might, as symbol of the whole,
The dome-crowned presence of the Capitol.
I envy those whose tattered standards waved
Within the city which their valor saved:
The Eastern heroes and their Western peers,
The holy joy that glittered in their tears,
As thronging upward to the nation's throne
They knelt and sobbed and kissed the very stone.
And thou brave Army, that hast borne the brunt
Of stern repulse so often on thy front—
Thou who hast rallied from each stunning blow
With godlike patience, facing still the foe,

Thou moving pivot of the deadly fight
Whose steadfast centre held all things aright,
Twice saved us from the foe's audacious feet,
And drove him howling through his last retreat,
Hung on his steps until for peace he knelt
And sued for mercy which he never felt.
I thank just fortune that it was thy fate
Alone to hurl the traitors from their state;
Alone to make their capital thy prize,
And watch the treason close its bloody eyes,
O, roll, Potomac, prouder of thy name,
Touched by the splendor of thy army's fame,
Thrill with the steps of thy returning braves!
Wail through thy margins of uncounted graves!
Laugh at the echo of thy soldiers' shout!
Whisper their story to the lands about!
Yes, feel each passion of the human soul,
But roll, great river, in thy glory roll!

Forget not here the nation's martyred chief,
Fallen for the gospel of your own belief,
Who e're he mounted to the people's throne
Asked for your prayers and joined in them his own;
I knew the man; I see him as he stands
With gifts of mercy in his outstretched hands;
A kindly light within his gentle eyes
Sad as the toil in which his heart grew wise;
His lips half-parted with the constant smile
That kindled truth, but foiled the deepest guile;

His head bent forward, and his willing ear
Divinely patient right and wrong to hear;
Great in his goodness, humble in his state,
Firm in his purpose, yet not passionate,
He led his people with a tender hand,
And won by love a sway beyond command.
Summoned by lot to mitigate a time
Frenzied with rage, unscrupulous with crime,
He bore his mission with so meek a heart
That heaven itself took up his weary part;
And when he faltered helped him ere he fell,
Eking his efforts out by miracle.
No king this man by grace of God's intent!
No, something better—freeman—President!
A nature modeled on a higher plan,
Lord of himself, an inborn gentleman.

Pass by his fate; forget the closing strife
In the vast memories of his noble life;
Forget the scene, the bravo stealing nigh,
The pistol shot, the new-made widow's cry,
The palsied people and the tears that ran
O'er half a world to mourn a single man.
But O remember while the mind can hold
One record sacred to the days of old,
The gentle heart that beats its life away
Just as young morning donned his robe of **gray**,
Stole through the tears beneath his golden **tread**,
And touched in vain the eyelids of the dead!

Remember him as one who died for right,
With victories' trophies glittering in his sight;
His mission finished, and the settled end
Assured, and owned by stranger foe and friend,
Nothing was left him but to taste the sweet
Of triumph—sitting in the Nation's seat.
And for that triumph Heaven prepared its courts,
And cleared its champaigns for unwonted sports;
Summoned the spirits of the noble dead
Who fell in battle for the cause he led.
Soldiers and chiefs awakened from the clay
And ranged their legions in the old array;
There LYON lead and KEARNEY rode amain,
And skilled MCPHERSON drew his bridle-rein;
Brave REYNOLDS marshaled his undaunted corps,
And SEDGWICK pressed to reach the front once more;
The star of MITCHELL glittered over all,
And STEVENS answered RENO's bugle call;
BAYARD looked worthy of his knightly name,
And MANSFIELD's eyes were bright with battle flame;
LANDERS' grand brow was flushed with eager ire,
And STRONG arose from WAGNER's roaring fire;
There gallant BUFORD in the van was seen,
And COCHRAN waved his flag of Irish green;
BIRNEY's clear eyes were radiant with his faith;
WINTHROP and GREBLE smiled at baffled Death!
Down SHAW's dark front a solemn purpose ran—
The slave's resolve to prove himself—mere man.
The heroes courage for that humble hope
Was all that winged him up the bloody slope.

There burly NELSON blustered through his men,
And RICHARDSON deployed his lines again;
BAKER looked thoughtful! WARDSWORTH's liberal hand
Pointed right forward; and the sharp command
Of SMITH's mild valor bore his soldiers on,
As when it rang o'er fated DONELSON!

All these, and more, before the martyr's gaze,
Passed through the shouts of Heaven's tumultuous
    praise;
The sound of clarions, and the choral songs
Of rapture bursting from the seraph throngs,
Passed like a pageant from the evening skies,
But left a picture on celestial eyes,
Whose tints shall deepen as the days increase,
And shine a marvel in that Realm of Peace.

MY MISSION.

Help me, O God! to do the work
    Before me set;
Let me not falter in the step
    Scarce taken yet.

If trials should beset my path
    Make me content—
Willing to bear all burdens which
    By Thee are sent.

Through weary moments, which come through
  The life to all,
Be Thou my guide, and lead me on
  Lest I should fall.

If I grow weary marking out
  My own life-track,
Strengthen me onward—I would have
  No turning back.

If I have worshipped earthly shrines,
  Oh, God! forgive!
Make me for other things than earth
  To hope and live.

Deal gently with the erring heart
  Unto me given;
Make it a pure and fitting thing
  For yonder Heaven.

THE COMMON SOLDIER.

BY O. P.

Nobody cared when he went to war
  But the woman who cried on his shoulder;
Nobody decked him with immortelles—
  He was only a common soldier.

Nobody packed in a common trunk
  Folded raiment and officer's fare;

A knapsack held all the new recruit
  Might own, or love, or eat, or wear.

Nobody gave him a good-bye fete,
  With sparkling jest and flower-crowned wine;
Two or three friends on the sidewalk stood,
  Watching for Jones, the fourth in line.

Nobody cared how the battle went
  With the man who fought till the bullet sped
Through the coat undecked with leaf or star—
  Only a common soldier left for dead.

The cool rain bathed the fevered wound,
  And the clouds wept the livelong night;
A pitying lotion Nature gave
  Till help might come with morning light.

Such help as the knife of the surgeon gives,
  Cleaving the gallant arm from the shoulder;
And another name swells the pension list
  For the meagre pay of a common soldier.

See, over yonder, all day he stands;
  An empty sleeve in the soft wind sways,
As he holds the lonely left hand out
  For charity, at the crossing-ways.

And this is how, with bitter shame,
  He begs his bread and hardly lives;
So wearily ekes out the sum
  A proud and grateful (?) nation gives.

What matter how he served the guns
   When plume and sash were over yonder?
What matter though he bore the flag
   Through blinding smoke and battle thunder?

What matter though a wife and child
   Cry softly for the good arm rent,
And wonder why that random shot
   To him, their own beloved, was sent?

Oh, patriot hearts! wipe out this stain;
   Give jeweled cup and sword no more;
But let no Common Soldier blush
   To own the Loyal Blue he wore.

Shout long and loud for victory won,
   By chief and leader staunch and true;
But don't forget the boys that fought—
   Shout for the Common Soldier too.

THE SOLDIER'S LETTER.

The balmy southern night is slowly falling
   O'er vale and mountain's brow,
And wrapping in its solemn dusky mantle
   One lone encampment now:
Within his tent your soldier-boy is seated,
   Writing these lines to thee,
And this shall be the burden of my letter—
   Dear Mother, pray for me.

STANZAS—BUILDING ON THE SAND.

'Tis well to woo, 'tis well to wed,
　For so the world hath done,
Since myrtles grew and roses blew,
　And morning brought the sun.
But have a care ye young and fair,
　Be sure you pledge with truth;
Be certain that your love will wear
　Beyond the days of youth!
For if you give not heart for heart
　As well as hand for hand,
You'll find you've played an unwise part
　And "built upon the sand."

'Tis well to save, 'tis well to have
　A goodly store of gold,
And hold enough of shining stuff,
　For charity is cold.
But place not all your hope and trust
　On what the deep mine brings;
We cannot live with yellow dust
　Unmixed with purer things,
And he who piles up dust alone,
　Will often have to stand
Beside his coffer chest and own,
　He "built upon the sand."

'Tis good to speak in kindly guise,
　And sooth where'ere you can;
Fair speech should bind the human mind,
　And love like man and man.

But stay not at the gentle words,
  Let deeds with language dwell;
The one who pities starving birds
  Should scatter crumbs as well.
The mercy that is warm and true
  Must lend a helping hand,
For those that talk and fail to do
  But "build upon the sand."

ON PICKET.

Within a green and shadowy wood,
Circled with spring, alone I stood;
The nook was peaceful, fair and good.
The wild plum blossoms lured the bees,
The birds sang mildly in the trees;
Magnolia scents were on the breeze;
All else was silent; but the ear
Caught sounds of distant bugle clear,
And heard the whistling bullets near;
When, from the winding river's shore
The rebel guns began to roar,
And our's, to answer, thundering o'er;
And echoed from the wooded hill —
Repeated and repeated still —
Through all my soul they seemed to thrill;
For, as their rattling storm awoke,
And loud and fast the discord broke,
In loud and trenchant *words* they spoke:

" *We hate!* " boomed fiercely o'er the tide;
" We fear not!" from the other side.
" *We strike!* " the rebel guns replied.
   Quick roared our answer: " We defend!"
" *Our rights* " the battle sounds contend,
" The rights of all!" we answer send:
" *We conquer!* " rolled across the wave;
" We persevere," our answer gave;
" *Our chivalry!* " they wildly rave.
   Of block and lash and overseer,
   And dark, mild faces pale with fear;
   Of baying hell-hounds panting near.
   But then the gentle story told,
   My childhood in the days of old
   Rang out its lessons manifold.
   O, prodigal and lost! arise
   And read the welcome blest that lies
   In a kind Father's patient eyes!
   Thy elder brother grudges not,
   The lost and found shall share his lot,
   And wrong in concord be forgot.
   Thus mused I as the hours went by,
   Till the relieving guard drew nigh,
   And then was challenge and reply.
   And as I hastened back to line,
   It seemed an omen half divine
   That " concord " was the countersign.
" *Ours are the brave!* "   " Be *ours* the free!"
" *Be ours the slave; the masters we!* "
" On us no more their blood shall be!"

And when some magic word is spoken,
By which a wizard spell is broken,
There was a silence at that token.
The wild birds dared once more to sing,
I heard the pine boughs whispering,
And trickling of a silver spring.
Then, crashing forth with smoke and din,
Once more the rattling sounds begin;
Our iron lips roll forth, " we win!"
And, dull and wavering in the gale,
That rushes in gusts across the vale,
Came back the faint reply, " *we fail!*"
And then a word, both stern and sad,
From throat of huge Columbiad:
" Blind fools and traitors! ye are mad."
Again the rebel answer came,
Muffled and slow — as if in shame:
" *All — all is lost!*" in smoke and flame.
Now, bold and strong, and stern as fate,
The Union guns send forth: " We wait!"
Faint comes the distant cry: " *Too late!*"
" Return! return," our cannon said;
And, as the smoke rolled overhead,
" We dare not!" was the answer dread.
Then came a sound both loud and clear —
A God-like word of hope and cheer:
" Forgiveness!" echoed far and near.
I thought of Shiloh's tainted air —
Of Richmond's prisons foul and bare,
And murdered heroes, young and fair.

THE DYING SOLDIER.

The setting sun threw golden rays on lovely southern
    flowers;
And nature donned her brightest robes, enhanced by
    summer showers.
The crimson clouds were all at rest in skies of deepest
    blue,
And every shrub and waving tree assumed its bright-
    est hue.
Alas that such a glorious spot rebellious fruit should
    yield,
That beauties such as these should cluster round the
    gory battle field;
The holy angels well might weep, at such a horrid
    strife,
When brothers raised their blood stained hands to take
    a brother's life.
With flashing eyes that glowed with hate, and hearts
    that would not fail,
They stood and faced the cannon's mouth while balls
    flew thick as hail;
Then hand to hand the contest came, and hotter grew
    the fight,
Until the stars and stripes, once more, burst on their
    gladdened sight.
The booming cannon long had ceased its sullen deadly
    roar,
And men whose hearts beat high with hope lay swel-
    tering in their gore.

Blood ran in streams, all o'er the field the dead lay
    piled around,
For death in every shape and form went rushing o'er
    the ground.
With glazing eye and labored breath the wounded sol-
    dier lay,
And sought to send some parting word to loved ones
    far away;
The day he came his mother kissed her darling's lofty
    brow—
His father blessed his only son, and he was dying now.
The evening breeze was wafted in with songs of happy
    birds,
While friends bent o'er and listened to his faintly
    whispered words:
"Tell my father that I bless him, and with my latest
    breath
Thank God and him I do not die a cringing coward's
    death;
My mother, oh, my mother! how I love you in this
    hour!
May God forever bless you, and shield you by his
    power;
My heart bled when I started, to hear your trembling
    sigh;
Oh, mother, mother! how I long to kiss you ere I die.
Tell my sister not to mourn, but comfort those at
    home,
And my parents will not have to bear this grief all
    alone.

And bear this ring to Jessie, there's much I wish to
    say,
But I hear the angels calling and I must haste away."
He faintly smiled, then tried to pray, then vainly
    gasped for breath,
We stood and gazed in silent awe there all alone with
    death;
The curls lay thickly o'er his brow, the noble heart
    was still—
He rests beneath a shady tree—a mark of southern
    skill.

NO MORE DEATH.

BY DR. ALEXANDER CLARKE.

WHEN winter is over and gone, and the time of the
singing of birds is come, when the grass is beginning
to spring forth and the flowers are soon to appear—
when everything seems to have a pulse, a breath and
a voice, we are apt to forget that the summer will
begin so soon to wither all this tender beauty, and
that autumn will chill and despoil what spring brings
to our eyes and souls in nature; and that another winter with shroud and silence for all its outward coming
life. But, as sure as there is change in the grass, and
leaves and flowers, so is there change in these bodies
of clay. As the growing grain, which so soon ripens

and is reaped, so our terrestrial forms grow up from the dust, in the dust shall be leveled and buried again.

Death comes to us as a light wind, wandering through groves of bloom, detaching the delicate blossoms from the tree; comes to us as a sweeping blast, crashing the tree to the earth.

"Leaves have their time to fall,
    And flowers to wither at the north wind's breath,
And stars to set—but all—
    Thou hast all seasons for thine own oh Death!"

Whatever of promise and beauty we see, yet this is a dying world. Immortality has no place under the circuit of the sun. That which is deathless and ever blooming is far beyond these hills—mortality is here; immortality is yonder. Corruption is now; incorruption is by and by, and forever. "Neither can they die any more" is not spoken of flowers, or of leaves, or grain, or trees, or present forms of men. For these all die; it is the divine prediction of something future. It compasses an eternal fact, and brings it to the soul. Every moment some child of Adam hurries away from earth. The Eden gate which opened toward tears and toils and homelessness has never yet been closed. The wages of sin is the whole world's currency. Each swing of the pendulum is the seal setting of some death warrant.

Human beings die in number beyond the tickings of the clock, by day and night, on and on, the years and centuries through. Going — dying! dead and gone! This is the record of the swinging pendulum. Summer and winter, there and here; of old and new; as Time's vibrations mark the nearing judgment and eternity — it is death, death! one by one from first to last — every moment another death. Somewhere a hurried, gasping, closing breath — father, mother, sister, brother, husband, wife, or darling child.

Even in this early spring Sabbath, only put your ear to the ground, and you might hear from every direction the measured step of men who carry a corpse to its burial. The gate through which Adam and Eve were driven for disobedience has neither locks, nor bolts, nor bars. Disease enters the securest home, as a thief in the dark, and brings out the best treasure of all. The parsonage and prison are alike exposed. The pale, cold faces of rich and poor are the same in the coffin.

Tears have no sects or schools. There is unity in grief and in the grave. Who can stay the strong arm of death? Who can forbid his touch upon a nearest and dearest friend? When sickness comes you cannot turn away and say, "thou shalt not enter." When paralysis crosses your threshold, and seizes you by the arm, of what avail to say, "unwelcome intruder, stand off!" Can you say to pain, "thou shalt not come nigh me nor mine"?

Can you face Death and defy his darts? Whatever your courage, your position, your influence, your choice, you shall one day be thrown prostrate and overcome and put in silence in the dust. Where is the scholar, or the teacher, the physician, or the minister, who can enter the death chamber and pronounce the *Talitha Cumi* of resurrection? Where is the mighty one among us now who can halt the funeral procession, look down upon the pulseless clay, and say arise?

The voice of death sounds everywhere abroad; but the word of life is only in the gospel. "The wages of sin is death," but Jesus Christ is the resurrection and the life. Death springs from the ground and claims the universal race, but life stoops from the skies and leads captivity captive. "Death is swallowed up in victory," and this is victory—even our faith. Each season speaks of death; the drooping spring blossom, the scorched leaf of summer, the ripe sheaf, and the fallen fruit of autumn, the bare drear ground and frozen snow of winter—all tell us of death. Storms and shadows, the lightning that scars and burns, the flood that drowns and devastates, the cold sea wave dampning the shore, ebbing tides and crumbling rocks, up torn trees and garnered harvests—all are messengers to us of death. The sceptered monarch reigns over earth and sea, he cuts his way into every city, into every island, into every community, into every home. In almost every family a vacant chair, an empty cradle. In every garden a faded rose, in every forest a fallen tree, on every tree a shattered bough, on every bough a withered leaf. In all the old tunes we sing there are rests and silences, in every harp we take up there is a broken string. Just west of San

Francisco, toward the sea, is Lone Mountain Cemetery, A rounded hill covered with evergreens and marble. The winds from the ocean blow among the quivering leaves, and make sad music as of invisible choirs chanting requiems for the dead. The sun sinks beyond the farthest circle of graves, and the darkness creeps up from the land and the sea, and the white marble and the bright evergreen are alike concealed in the midnight. But soon the east is kindled by the sunrise and the new day smiles all abroad; there is light once more, but no life. By and by our Son of Righteousness shall arise with healing in his wings, and all that are in their graves shall come forth. There shall be an eternal morning. But, here again, "the second Adam is a quickening spirit;" Jesus Christ who tasted death for every man is the conqueror of death. The grave is but the slumber ground for waking into glory.

Death is but a sleep from which the sleeper shall awaken in the morning. The sunset becomes the sure sunrise, Eastward and forever! The truth of the resurrection is here, and it shall burst in music upon the sleeping saints of God. Now, we must die; but for a saint to die is eternal gain. The complete destruction of death is at hand. The mighty God, who holds all worlds in their places, shall redeem His people from the grave's dominion. He is able. He has promised. And it shall be. Amen! and amen! The time for unlocking of sepulchres, for the rolling away of the great stone, is coming. It is a divine fact wrought into this world's grandest biography already. For, now is Christ risen! We are started in a pathway that leads through the grave's dark portals to light and immortality, to thrones and principalities and power. Though we die, we shall live again. Though we have toil and trouble for awhile, we shall be kings and priests unto God forever. Death is here, to be sure, greedy for us — grasping for us; but, brethren, these blessed spirit wings, they shall bear us to life up yonder, and we shall live forevermore. There shall be no more crying nor any more pain; nor any more death. Pilgrims and strangers here, but yonder friends and companions with Jesus. That which is sown in weakness, shall be raised in power. Man was not made to die, but live. God does not love death, nor does He desire this gloomy death perpetuated. This desolation and ruin in the great temple of humanity are the results of sin. Justice from the beginning of transgression demands the execution of the sentence: "In the day thou eatest thereof, thou shalt surely die!" This world was made with a garden, and no sepulchre. But, blessed be God! in a New Testament garden there is a new sepulchre! These eyes were not made to weep, but to sparkle with gladness. Do your lips ever murmur? They were formed to speak praise. Do you get sick? You were made to be healthful. Do you die? You were made to live, and these consequences of sin, the divine Savior will utterly overcome, so that you cannot die.

The day of Christ's final victory is coming nearer and nearer every hour. "I will ransom from the power of the grave; I will redeem from the power of the grave; I will redeem from death." "O, grave I will be thy destruction!" There is for us a better life and a better time. Like the cadence of an angel song, and yet with the power of the omnipotent, come the thought of our departed loved ones. "Neither can they die any more." We look up, march forward and take strength. The heart of mercy bounds the victor thrill of the resurrection. The arm that broke the grave's bars down is still outsretched to conquer for all the saints a full salvation. The death reign shall be ended, Satan shall be bound; our faith shall overcome the world and have the victory. Notice, it is not "neither shall" or "neither may," but "neither can they die any more." Death is now the law, then it will be an absolute impossibility. Blessed home, blessed life, resurrection is only the lowest round of this ladder, whose foot is planted by the open grave, and whose top rests upon the throne.

Resurrection, ascension and eternal glory! New Jerusalem shall never crumble down. The white robes shall never need cleaning or renewal. The glass through which we now see darkly, shall be thrown aside, and we shall behold Jesus face to face, and be like him.

TOBACCO.

I.

Come old and young and hear me tell
How strong tobacco smokers smell,
Who love to smoke their pipes so well,
That for tobacco they would sell
Their right to social union.

II.

They always scent the atmosphere,
And you may know when they are near,
Though not a word from them you hear.
Their breath grows stronger every year,
While in the smoking union.

III.

They clean their pipe stems with a wire,
Then fill the bowl and put in fire,
And smoke till it does quite expire,
Nor do they ever seem to tire,
In this laborious union.

IV.

Sometimes from three to six you'll see
Collected in one company,
And every fellow in good glee;
They then must have a smoking spree—
A fetid smoking union.

V.

And then the fumes and smoke will rise,
Like morning mist toward the skies;
Then woe to him who has weak eyes,
Unless he takes his leave and flies
Away from such a union.

VI.

With impudence they oft' presume
To vex all persons in the room,
Who can't endure tobacco fume—
And they must bear this wretched doom,
Or, leave this smoking union.

VII.

Some keep the money from the poor,
And send the hungry from the door,
And haste away to some one's store,
And spend it for tobacco more,
To burn in smoking union.

VIII.

Those who in utter darkness lie,
May in their error live and die,
Before those persons e'er will try
Them with the gospel to supply,
To teach them heavenly union.

IX.

I wonder how such folks can say
They have religion every day,

And love the Lord and love to pray
When they his money smoke away
In guilty conscience, union.

X.

There are some who tobacco chew,
And though it often makes them spew,
And makes them drunk as Bacchus, too,
The practice they will still pursue,
At the expense of social union.

XI.

Sometimes within their neighbor's door
They'll cast their quids, some three or four,
And spit on carpet, hearth and floor,
Sometimes a gill, or even more,
And talk of social union.

XII.

Oft times within the church you'll view
That person's there will sit and chew,
And spit upon the floor or pew
Until it spreads a foot or two,
And sing of heavenly union.

XIII.

The quid is oft so large within
The juice runs out and stains the chin;
And then I always have to grin,
And think there is no little sin
In this tobacco union.

WELCOME TO THE NATIONS.

BY OLIVER WENDELL HOLMES.

Bright on the banners of lilly and rose,
  Lo! the last sun of our century sets!
Wreathe the black cannon that scowled on our foes;
  All but her friendships the Nation forgets;
  All but her friends and their welcome forgets;
These are around her.   But where are her foes?
  Lo! while the sun of her century sets,
Peace, with her garlands of lilly and rose.

Welcome! a shout like the war-trumpet swell
  Wakes the wild echoes that slumber around;
Welcome? it quivers from Liberty's bell;
  Welcome! the walls of her temple resound.
  Hark! the gray walls of her temple resound;
Fade the fair voices o'r hill-side and dell.
  Welcome! still whispers the echoes around;
Welcome! still trembles on Liberty's bell.

Thrones of the Continents! Isles of the Sea!
  Yours are the garlands of peace we entwine;
Welcome, once more, to the land of the Free,
  Shadowed alike by the palm and the pine,
  Softly they murmur, the palm and the pine:
"Hushed is our strife, in the land of the Free."
  Over your children their branches entwine,
Thrones of the Continents! Isles of the Sea!

21

FATHER, IS THIS THE WAY?

I.

Father, is this the way?
This narrow, rugged path—the way my feet must go?
I see no sheltering tree, no green branch waving low
O'er the rough defile, while fervid is the glow
Of cloudless noonday sun—and fears distress me so;
Father, is this the way?

II.

Father, is this the way?
Is this the road that brings me nearer Thee?
Is there no other way?   Far lovelier paths I see—
Flower-strewn and shady walks—soft winding through
    the lea,
While this is straight and steep — this one marked
    out for me.
Is there no other way?

III.

Father is this the way?
I fear my faltering feet will slip—that I shall fall
Back in the miry pit that held me long in thrall:
I dread to taste again the wormwood and the gall.
Father, O! hear my cry—answer my earnest call—
Is there no other way?

IV.

Father, is this the way?
Must I this burden bear, far up the giddy height
Whose top, like jasper walls, is bathed in crystal
    light?
So steep, so far, it seems to my imperfect sight,
'Twere vain to try to reach it ere 'tis lost in night.
Is there no other way?

V.

Father, is this the way?
Ah, yes! I scan the path and see *Thy foot-prints*
    there,
And lo! great shadowy rocks, shielding from sun
    and air,
Quite unperceived before, I find, for rest and prayer,
With angels waiting near the message home to bear.
Father, I know the way.

VI.

Father, I love the way!
And light my burden seems, and firm my onward
    tread,
While upland breezes float flower perfumed round
    my head;
From living springs my thirsty soul is sweetly fed;
Angels attend my steps, and every fear has fled.
Father, I love the way!

HOME.

BY TIRZAH H.

Home! what a source of pleasure's there,
Where we the joys of friends may share,
And join them in their social glee
With hearts from care and sorrow free.

Home! says the traveler, far away,
When shall I see that happy day,
When I at HOME shall happy be—
From this fatigue and journey free.

Home! says the soldier; *Home* once more
From weary march and cannon roar;
Home to my friends, who still prove true
To the dear Old Flag—*Red White and Blue.*

Home! says the christian, and his eye
Turns to the heavens so bright on high,
Where HE, when his sad life is o'er,
Will meet with those who've gone before.

Home has a charm for every care,
For all who this sweet comfort share;
Their broken hearts may find relief,
And drive away the sorest grief.

LIFE'S LOT.

I know not if the dark or bright,
  Shall be my lot;
If that wherein my hopes delight,
  Be best or not.

It may be mine to drag for years,
  Toil's heavy chain;
Or day and night my meat be tears,
  On bed of pain.

Dear faces may surround my hearth,
  With smiles and glee;
Or I my dwell along and mirth
  Be strange to me.

My bark is wafted to the strand,
  By breath divine;
And on the helm there 's a hand
  Other than mine.

One who has known in storms to sail,
  I have on board;
Above the raging of the gale
  I hear my Lord.

He holds me with the billows' smile —
  I shall not fail;
If sharp, 'tis short — if long, 'tis light,
  He tempers all.

Safe to the land — safe to the land,
  The end is this:
And then with Him go hand in hand
  Far into bliss.

CHRISTMAS COMING.

Of all the days throughout the year,
  The gladdest day and best;
Comes in the heart of winter,
  When nature is at rest.

When the days are the shortest,
  And the nights are dark and long;
And only of the singing bird,
  The robin pipes his song.

When not a flower is on the hill,
  Nor a green leaf in the tree;
And only the holly and ivy
  Are beautiful to see.

Then cometh the best day of the year,
  The blessed day of all;
When Jesus Christ, the Savior,
  Was born in the oxens' stall.

Not amid gold and purple,
  In pomp of worldly pride;
With chancelors and archbishops
  And ladies on every side.

But, all among the oxen,
  Those plodding and patient things;
Was born in the depth of winter,
  The King of earthly kings.

NO ROSE WITHOUT A THORN.

No rose without a thorn,
Without the husk, no corn;
No nut without the shell,
Without the hill no dell.

No joy without some woe,
No scene all bright below;
Some bitter with the sweet,
No bone without the meat.

No rose without the thorn,
Without the night no morn;
No star without the night,
No Luna's welcome light.

No life but has its pain,
The sunshine brings the rain;
No love without its cross,
No gold without some dross,

No rose without a thorn,
No face of beauty born
But has imperfect spot,
The thorns in fairest lot.

MY PSALM.

BY J. G. WHITTIER.

I mourn no more my vanished years,
    Beneath a tender rain;
An April rain of smiles and tears,
    My heart is young again.

The West winds blow and singing low,
    I hear the glad streams run;
The windows of my soul I throw
    Wide open to the sun.

No longer forward nor behind,
    I look in hope or fear;
But grateful take the good I find,
    The best of now and here.

I plow no more the desert land,
    To harvest weed and tare;
The manna dropping from God's hand,
    Rebukes my painful care.

I break my pilgrim staff, I lay
    Aside the toiling oar;
The angel sought so far away,
    I welcome to my door.

The airs of spring may never play
    Among the ripening corn;
Nor freshness of the flowers of May
    Blow through the autumn morn.

Yet shall the blue-eyed gentian look,
  Through fringed lids to heaven;
And the pale aster, in the brook
  Shall see its image given.

The woods shall wear their robes of praise,
  The South wind softly sigh;
And sweet calm days in golden haze,
  Melt down the amber sky.

Not less shall manly deed and word,
  Rebuke an age of wrong;
The graven flowers that 'neath the sword,
  Make not the blade less strong.

But smiting hands shall learn to heal,
  To build as to destroy;
Nor less my heart for others feel,
  That I the more enjoy.

All as God wills who wisely heeds,
  To give or to withhold;
And knoweth more of all my needs,
  Than all my prayers have told.

Enough that blessings undeserved,
  Have marked my erring track;
That wheresoe'er my feet have swerved,
  His chastening turned me back.

That more and more of Providence,
　Of love, is understood;
Making the springs of time and sense,
　Sweet with eternal good.

That death seems but a covered way,
　Which opens into light;
Wherein no blinded child can stray,
　Beyond the Father's sight.

That care and trial seem at last,
　Through memory's sunset air,
Like mountain's ranges over-past,
　In purple distance fair.

That all the jarring notes of life,
　Seem blending in a psalm,
And all the angels of its strife,
　Slow sounding into calm.

And so the shadows fall apart,
　And so the West winds play,
And all the windows of my heart
　I open to the day.

COAL HILL OPPOSITE GREENVILLE, PA.

Bold mount whose winter blasted side
  Sweeps up toward the midnight moon,
What histories in thy depths abide,
  And will till comes the shock of doom!
The wind-sung shadows sweep about
  Thy rocky ramparts, wild and cold,
Like dusky banners night flings out,
  And leaves the stealthy morn to fold.

Through thy umbrageous aisles of old
  Full many a hymn the wild winds sung;
And many a savage war-whoop rolled
  Through lonely depths with darkness hung,
And many a screaming wild bird swept;
  There crawled the snake, and hissed his spite
Around his bramble-matted nest;
  And there the panthers howled at night,
And storm-rocked eagles sunk to rest.

But time hath chased the shades of old;
  A full free breath of life hath blown,
And riches long in depths withheld
  Send their broad smoke wreaths round thy throne.
O mount, forever proudly stand,
  Though man has scarred thy stately form,
For thou art in thy silence grand,
  A page to read in calm or storm.
How many eyes that gazed from thee,
  Once bright with boyhood's dreams and trust,
Have come, as mine have come, to see
  Much once beloved returned to dust.

SWEET TWILIGIIT IIOUR.

Sweet twilight hour, I love thee well,
    Far better than all hours beside,
For in thy rich and softened light
    The busy cares of day I hide.
Thy gentle light, like smiles of love,
    Rests on each object that I see,
And beautiful they then appear
    Clothed with new beauty flower and tree.

If far away to yonder hill
    In listless gaze I turn my eyes,
Thy deepening shadows blend in one
    The trees that from its summit rise;
The mighty ocean with its waves
    Seems murmuring music to my ear,
As in thy still and quiet hour
    Methinks its cadences I hear.

Sweet twilight hour, how fraught thou art,
    With power to sooth the weary soul,
To elevate our hearts, and cause
    Serenest thought through them to roll;
Each note of music and each sound,
    At thine all hallowed hour,
More rich in melody appears,
    And greater in his power.

Sweet twilight hour how many a tale
    Of love thou oft dost tell,

Of whispering zephyrs wooing love
  In some enchanting dell.

'Tis then I love to hie myself
  To some sequestered spot,
And feel thy cool air fan my brow,
  While cares are all forgot.

'Tis then I love to hold commune
  With God and nature too,
To feel his spirit brooding o'er,
  As falls the gentle evening dew;
To feel my soul communing with
  The spirit of the air,
And realize that God is near,
  Around, yet everywhere.

FREE.

By the blood our fathers shed,
By the graves of martyred dead,
By the land we dearly love,
By the stars that shine above,
            We are free.

By our mountains and our hills,
By our rivers and our rills,

By our friends and firesides dear,
By our birthright bright and clear,
   We are free.

By the flag that floats afar,
By the thunder tones of war,
By the fields so nobly won,
By the deeds of glory done,
   We are free.

FOR YOU.

BY REV. H. B. HARTZLER.

There is for you a sphere of toil,
 And God would have you fill it;
A field of rich and fruitful soil
 Awaits your hand to till it.

There is somewhere a mine of gold
 Beneath the rocks that bind it,
Whose hiding-place the mountains hold,
 And none but you may find it.

There is somewhere a tuneful lyre
 That waits your touch to wake it,
Whose music will your heart inspire,
 And bless the hands that take it.

There is somewhere a burden laid
  On arms too weak to bear it,
And wistful eyes and heart dismayed
  Look up to you to share it.

Then train your hand for fruitful toil
  Upon the field of labor;
Nor wait for fortune's hazard spoil
  On fancy's dazzling Tabor.

With heart and mind alert and strong,
  ·Confront your lot and take it;
While God is true and chance is wrong,
  Your life is what you make it.

CLOUDS AND SUNSHINE.

Sweet in nature to behold them,
  Cloud and sunshine, light and shade,
God in beauty doth unfold them,
  Earth by each is fairer made.
Never day so darkly clouded
  But above in beauty fair,
Though from earthly vision shrouded,
  Bright the sun was shining there.

Sorrow clouds will gather o'er us,
  And the sun of joy is dim;
Christ hath trod the vale before us,
  Trusting, let us follow Him.

Never sorrow hath He given
  But some cause for joy remain;
Faith looks up, the cloud when riven
  Will reveal the sun again.

Clouds and sunshine changing ever
  Scenes through which we journey now,
But there falls a shadow never
  Where the happy spirits bow.
Could we in the light of heaven
  View the way through which we go,
Why our darkened hours are given,
  Why our trials we might know.

LINES ON A SKELETON.

Behold this ruin! 'Twas a skull
Once, of etherial spirit full;
This narrow cell was life's retreat;
This space was thought's myterious seat.
What beauteous visions filled this spot!
What dreams of pleasure, long forgot;
Nor hope, nor joy, nor love, nor fear,
Have left no trace of record here.

Beneath this mouldering canopy
Once shone the bright and busy eye;
But start not at the dismal void—
If social love that eye employed—

If with no lawless fire it gleamed,
But through the dew of kindness beamed—
That eye shall be forever bright
When stars and sun are sunk in night.

Within this hollow cavern hung
The ready, swift, and tuneful tongue;
If falsehood's honey it disdained,
And where it could not praise, was chained;
If bold in virtue's cause it spoke,
Yet gentle concord never broke;
This silent tongue shall plead for thee
When time unveils eternity.

Say, did those fingers delve the mine?
Or, with envied rubies shine?
To hew the rock or wear the gem,
Can little now avail to them?
But if the page of truth they sought,
Or comfort to the mourner brought,
These hands a richer meed shall claim
Than all that wait on wealth or fame.

Avails it whether bare or shod
These feet the depths of duty trod?
If from the halls of ease they fled,
To seek affliction's humble shed;
If grandeur's guilty bribe they spurned,
And home to virtue's cot returned;
These feet with angels' wings shall vie,
And tread the palace of the sky.

22

LINES.

Alone I walked the ocean's strand,
A pearl shell was in my hand;
I stopped and wrote upon the sand
    My name, the year, the day.

As ownward from that spot I passed
One lingering look behind me cast;
A wave came dashing, high and full,
    And washed those lines away.

So, methought, 'twould shortly be,
When every trace and memory of me,
A wave of the dark oblivious sea
    Would wash those lines away.

THE BETHEL DREAM.

The sun behind Judea's hills
    Had calmly sunk to rest,
And bright its Iris banner streamed
    Within the crimsoned west.

The silver-sandaled feet of day
    Had sought the hills of blue,
And seraphs the door that hides
    The spirit world from view.

Weary the Bethel dreamer stood
  Upon the shadowy plain,
To watch, perchance, the sunbeams glide
  Away from earth again.

While stars climbed up the azure dome,
  And silently did stray,
Amid the trembling ether depths,
  To hill-tops bare and gray.

Exhausted on the earth he sank—
  His pillow 'twas of stone;
As from the sapphire halls above
  His ladder down was thrown.

From lowly earth to vaulted skies,
  From Heaven's jasper wall,
Adown the burnished rounds of gold
  The angel's foot-beats fall.

Our hopes, resolves, and prayers—
  The bribe we thrust away—
Methinks *these* are the steps that lead
  Us up the shining way.

The vision fades, the dream departs,
  The ladder is withdrawn;
The stony pillow but remains,
  And the angels, too, have gone.

No crown for us but one of thorns;
  No robes save those of clay;
What wonder that to earth we cling,
  E'en though we aspire to pray?

JUST ELEVEN.

Three years ago to-day,
  We raised our hands to heaven,
And on the rolls of muster
  Our names were thirty-seven.
There were just a thousand bayonets,
  And the swords were thirty-seven
As we took the oath of service
  With our right hands raised to heaven.

O 'twas a gallant day
  In memory still adored,
That day of our sunlight nupitials,
  With the musket and the sword.
Shrill rang the fife the bugles blared,
  And beneath a cloudless heaven
Twinkled a thousand bayonets,
  And the swords were thirty-seven.

Of the thousand stalwart bayonets
  Two hundred march to-day;
Hundreds lie in Virginia's swamps,
  And hundreds in Maryland clay.
And other hundreds less happy, drag
  Their shattered limbs around,
And envy the deep long blessed sleep
  Of the battle field's holy ground.

For the swords, one night a week ago,
  The remnant just eleven,

Gathered around a banqueting board,
  With seats for thirty-seven.
There were two limped in on crutches,
  And two had each but a hand
To pour the wine and raise the cup,
  As we toasted "Our flag and land."

And the room seemed filled with whispers
  As we looked at the vacant seats,
And with choking throats we pushed aside
  The rich, but untasted meats;
Then in silence we brimed our glasses,
  As we rose up just eleven,
And bowed as we drank to the loved and dead,
  Who had made us thirty-seven.

LINES.

Flowers on the graves of loved ones
  They of worth affection still,
The tablet marks the sacred spot
  But holds no mystic spell.
It speaks not of remembrance still,
  Nor of the falling tear,
Nor of the lonely heart that decks
  With flowers the loved one's bier.

Flowers on the graves of loved ones,
  Show a kind and tender care,
And they tell the stranger passing,
  That a loved one's sleeping there.
Yes, they speak of kind devotion,
  And of friendship, noble, true,
For they prove the living ever
  Keep their dead, their loved in view.

Flowers on the graves of loved ones,
  Speak as can no sculptured art,
And the grave that's decked with flowers
  Show the work of loving hearts;
Stops the stranger and he lingers
  Long to view that sacred mound,
For he feels where love has labored
  That it must be hallowed ground.

Flowers on the graves of loved ones
  Prove communion, holy, sweet,
For they show the dead and living
  Beyond the vale each other greet.
Yes they're still the loved companions,
  Not in form but spirit true,
And these little acts of kindness,
  They bring back the loved to view.

"JESUS ONLY."

Christian are you sad and weary,
Lone and desolate and dreary?
Have the clouds obscured thy vision
Of the golden fields elysian?
  Look about thee, none can help!
When thou 'rt sad, dejected, lonely,
  None can drive away the clouds;
None can help but " Jesus only."

When upon the raging water,
Peter's faith began to falter —
On that dark and troubled sea,
Wild, tempestuous Gallilee!
  Peter saw that none could help,
On the water bleak and lonely;
  Raised his voice in prayer, and saw
Right before him " Jesus only."

He can calm the stormy billow —
Make as down thy dying pillow;
Calm the pulse and still the fever
Of the penitent believer;
  Then above thee look for help,
When the heart is sad and lonely;
  None can bid thy heart rejoice
With delight, save " Jesus only."

When the earth shall part asunder,
As the trumpet's awful thunder

Shall proclaim that Time is ending,
With eternity is blending;
When mankind its sentence waits,
Christian, thou shalt not feel lonely;
For, upon the judgment seat
Who shall sit, but "Jesus only."

THE PARSON GOING TO MILL.

The parson sat in his house one day,
While the winter storm did rage;
High-rapt he drank in lofty thought
From Hooker's classic page.
But, as he sat, and holy dreams
Into his heart did steal,
His sweet wife opened the door and said:
"My dear, we have no meal."

With saddened brow and heavy sigh,
He laid aside his book;
And with a meek, despairing eye
Upon the hearth did look.
"My people think that I must break
To them the bread of heaven;
But they 'll not give me bread enough
Three whole days out of seven."

But hunger is a serious thing,
   And it is sad to hear
Sweet children's mournful cry for bread,
   Loud ringing in your ear.
So, straight he mounted his old horse,
   With meek and chastened will;
And on his meal bag, patched and coarse,
   He journeyed to the mill.

The miller bowed to him, and said:
   " Sir, by your church-steeple,
I vow I give you praise for this —
   But none to your church-people!"
The parson mounted his old horse,
   He had no time to lag,
And rode like a hero to his home,
   Right on his old meal bag.

But as he rode, he overtook
   A proud and wealthy layman,
Who with a close astonished gaze
   The parson's bag did scan.
" My reverend friend, the truth to tell,
   It makes me feel quite wroth,
To see you compromise this way,
   The honor of your cloth.

" Why told you not, my honored friend,
   Your meal was running low;
What will the neighbors think of us,
   If to the mill you go?"

" My wealthy friend," the parson said,
  " You must not reason so,
For 'tis a fixed and settled thing,
  My meal *is always low.*

" If my dear people wish to know
  How to promote my bliss,
I'll simply say, a bag of meal
  Will never be amiss.
Just keep the store-room well supplied,
  And I will be right still,
But if the meal gives out again,
  I must go to the mill."

MORAL.

Laymen! it needs no miracle,
  No hard laborious toil;
To make the parson's meal-bag
  Like the widow's cruise of oil.
Pour forth into his wife's store-room,
  Your gifts right plentiful;
The miracle is simply this:
  To keep it alawys full.

IN MEMORY OF FATHER AND MOTHER.

BY SISTER LIZZIE.

FATHER.

Of that grand life, it might be said
He walked by faith, as day by day
Death's shadows darkened round him,
Yet his faith was firm that God would take him
When his weary pilgrimage was o'er.
Even now, after the lapse of many years,
Memory brings back the dear familiar face
In its accustomed place, just where
The evening light would linger ere 'twas hid
Behind the western hills.
Across the meadows, and the woodland cool and dim,
The dim outlines of the old white church were seen,
Where he had worshiped ere disease
Had stripped him of his strength;
And just beyond, upon the grassy slope
Of the green hill-side, were the graves
Of many a dear one gone before,
And where he, too, hoped soon to be at rest.
After a life of care and toil it would be sweet
In peace to sleep.

There came a day when he was missed
From the old window seat—
When in a darkened room he lay,
So pale and still, save for the hollow cough
That told his work on earth was done.

It was not long, only a few short weeks,
And then death called for him,
And found him ready, waiting to go home,
Leaving the rich legacy of a life well spent.

MOTHER.

Dear Mother, many a fleeting year
  Has hurried by
Since in thy shroud and on thy bier
  I saw thee lie,
And, dear mother, it seems to me
  A weary way.
My heart oft wanders from its guide—
  My feet will stray.
O, might I know the perfect peace
  Which now is thine;
O, might I go and dwell with thee—
  Thy home be mine.
Yet, let me learn to bide my time
  With patient heart,
And let me labor faithfully
  Till I depart;
For life, with all its hopes and fears,
  Will soon be o'er,
And then thy loved ones may behold
  Thy face once more.

FAMILY GATHERING.

Yes, they all came home together
  To the old house on the farm;
Fathers, mothers, little chidren—
  But the day had lost a charm.
Oh! the places 'round the fireside!
  Places that the stranger fills:
Oh! the cold and dreary north-wind
  'Round the graves at Malvern Hill!

Out upon the bleak brown hill-side,
  Where the restless pine trees moan,
One is lying in their shadow,
  Through this autumn light alone.
With his soldier-cloak around him
  He is resting from the strife,
But we could not smooth his pillow—
  Could not cheer the parting life.

One more, wounded at Antietam,
  In his boyhood stricken down—
Clay-cold cheek, and brow of marble
  Resting on its laurel crown;
Slowly, tenderly, they brought him
  In New England soil to rest,
So we wreathed the white immortelles
  And laid them on his breast.

Hark! the chime of soft sweet voices,
  Music ringing through the hall;

But a sound no tongue can utter,
  Murmuring through its rise and fall,
Like the far-off noise of armies—
  Like the hollow roll of drums;
From that dim, blue line of waters,
  Sadly, plaintively, it comes.

Blind and foolish we who murmur;
  Holy, powerful and calm
God is guiding on the people,
  Though we may not feel his arm.
Something clearer than the star-light
  Sleeps upon those quiet graves—
Glows above the blue Potomac,
  Glows above its storied waves.

In their watches on the mountain
  They have seen his rising star;
They have looked upon his beauty;
  He is with them where they are.
So we kept a glad Thanksgiving
  In this year of grief and care.
And we heard their spirit voices
  When we said our evening prayer.

A TEACHER'S DREAM.

The weary teacher sat alone
  While twilight gathered on;
And not a sound was heard around—
  The girls and boys were gone.

Another round, another round
  Of labor thrown away;
Another chain of care and pain
  Draged through a tedious day.

"Of no avail is patient toil,
  Love's strength is vainly spent,
Alas," he said, and bowed his head,
  In lonely discontent.

But rising soon a saddened face,
  He started back aghast,
The room by strange and wondrous change
  Grew to proportions vast.

It seemed a senate hall, and one
  Addressed a listening throng;
Each burning word all bosoms stirred—
  Applause rose loud and long.

The sad spectator thought he knew
  The speaker's voice and look,
"And for his name," he said, "the same
  Is on my record book."

Slow disappeared the senate hall,
  A church rose in its place;
A preacher there outpoured a prayer
  Invoking Heaven's grace;

And though he spoke in solemn tone,
  And though his hair was gray,
The teacher's thought was strangely wrought,
  "I whipped that boy to-day."

The church was gone—a chamber dim,
  Was next obscurely shown;
There among his books, with earnest looks
  An author sat alone.

"My idlest lad!" the teacher said,
  Filled with a new surprise;
Shall I behold his name enrolled
  Among the great and wise?"

Now rising humbly to the view
  A cottage was descried;
A mother's face illumed the place,
  Her spirit sanctified.

"A miracle!" the teacher cried,
  "This matron well I know,
Was but a wild and careless child,
  Not half an hour ago.

And when she to her children speaks
  Of duty's golden rule,

Her lips repeat in accents sweet
  My words to her at school."

The scene was changed again, and lo!
  The school house rude and old;
Upon the wall did darkness fall—
  The evening air was cold.

"A dream!" the sleeper wakening said,
  And paced along the floor;
Then whistling slow, and soft and low,
  He locked the school house door.

And walking home his heart was full
  Of peace and trust and love and praise,
And singing slow and soft and low,
  He murmured, "After many days."

THE OLD MUSKET.

It has hung for many years
  Against the farm-house wall.
And a dingy rust has thrown
  Its mantle over all.
'T was a grandsire's hand did wield
  This weapon long ago,
And the barrel is worn with lead
  That sped against the foe.

Oftentimes did the old man,
  Long since gone to his rest,
Take the old piece fondly down
  And press it to his breast;
'T was a well-tried friend, he said,
  In many a bloody fight —
Then of Bunker Hill he told,
  And trembling clutched it tight.

How his dear face brightened up
  As he marched o'er the floor,
While his thoughts dwelt proudly on
  Those glowing scenes of yore;
When his bleeding country bade
  Him join the noble band,
That dismayed and shattered drove
  The hirelings from our land.

It has hung for many years
  Against the farm-house wall,
And a dingy rust has thrown
  Its mantle over all;
But I prize the old worn piece,
  For his sake who has gone,
And the fancies fond and pure
  That at its sight are born.

"THE WINE-CUP DID IT ALL."

*[The last words of a young man who was hung in England for
the murder of a younger brother while in a fit of intoxication.]*

I.

The drop was ready, and the crowd
  Stood breathless in the sun,
While pealed the prison bell most loud
  The appointed hour of one;
Some eyes were wild, and some were wet,
  And some were closed to pray:
" Prisoner, we wait a moment yet
  If you have aught to say."

II.

The young man looked upon the drop,
  Then cast a wistful eye
Toward his father's chimney top
  And native village nigh;
The vanished joys of early years,
  He dimly did recall,
Then said with quivering lip and tears:
  " The wine-cup did it all."

III.

" I struck the blow — the proof is clear —
  But give to me my due,
My brother was as dear to me
  As any one to you;

Upon his fair and tender brow
  My warmest kiss did fall—
I loved him then, I love him **now**:
  The wine-cup did it all."

IV.

They bore his form — of friends **bereft,**
  Where riteless graves were found,
And there the twilight sunshine left
  The shadow on his mound;
And often there, by moonlight **dim,**
  The village lads recall
His hapless fate, and say of him:
  " The wine-cup did it all."

THE SHORE OF MEMORY.

Wandering on the shore of **Memory,**
  Gathering up the fragments **cast**
By the surging waves of feeling
  From the ocean of the past.

Here a shell and there a pebble,
  With its edges worn away
By the rolling of the waters—
  By the dashing of the spray.

Some lie smooth and many-tinted
    High upon the glistening sand,
Others sharp and freshly scattered—
    Wound when taken in the hand.

Here are wreaths of bygone treasures,
    Garnered in our early years—
Garnered now in hidden caverns,
    Crusted with the salt of tears.

Joy that vanished ere 'twas tasted
    Is but sea-weed wet with spray;
Eagerly we seek to grasp it,
    Lo! its beauties fade away.

Though temptations without number
    Throng and bar thy narrow way,
There's an eye that cannot slumber,
    There's an arm shall be thy stay.

Then be strong, whate'er betide thee—
    All of joy or all of bliss—
Shall not God himself beside thee
    Soothe the storm with " Peace, be still."

SHEAVES.

In the courts of the Master's Temple
  Shall listless footsteps fall,
And banners that no breeze has touched
  Hang drooping from the wall;
Shall we sit idly waiting
  Some summons from afar,
While here in the lanes and byways
  The faint and suffering are?
From the arid hills, from the valleys, swept
  By the dark simoon of sin,
With the Words of Love our hearts have kept
  We gather the children in—
From the haunts where sorrow and crime have rule
  We gather them in to the Sabbath School.

Oh! the weary, weary children,
  Who, knowing no home ties,
Grow up in their haunts of misery,
  Cunning and sad and wise:
Oh! the outcast, sorrowing children,
  Whom no kind hand hath led,
Whose bleeding feet a flinty path
  Pain racked and suffering tread,
From the drunkard's home, from the miser's grasp,
  With their pallid cheeks and thin—
From the outlaw's lair with their stolid eyes
  We gather them fondly in,
And patiently teach the Saviour's rule
Of love to all in the mission school.

We yield the gospel's sweet repose
  To hearts where hope is dead,
And bid them join their song with those
  Of children gently led,
Who know the blissful story
  How Jesus died to save,
And the joys of saints and glory—
  The rest beyond the grave;
From the storm and strife of a crimson stained life,
  From the dews where their feet have been,
From the pains they bear in want's grim fare,
  We gather the children in,
And patiently teach love's golden rule
To rich and poor in the Sabbath School.

From the frivolous homes of fashion,
  From the haunts where lust of gain,
That one absorbing passion,
  Leads forth corruption's train;
From envy, and hate, and malice,
  And all unkindly thought,
We would shield the heir of the palace
  And the child of the humblest cot;
From the binding ties of the worldly wise,
  Their aching hearts to win,
To the home of peace where bickerings cease
  We gather them fondly in,
And hope and love hold joyous rule,
O'er the rich and poor in the Sabbath School.

Come over and help us ye who sit
  At ease by the temple's gate,
The fields are white to the harvest yet,
  What sheaves for the sickle wait!
The time will come when you'll look with **pain**
  O'er the master's fallow ground,
And weep in vain for the wasted grain
  That should be in your garners found;
How blest a toil from the world's turmoil,
  We gather this infant choir,
On the heart's cold shrine with touch divine
  To kindle the sacred fire,
And earnestly teach the Saviour's rule
Of love to all in the Sabbath School.

www.ingramcontent.com/pod-product-compliance
Lightning Source LLC
Chambersburg PA
CBHW021746110726
47902CB00006B/1419